D1559459

Tha Last of My Kind

of

MARCELLUS ALLEN

ISBN: 978-1-48359-363-0

This one is for my best friend Darius 'Lil Boobis" Perry, R.I.P. my nigga. I think about you every day and that makes me go harder! Ima do this for us! Lanes for ever.

I also dedicate this to all the real men and women behind the walls, keep dreaming and never give up on yourself.

Last but not least, I dedicate this to all the Black people that that have lost their lives in the streetz. Rather from the police, enemies, gang wars or drug wars, its all senseless at the end of the day. Ask ya dead homies mother or kids and see what they say.

-Tayari

ACKNOWLEDGEMENTS & SHOUT OUTS

First I must thank God for allowing me to live this long [26 years lol] when I should of been dead. Thank you for all the blessings you keep raining down on me when I know I don't deserve nothing but death. I thank you for the team of loyal people you blessed my life with. MOTHER: I love u with all my heart, without you I'm nothing. When nobody's there you're always there. No matter what I do, what they say, what charges they put on my indictments, you never leave my side! JAQUES: Lil bro without you this book or company would never exist. Only few people actually believed in me and even fewer actually put some money up. Without you I would be lost, just another person in prison with a dream and some talent. I'll take a bullet for you-literally. This our year! LASHAHRI: I don't even know where to start with you, I could write a whole book about what you mean to me/ have done for me. How many pages have you typed? Edited? Re-edited? I done lost count on how many phone calls you've made for me concerning this book. From calling manufacturers, magazines, editors and everybody else. Without you I would be lost personally and book wise. You're the true definition of a best friend. I'll die for you literally. I don't think nobody has more faith in me than you do. You see things in me that I don't realize till years later. I told you 2017 would be our year, just watch. And once I win this appeal we really going all the way. LEESA: Lil sis you damn near typed the whole book! Made countless phone calls and whatever else was needed to get this book out. We been pushing this joint sense 2014, it's our year! You're the first person to read this book and the first to motivate me to keep going. I luv you with all my heart and I'm 100% proud of you and your accomplishments. GOTTI- I luv you big bro I've spent my whole life tryna be like you, Drex and Elijah. It's always hard to reach you on the phone because you out getting that money, but you ain't never not came through! When money is needed I know who to call lol I did this for us big bro. DREX and ELIJAH: I luv yall to death. When I really need yall, yall always come through. A Elijah, remember when you said you was gone pull a rabbit out the hat for me? And the next day you had 10 thousand for my lawyer! Drex you didn't miss one day of my trial! If somebody ever needa take a bullet for yall, don't look around cause I'll already be stepping in front of yall.

SPIKE AKA NON-STOP: You one of the last homies i still address as 'big homie', i luv u to death. Keep living in ATL and making those beats, let the homies hate. How many niggaz from Portland got their beats on #1 singles? Or got Rick Ross or L.A. Reid # in their phones? You ain't gotta pick up no hammers no more, I'll do it for you. Lanes!

LAY-G [NEW JERSEY]: What's poppin 5? we sitting in the cell together right now but we'll be on one of those islands in a minute! we bout to take over this publishing game in 2017 just like i said! Too many of these authors be writing some straight trash! we can tell they aint from the streets! Got hood niggaz jumping outta airplanes with Gucci parachutes with silencers! lol where they do that at? we taking this Lay em down publications international; nuff said.

Shout outs to my bro Nellc! they know if they want you dead then they gotta get me first [if they smart]. CHILL-luv u relative, keep grinding.. RESPECT-stay focused and real.. LIL GHOST-stay trill and out the way.

BLEED- you still my main manz I could never beef with u, we'll figure it out much luv.. LOLITA- thanks for those chapters you typed.. MY GRANDPARENTS- yall raised me right, nothings yall fault. I'll be back in L.A. soon. luv yall.. UNCLE CORNBREAD: luv u to death and u always come thru for me.. TYCKOON BOOYOW- what's good relative? u know what it is with us. Hold ya head up down there in the pen in Washington. Mob up or lay down! We started this... G'EARL: baby bro i luv u to death. I'm sorry I'm not there. When you turn 18 Ima make sure u have everything u need to prosper in life...

TO ALL MY HOMIES NATION WIDE- that I've never met, get at me!.. SQUEEZE- I see you.. TO ALL MY TRIPPLE O HOMIES- we luv yall on the west. LIL BLEEV- you was the main homie motivating me in county, good looking.. GEE-- what's hood big bro? i know u see we winning now, finish that book.. PACKIE- what's hood?.. J-GROOVE- what's mobbin relative? It's our turn. mob up or lay down, we started this. blatttttt! SHOUT OUT TO MY FUTURE WIFE- i haven't met u yet, what's been taking u so long? Hurry up and find me. SHOUT OUT TO MY TWO CITYS- PORTLAND and L.A. they gone luv this down on Figueroa St.

R.I.P. LIST: MY FATHER [MARCELLUS ALLEN]. -JERMAINE DAVIS. -LIL BOOBIS, TURK, STIX, BACK SEAN, CAM, F.T., DRAGON, GHOST, DARSHAWN, SMASH, DICKY, OVERDOSE, TAYDA MO-B, LIL CHUCK, AND COMRADE GEORGE JACKSON! AND EVERYYBODY ELSE WE LOST IN THE STRUGGLE.

LIL ACKTIVE/OSO- TO EVERYBODY IN THE STREETZ

TAYARI KENYATTA-SHAKUR- TO ALL MY NEW AFRIKANS

CHAPTER 1

Now They Gone See Why They Call Me O-Dawg.

Sluuurp, slurrrp, is the sound Tamia's mouth makes as her head bops up and down on O-Dawg's dick.

"Awwwww fuck, you bout to make a nigga nut already!" O-Dawg moans as he palms her ass cheeks. He has her ass naked on her knees on the couch.

"You like this Daddy?" Tamia starts to jack him off real slow, then starts to lick his head at the same time.

"Hell yeah! Awww, put it back in your mouth and stop playin!" O-Dawg now gripping the back of her head trying to force her all the way back down.

"Patience....good things come to those that wait", then she slips his whole 8 inches down her throat.

Ssluuurp! Sluuurpp! She's now slurping louder and bopping faster than before. Up and down, up and down. She then pulls her signature move. She scoots closer, lifts her ass higher in the air, and swallows his dick slowly, inch by inch until the head is touching her throat. Once her throat

1

fully accepts it she relaxes her muscles and starts to kiss his pelvic area. She knows this drives him crazy every time so she wasn't surprised when he yelled,

"Fuck you know I love when you do that shit! I don't know how the fuck you do that! I'm about to nut in yo mouth." Tamia's only response was nodding her head because she was fully concentrated in her zone.

She started to taste his pre-cum and knew it was time to perform the final act of her trick. She slid about an inch of his dick out of her throat, then started humming.

"Mmmnnn, mmnnn." She does this for about 10 seconds then she heard him say

"I'm about to bust!" She immediately starts gobbling that inch she released moments earlier. Up and down, up and down fast as she can possibly go, only that one inch though cause she keeps the other 7 inches down her throat. O-Dawg grips the back of her head and pushes it all the way down as he roars,

"Awww fuck!" while he's cumming.

Tamia let her mouth get full with cum until he's done squirting. Once she feels him release his grip on her head she starts swallowing every last drop. She slowly slides his dick out her mouth inch-by-inch until she gets to the head. Then she starts sucking on the head while squeezing his dick to make sure she got everything out of the hole. Just when O-Dawg thought she was done she starts gobbling up and down, up and down making slushing sounds. Sluuurp! Sluuurp! Once he's fully erect again she takes it out and kisses the head.

"You all better Daddy?" She asks while she's still stroking him with her hand.

"Hell yeah, you know you got the best head in the town, I still ain't got used to it, probably never will."

"Well won't you give a bitch a reward for that super head performance I just put down? I need some of that dick before you leave." O-Dawg looks at his canary yellow diamond Rolex watch.

"Its 10:42, I'm leaving at 11:15 so come on."

"Let me go get my Bobby Valentino CD out the room, and take those clothes off before I get back." O-Dawg just stares at her gigantic ass cheeks wobbling one cheek at a time as she walks away, he feels himself getting all the way back hard.

Tamia is a sight to see, at 5'7, long hair, half Dominican with a small chest but humongous ass, she keeps niggas, even bitches trying their best to get in her panties. Once she comes back to the living room she replies,

"Why you still ain't took them clothes off?" She flicks the light switch so it's dim, with only a small lamp on in the corner. She walks to the surround system and starts pushing buttons to put the CD in. She then bends over to put it in and sees him staring at her ass, so she puts on a little show and bends over more than necessary with her legs spread so he can see her fat shaved pussy.

"You see something you like?" As soon as he was responding he heard a loud bang coming from the door. In that split second he yanked his pants up and reached for his .40 caliber pistol laying on the ground. A second loud bang happened and the door flew open with two masked gunmen coming through. Everything seemed to happen in slow motion, at the same time for O-Dawg. Him seeing Tamia scream, him seeing the two shooters lift their guns in her direction. Why are they aiming at her? Who are they? Oh shit it's too dark for them to fully see, they don't know where we exactly at, they're going off sound. All these questions and realizations went through his mind in less than two seconds, then he made up his mind.

Boc! Boc! Boc! He starts letting his burner go off recklessly. Boom! Boom! Boom! Boom! The attackers return fire with what sound like a .45

caliber pistol. Boc! Boc! O-Dawg now running towards the bedroom while he fires behind him blindly, just aiming in their direction. Boom Boom! Boc! Boc! Boom! Boom! Boom! Boom! A bullet hits the wall in front of him and particles start flying just as he is turning left into the bedroom. He closes the door and locks it immediately. Then he rushes to the window and opens it, "thank God it leads to the parking lot" he starts to think. Soon as he is half way out, shots start flying through the door.

Boom! Boom! Boom!

"Fuck these niggas is on me!" Boc! Boc! He returns fire aiming at the door.

"That should hold em for a minute." Then he falls out the window onto the ground, his gun landing a few feet away from him. He hears the door being kicked open, grabs his pistol and starts running towards his car. Boom! Boom! Boom! He hears behind him as he stretches his arm out shooting blind. Boc! Boc! He keeps running, then looks behind him because the shooting has stopped, he sees no one.

He takes his car keys out, pushes the automatic unlock button and hops in his all red 745 B.M.W. As the tires are screeching out of the parking lot and his breathing is still not normal, he grabs his I-Phone.

"Call Boobie," "Calling Boobie cell phone now" the Siri voice replies. He looks in his rear-view to make sure nobody's behind him as the phone rings.

"What's mobbing?" he hears a deep, raspy voice come through the phone.

"Blood I just got served! Niggas kicked down Mia's door and got to bustin! I got to running and clacking back and got the fuck up outta there!" O-Dawg started yelling and talking fast, which is saying a lot because his normal speech pattern is already too fast.

"Hold on nigga, slow down! Where you at right now? Anybody get hit? Tamia?" Boobie replied, now animated and alert.

"I don't know nigga! I'm driving down the street headed to the spot. Call everybody and tell them to get there right now! Tell em to keep their ears to the street, watch the news whatever. I'll call Tamia when I get to the house. Shit she's probably dead or getting questioned by detectives right now." O-Dawg yelled back into the phone and hung up, angry that this just happened to him.

"Fuck! Fuck! Fuck! He screams as he punches his steering wheel. Bitch ass niggas tried to get at me. Niggas aint even graze me, fucking rookies. Now they gone see why they call me O-Dawg. He pumps himself up as he drives.

CHAPTER 2

If you stare at a picture long enough, even the most perfect picture you'll find something is wrong.

A few hours later inside O-Dawg's home in the suburbs of Beaverton, all the heads of Mob Life were present debating the situation.

"Look relative, some shit just aint adding up. 1ˢᵗ, is Tamia, did she set you up? I know a lot of fundamental shit points her direction. Like how would they know you were there? And at the right time? But what really gets to me is the lights situation. Soon as she flicks em off niggas rush the spot. That alone is suspicious, like it was a signal." Gotti says who is O-Dawg's favorite cousin and the most complex thinker out the bunch.

"I feel you my nigga, but I just don't see her doing something like-"

"Hold on, hold on nigga" Gotti cuts off O-Dawg.

"I'm not finished making my points. I don't feel she did it either; now let me tell you why. How much money and work you keep over there?"

"About 50 racks and half a brick!" O-Dawg replies getting animated because he just realized he might have lost his money. This is his first time coming to this conclusion.

"Fuck Blood! Hold that thought, I gotta call this bitch real quick!" O-Dawg yells as he's pulling his phone out his pocket. "Call Tamia."

While it's ringing he puts it on speakerphone.

"Hello, baby can you hear me? Are you okay?" Tamia's voice fills the room,

"Yeah I'm good, what's going on that way?" replies O-Dawg.

"It's hot right now, detectives all in my face talking bout some shooting and they found like 30 shell casings. I told em some nigga I just met at the club came over and we must have been followed by some jack-boys, but let me call you later when I get these pigs out my house baby."

"Hold on Tamia, did they get my shit?" O-Dawg asks with his heart beating fast during the silence.

"Naw, I had to tell them aint no shooters hiding in my bags and cabinets. They some nosey muthafuckas." Tamia answers.

"Wheew! Aight baby, hit me later when they leave and good looking, but we gone have to talk." Then he hangs up the phone.

"What y'all think? Y'all think she's lying?"

"Hold on bro....aight good looking baby, I'll see you later." Gotti responds in his phone then hangs up."

"That was Traci, she said the pigs is at Mia's house deep and word is you got popped at her house. But she said aint no word on who the niggas is." Gotti gives the room the news.

"Anyways like I was saying before you called her, if she set it up she would have gave them the keys. She could have left it unlocked or called them when you were sleep. But really she could have had the niggas already waiting in the closet before you got there. Not to mention yo money and dope woulda been gone, ya feel me?" Gotti asks.

"Check this out son!" Jersey Joe interrupts him. "I know I'm the newest nigga to the circle and all, but I'm here for a reason B. Y'all West Coat niggas kill me son, with all this sitting around debating and shit. Yo if we was back home in jersey son, everybody a be laid the fuck out, bleeding out they mouth. Word to my motha, y'all kill me with this talking shit. Look blood, this shit aint algebra. It's simple as fuck B! We go over there murk da bitch, try to make her talk, if not kill her anyways. Whoever on the shit list they the ones that's food yo. Aint no innocents in this game. So if we murk a few extra niggas what's the harm? They gone be food anyways! Better them now, then us later. Talking about, oh she hit the lights! She coulda gave em a key, what about your money, she wouldn't do anything like that! Y'all sound like a bunch of republicans' son, kill me dead if I'm lying." Jersey Joe stated, then relaxed in his chair like he just said the smartest thing ever said and couldn't believe he had to say it out loud.

Boobie just stares at him then looks at Burnside and says

"What's up with yo wild ass relative? Where you find him at? He'll fuck around and have us all in the feds. You need to explain to him this is Portland, Oregon. Not fucking New Jersey Drive. The town is too small and filled with snitches. We start clapping at everybody on some wild shit we liable to get told on. Fuck round and hit one of these white people. Shit all these oh dry snitchin ass niggas on Facebook and twitter." Boobie schools Joe, while looking around for support. This really pisses Jersey Joe off.

"Yo son y'all tellin me y'all scared of some snitches? Aint it supposed to be the other way around? Fuck they do that at? Fuck a snitch nigga! We kill rats where I'm from son. Aint no snitch or cracker gone have me in the house scared hiding. Fuck the feds too, catch me if they can. Blow the top off they muthafuckin noodles too, police aint exempt!" Jersey Joe rants and is getting madder by the second. Finally Burnside speaks up.

"Look Boobie, O-Dawg, you too Gotti. Imma have to side with my relative on this one, far as action go. Jersey on some real shit what Boobie told you is real. I say we kill everybody, but not on some flamboyant shit. And damn sho not no feds, Joe shut yo dumb ass up blood. That's why you down here now, shooting everybody back in Jersey. O-Dawg, real shit we been getting money for a lil too long without violence, you know niggas only respect murder. I know we came up wild and earned everything we got. But niggas got short term memory, its time you let me off the leash. I got a real good feeling it was Butta and them Gutta Squad crabs. I bet they still hot about that shit at the Blue Fontaine."

Burnside was referring to the incident 3 months ago where he was hugged up on the wall with this thick red-bone named Felicia. As he was rubbing his hands on her ass he saw Half-dead making his way across the dance floor in his direction. Moments later he was grabbing Felicia arm and screaming

"Bitch what the fuck is you doing in here hugged up lookin like a hoe? Bitch get home to my son, now!" She yanked her arm away and screamed

"Nigga you aint my man! And your son is at moms' house for the night, so go back to your groupie hoes and let me be."

"Bitch!" he was yelling while trying to pull her away. Burnside finally stepped in.

"Look blood, she aint tryna to leave with you. You fucking up the mood and shit. Far as your family go I aint got nothing to say about that. But tonight she fuckin with the kid so just fall back my nigga." Half-dead steps in his face.

"Bitch nigga don't ever blood me again. Don't worry about mines slob ass nigga. I don't give a fuck who you suppose to be nigga I know the real you."

At that instant Burnside hit em upside the heat with his Rose bottle shattering it into pieces. Soon as Half-dead hit the ground he started getting stomped by a group of mob niggas. Seconds later Dirty Dan sees what's going on and has to rescue Half-dead. So he pulls out his 9mm and starts shooting in the air. Boom! Boom! Boom! The crowd breaks up and everybody in the club starts running and falling....

"Yeah yo I told you we shoulda murdered all them niggas back then son, now look! They at us." Jersey Joe tries to make his point again.

"Aight! Look blood this is what we gone do." O-Dawg cuts off jersey Joe before he gets started on another one of his kill everybody theories.

"Imma call this nigga Butta and check his temperature. If he sounds surprised that means he thinks I'm dead or at least in the hospital. If he starts immediately denying shit, he guilty. Imma try to bring up past situations so I can bait him to admit to the shit. My brother taught me: "If you stare at a picture long enough, even the most perfect picture, you'll find something is wrong."

"Joe and Burnside, no matter what this bitch ass nigga say, don't say nothing!" O-Dawg instructed them while the phone is ringing on speakerphone. "I'm not a star! Somebody lied, I got a choppa in the car don't let me make it outside." Rick Ross gruff voice is blasting out the speakerphone.

"Who dis?" A voice interrupts the music.

"This Butta?" Replies O-Dawg.

"Yeah this Butta, you called my phone."

"Look my nigga, this O-Dawg."

"O-Dawg? What you calling my phone for? We don't rock like that, must be about some money." Butta responds with cockiness in his voice.

"Naw, this ain't bout no money blood. This about me addressing some rumors before I react to them. I'm sure you know some bitch niggas tried to get at me a couple hours ago. Now the funny thing is, word is them was yo niggas, which means you sent them. I told my niggas like hell naw, that wasn't Gutta squad niggas. Them had to be some rookies the way the shit played out. Plus you know how I get down, so you know you'd have to make that one chance count. But on top of everything, we ain't got no issue with each other. I know ever since high school we been kinda distance over me fucking yo bitch Charlene. But shit I'm sure by now you know you can't be mad at the nigga, you gotta blame the bitch." O-Dawg replies with sarcasm to try to get a raise out of him.

"Ay watch yo mouth cuz, that's my baby mom you taking about. Plus when you so called fucked her we had just broke up so that wasn't on me. Now far as that other shit, I don't know nothing about that." You can hear the hostility coming out of Butta's voice.

"I already know my nigga, that's what I was telling Burnside. You know how he is though. Then of course you could be mad that I had to lower my prices on them bricks cause we got so many and too much money. I remember you saying I put a black eye in the game. Then to top it off my niggas had to whoop on Half-dead for trying to be captain save a hoe! And ya'll never got no get back which made ya'll look soft. So I'm pretty sure that's why the streets is putting yo name in the blender, but like I said I don't really believe you had no parts. Too violent, not really yo style." O-Dawg laid it on thick with cockiness and belittling Butta at the same time. The room and phone went quiet for 5 seconds before Butta's voice blasted through the phone.

"You bitch ass slob nigga! Yeah that was my niggas that came through to rock yo ass and you would be sleep right now if you didn't turn pussy and haul ass like the hoe you is. You don't even live up to half yo name pussy! Talking bout violence? When the last time you bust yo gun? Nigga you got way to big for your britches bitch! We tried to be on some coo shit, some get money shit. But ya'll way to disrespectful on that side so it is what it is." O-Dawg just smirked at Boobie before he responded.

"You know what Butta? On some real shit, you got a point." At that moment Burnside hopped up to grab the phone but O-Dawg pushed him back and put his finger to his lips to symbolize silence.

"Like I was saying I feel where you coming from." Jersey Joe is staring at O-Dawg with pure disgust.

"If I was in yo shoes I woulda did the same thing, real talk. Look my nigga we about money over here not egos and bullshit murders. That's for the kids and wannabees. So look ya'll got ya'll get back. No harm, no foul. Lets just dead all this shit before it gets outta hand. Cause how it look right now we all headed to jail or the graveyard. Plus I'm on some rap shit, I'm almost out the game, ya'll can have this shit in a few more months."

Butta couldn't believe his ears.

"So you telling me you willing to squash the beef just like that? That shit almost don't sound right, but I know you been on some fall back just rapping shit. We can kill all the bullshit, but you gotta keep yo niggas in check and get back to the regular prices. Like I been saying, you fucking the game up with that 17 a key shit. This aint 2005 nigga, and you don't know the real Big Meech either. On some real nigga shit, have yo man Burnside shake hands and apologize to my nigga Half-dead if you really serious." Butta had it on thick now. He's been waiting for years to finally get back at O-Dawg and he wasn't wasting the opportunity. He knew in his heart that O-Dawg was a bitch hiding behind his money and an old reputation. He felt it was time for him to be sitting on the throne, his time was finally here.

"Aight my nigga imma holla at Burnside. Consider the prices back to normal and from now on if an issue arises lets handle it like men, on some boss shit." O-Dawg swallowed his pride and replied. Butta just couldn't let this opportunity pass,

"Aight cuzz, you c-safe out here and stick to your word." Butta just blatantly disrespected him.

"Butta my word is all I got and you got my word." O-Dawg just sealed the deal on the truce and lost respect in the process. Butta disconnected the call. O-Dawg looked up and everybody was staring at him dumbfounded. All except Boobie, he was smirking.

Burnside broke the silence. "Nigga on the Mob I aint apologizing! What the fuck kinda shit you on nigga?" O-Dawg stared deep in his eyes.

"I'm on some smart shit, some next level shit. You stay here when everybody else leave, we gone talk about yo apology then. The rest of ya'll stay low-key and get money. I aint never steered ya'll wrong before have I? Leave them niggas alone. No retaliation, bring the prices back up to 23 grand a piece for the time being. We still going to Magic Monroes in two weeks. Fuck with some strippers and celebrate our wealth, fuck them broke niggas. I'm bout to go to sleep, it's been a long day. Ya'll stay in contact and remember what I said." O-Dawg instructed.

They all got up one by one to shake em up and leave. Boobie, Gotti, Jersey Joe, then Burnside. None of them made eye contact. They all was thinking the same thing, their leader had turned soft. When Burnside was walking out the room O-Dawg said,

"You stay here a while, we need to discuss yo apology."

"You serious blood?" Burnside really couldn't believe he was serious.

"Yeah nigga I am, now sit down."

CHAPTER 3

It comes a time in a man's life when he has to decide if he's a man or not.

"**M**arshawn! Marshawn! Wake up, nigga I know you hear me! Wake up!" Olay yells as she's pushing O-Dawg's shoulders while he's playing sleep in the bed. He's a light sleeper, he's been up since she started getting dressed 45 minutes ago. He knew this moment would come, but he was hoping on delaying it until much later.

"Why are you pushing me and yelling this early in the morning? What time is it?" He said then grabbed his I-phone to check the time.

"It's 8:35am, way too early, what do you want?" Olay folds her arms before she responds. "Why you aint tell me you got shot at? You came in here last night like everything was normal, I knew something wasn't right, having meetings at midnight and shit. Since when do we keep secrets from each other?"

O-Dawg finally sits up because he knows it's time to face the situation. He just stares at her for about 10 seconds. She has on her red Nike golf shirt, beige pants, and a red Nike snap back. She has her hair in a ponytail. Even in her golf attire her beauty could not be ignored. She is 5"6, light skinned, hair down to her shoulder, with a petite body frame. But his favorite asset was her slanted eyes due to her having a mixture of Japanese in her. When she's mad and staring it makes her eyes really stand out in a exotic looking way.

"What are you staring at? Are you going to answer my question?" Her voice breaks his concentration.

"I was just sitting here thinking bout how beautiful you are. Like seriously you're a work of art. I'm surprised nobody's painted a portrait of you. Then when you get mad and stare with yo arms crossed it's priceless. Come here baby, come talk to daddy." She just stands there with her face still looking mad. Deep down inside she's smiling, she has a serious soft spot for him but can't let him off the hook that easy. So she replies

"Nigga I done heard it all before in the last what? 11, 12 years? But what I aint heard is an answer to my question! You sitting here procrastinating cause you know damn well you in the wrong. Nigga what was you doing at that bitch Tamia house in the first place?!" He knows he has to answer carefully and be persuasive because Olay rarely cusses, something he always teases her about it.

"So if I woulda got shot at in the Lloyd center or in my car it woulda been no issue right? You not concerned about if I'm gucci or not. All you want to know is why was I at the bitches house right? You come in here yelling at 8:30 in the morning over some bitch? Shit at least cook a nigga some breakfast, give me some head or summin got damn! But since you're so concerned about summin another bitch will never have, let me explain. It's a whole organization called the F.B.I. you've heard of them right? Anyways their calling in life is to lock up drug dealers. Now unless you've forgot how you got all those diamonds and clothes, let me remind you. I'm a drug dealer, I sell drugs.

Now, rule #1 never leave drugs or money where you sleep at. So that means I can't leave them here cause if so, then we're both going to jail. So we smart drug dealers use people's houses that we really don't care about, usually a bitch. So Tamia's house is one of the few that I use. I pay her rent, furnish the spot and whatever else. In exchange she holds my dope, money, guns, and whatever else I need her to. So to answer your question, I was going over there to pick up some dope. Some crabs kicked the door down and we had a shoot-out. They missed, I'm still alive. But what's my fuckin reward? My bitch waking me up yelling the next day talking bout some damn bitch!" O-Dawg responds while faking an attitude.

"Whatever nigga I know one thing, aint no female gone put her life on the line unless she in love with the nigga. So are you having sex with her Marshawn?" She asks, but while she's waiting Jay-z's voice blasts through the room.

"I got a special Ed plug I got it made, if Jeezy's paying LeBron I'm paying Dwayne wade."

"What's mobbin big bro? This early? Aight I'm on the way." O-Dawg hangs up and tells Olay "I gotta go baby, where you bout to go?" She smirks before she responded,

"To this nigga house where I keep my golf clubs at." This sets him on fire and if looks could kill she'd damn sho be dead.

"Aight keep playing with me and you gone fuck around and wake up dead, you and that nigga gone have permanent bunk beds in I.C.U."

"Whatever 'O-Dawg' you know where I'm going." She uses her hand to make quotation marks when she pronounces O-Dawg, the name she never calls him. She turns and leaves, He hears the door slam loud 30 seconds later.

"Stupid ass bitch." He mumbles as he's putting on his True Religion jeans.

ɚↄ

1 HOUR LATER

ɚↄ

Inside Jaxx's house, they're in the front room having a discussion concerning O-Dawg's current situation. Jaxx has on some red and black Chicago Bulls basketball shorts and a white tee. He puts his long dreadlocks in a ponytail, then leans back on the couch. 5 seconds pass, 10, 15, 20, then he finally speaks.

"It comes a time in a man's life when he has to decide if he's a man or not." He lets this game soak in on his younger brother for a few seconds.

"That time comes when he's facing a life sentence or when he has everybody's life in his hands, who follows him no matter the decision. Now with this dilemma a man is going to choose based off logic, the one who's still trying to become a man chooses based off his pride. Now I'm not telling you what to decide, cause I can't be a man for you. I'm simply telling you to weigh your options and respond according to what's logical. Do you care about what the streets are saying about you? Or what your family says about you? You care about money or murder? Do you love making music or running the streets? These are questions only you can answer. But just know whatever decision you make effects the life of others either way. So tell me that look I see in your eyes isn't revenge?" Jaxx laughs to himself for a few seconds.

"You might can trick everybody else with that bullshit, but I'm the one taught you the game. I taught you that look you're doing right now, sitting there playing innocent and shit."

O-Dawg can't understand how his brother can read his eyes so good when his face is showing the opposite. He's been fooling everybody else, but can never pull one over on Jaxx. So he just replies, "So it's 20 thangs in the bag right? How much I owe you?"

"You owe me 300 even, I like how you switched topics too." O-Dawg gets up with the bag.

"I aint switchin nuttin, I was done with that. I already told you I'm having Burnside make his apology known at Magic Monroes next weekend. Is you coming with us?" O-Dawg smirks because he knows Jaxx aint been to a club in the last 5 years. He admires his brothers' self-control and low-key lifestyle but he knows he could never do it. He's addicted to the spotlight, the bad bitches, and the reputation.

"Picture that." Jaxx replies.

"Aight big bro I'll holla in a couple days." O-Dawg stands on the porch and takes in his surroundings. Sees his 745 parked, nothing out of the usual. Then he spots an all-black Benz-C350 halfway down the block. He walks to his B.M.W., puts the duffle bag in the trunk and keeps walking. He hops in the passenger seat of the Benz and pulls out his phone.

"What's up daddy? I don't get no kiss?" Tamia asks from behind the steering wheel. O-Dawg just stares ahead until he sees a person jump inside his B.M.W. and drive off.

"Call Boobie" He tells the Siri command...

"Yeah you good blood aint nobody following you. I'mma hit you on the bat line later." Then disconnects the call.

"You can drive off now Mia." He says without even looking her way.

O-Dawg was deep in thought, thinking about what Jaxx was saying when Tamia interrupts his thoughts.

"You've been sitting there 10 minutes not saying shit, why the fuck you getting in my car with an attitude? You acting like a bitch did something to you!" O-Dawg finally looks at her for the first time. She has on some silk shorts that barley covers her thighs, and a black shirt with Marilyn Monroe on the front that stops just above her belly button. He looks at her butterfly belly ring then down to her expensive sandals. She's wearing her hair down today, his favorite. Her hair easily goes past her shoulders. Hands down she's a dime piece, un-debatable. He leans his seat back then replies,

"Tamia how did those niggaz know I was at yo house? How did they know to kick down the door as soon as the lights went out?" He's staring at the ceiling waiting on her to reply. Once he realizes it's been minutes since he asked his questions he looks at her. Tears are running down her face and she keeps having to wipe her eyes every few seconds.

"Why the fuck you crying? You know I hate that shit." He starts looking back at the ceiling shaking his head. He hears her sniffling before she responds,

"Fuck you nigga! I'm done with yo ass! All the shit I do for you, all the shit I take from you! And you gone sit here and accuse me of trying to kill the only nigga I've ever loved! Can you name one reason why I would do some shit like that? What would I gain? I would only hurt myself! I shoulda been left yo ass! I let you play house with that square golf playing bitch, I let you come and go and do whatever you want to me! But you know what MR. Big bad ass O-Dawg? You gone miss me when I'm gone, I guarantee that muthafucka! Oh and another thing! If I wanted to set you up I woulda done it way better than that.

I coulda had niggaz waiting in the closet or the room. Better yet I woulda had niggaz waiting by your car outside your brother's house. Cause that's when you got the most dope, then went and cleared yo safe out and lived my life happily ever after! Fuck you nigga! Once we get downtown to this condo we're supposed to be looking at together I'mma drop yo ass off. Matter-o-fact don't even come in. Cause yo ass aint never gone be welcome anyways! I fucking hate you! Selfish ass nigga, fuck you!" She screams as she's still wiping tears out her eyes even faster now. He feels like shit because he knows she's right. Her words are stinging deep in his heart.

"If I really thought you set me up you would be dead by now and you know it." That's his way of trying to correct what he said.

"I can't tell nigga. Everybody in the town knows who got at you and they aint dead." Tamia replied trying to hurt him with her words and it worked.

O-Dawg jumped in her face instantly.

"Bitch watch yo muthafuckin mouth, don't get besides yoself. I let you get away with all that other slick shit on the strength that I was wrong. Now you being disrespectful, questioning my manhood. You know of all people how I get down so miss me with that lame shit. And for the record, this is my muthafuckin car and like I said you woulda been dead. You my bitch and you aint going no damn where. Now hurry up and get to this condo so I can see it."

O-Dawg finally leans back in his seat then adds,

"Oh and by the way you look beautiful today, and don't think I didn't notice you wearing yo hair down for me today.

Tamia started shaking her head, "You're the only nigga I know that compliments and disrespects in the same sentence. You owe me a major apology too nigga! But all she hears is him mumble,

"What's up with everybody wanting an apology?" She just keeps driving waiting for him to speak again, but he doesn't.

10 minutes later she was parking in the lot reserved for the condominiums. She's in love already just at how you gotta pass through a security gate to reach the parking lot. She grabbed her purse off the backseat then slammed the door as she got out. O-Dawg is still sitting there staring at her walk away.

"Damn she got ass, I love this crazy bitch." He finally got out and followed her into the building. Inside the building Tamia is talking to one of the managers in the back office.

"So do you know when Mrs. Brown will be available to give us our tour of the condo? It was scheduled for 1:15 and its 1:25 now." Jaleesa Booker, as her name tag read is looking on the computer for the next time slot Mrs. Brown has and herself as well. She knows her co-worker won't be coming in due to her having the flu. She also knows her supervisor will be pissed if the vacant condo isn't leased out. What the hell she thinks, she could use the commission with all her school loans adding up.

"Ms. Rodgers, I have a 2:00 pm opening available. I'll be able to show you around and start the paperwork process if you decide this is where you want to live. Mrs. Brown is out with the flu for a few days." Jaleesa says holding her breath hoping Tamia would wait the extra 35 minutes.

"How about this Ms..." Tamia says as she's trying to read her name tag.

"You can just call me Jaleesa"

"Okay how about this Jaleesa, you let me go check the condo out by myself and I'll be done by 2:00, and if I like it then we can start the paperwork. That way I don't have to wait and you don't have to take on no extra work and you still get yo commission because technically you gave me the tour." Jaleesa started debating the situation. She knows it's against policy to not give a tour and especially to hand over keys that haven't been leased out. She looked around at the other cubicles, her co-workers were hard at work not paying any attention to them.

"Okay I'll give you the keys, then I'll be up there at 2:00 because technically I'm not supposed to hand them over. Its number 410, take the elevator to the fourth floor and it'll be one of the first ones." She says as she passes Tamia the keys.

"Thanks a lot, oh and my slow ass boyfriend should be walking up any minute, most likely. So just tell him how to find it if he comes in." Tamia just got mad again as she was mentioning O-Dawg. Their argument had slipped her mind the last 5 minutes.

"Aight what does he look like so I'll be able to stop him first before he talks to the wrong person?"

"Trust me you won't miss him. He wears Dolce & Gabbana prescription glasses, has waves, and a teardrop on his face. He'll probably have an attitude too." Tamia smirks as she states the last part.

"Okay I'll be on the lookout." She replied as Tamia walked away.

5 minutes later as Jaleesa is talking to herself reassuring herself her supervisor aint gone come in she sees O-Dawg approaching the office door looking confused. Jaleesa couldn't help but to stare and smile at what she sees. She was expecting something totally different. She had him pegged as a regular street looking dude. She started at the shoes like her mom taught her years ago. Black and gold Y.S.L. sneaker type shoes, she could tell the jeans were True religion because her cousin Delroy always has some on. His shirt wasn't too big or one of those skinny muscle type shirts she sees everybody wearing now days. She hates when niggaz wear them and skinny jeans, it's too feminine she feels like. The shirt was black and gold also with Y.S.L. going across the front. She sees all of his tattoos since his shirt is short sleeved. Once the Rolex came into view she knew who was paying for the condo. As their eyes connect she sees a D.G. in diamonds on the side of the frames.

"And this nigga got the nerves to have waves, with his fine ass." She mumbles to herself. They smile at each other as he closes the distance.

"Your here to see the condo with Ms. Rodgers right?"

"Right, how did you know? Never mind she obviously told you."

"Follow me this way please." Jaleesa replies as she's walking around her desk headed to the door. She doesn't want anybody to hear her or ask why he's there. As she walks past O-Dawg he checks her out from head to toe. This bitch bad, he thinks to himself. She got a fat ass too and know how to dress. O-Dawg is rarely attracted to dark skinned females, but for some reason she has his undivided attention.

Jaleesa is 5"7 today due to her 3 inch heels. Her natural hair touches the top of her shoulder. She has it straight down and he can tell it's natural. Green toe nails with some pretty feet, white skirt, and green sweater that fits tight on her, showing exactly how big her titties are. When she was talking he noticed her tongue ring as well. No tattoos or fat on her, she's always described as a thicker version of Gabrielle Union. Jaleesa leads him back to the main lobby and feels his eyes on her ass. Once in the lobby she introduces herself.

"How are you doing today? My name is Jaleesa. I gave Ms. Rodgers the key so y'all could look around while I finish up the rest of my workload. Your original tour host caught the flu so I'm filling in."

"Nice to meet you Jaleesa, I'm Marshawn. Can you give me directions on how to get there? I don't know why she didn't wait for me." He replies as he shakes her hand.

"Take the elevator to the fourth floor, its room 410. I forgot to tell Ms. Rodgers that the condo is fully furnished, if y'all decide to move in it all comes with the lease."

"I'll make sure to tell her. So if I move in how often will I get to see you? Sometimes I be having a bad day and I'm sure if I got to see your smile it would cheer me up." O-Dawg says trying to flirt with her. He noticed how she was checking him out from the moment he walked in. "If you're asking how many days I work a week, it's 5. Monday through Friday, 9am to 5pm. I only work in the manager's offices though. So unless it's concerning your lease or the condo is having problems, chances are you won't see me. Thank you for the compliment, but I'm sure your girlfriend's smile can get the job done."

"You're welcome, and Tamia isn't my girlfriend. She's a special lady friend, it's a difference."

"Well she specifically used the word boyfriend, but that's none of my business either way. I have to get back to work but I hope you like the condo

23

and decide to become a resident. I'll be up there a lil after 2:00 o'clock and nice meeting you." Jaleesa replies while walking away. She turns her head to see if he's still watching her. He is, so she switches a lil harder for him.

"Yeah she on me" He said to himself as he's getting on the elevator.

Once he found the condo and walked inside he immediately liked it. The whole floor has cream colored carpet covering the wood. Nice kitchen and the front room was big. There's also a patio you can access over by the closet in the corner of the front room.

"Tamia!" O-Dawg yelled her name loud so he could find her. "I'm back here in the room."

He walks through the hallway and passes a bathroom to reach the master bedroom. It has a queen size bed set in there and a fireplace.

"This is a long ways from the ville, do you like it baby?" O-Dawg asks hoping she's not still mad.

"Yup." She replies with an attitude. "I see another room to the left, plus it's a bathroom in here too." She added.

"So that's 2 bedrooms, 2 bathrooms. How much every month?"

"Its $2,000 a month, if you don't want to pay that much we can find a one bedroom, I'm sure they got some." She still had an attitude. She's looking at the dresser drawers and admiring the wood. She still hasn't made eye contact. Her attitude is irritating him but he knows it's his fault, so he has to suck up to her.

"We get all the furniture and shit if we move in. Do you like it? You wanna live here?" He asks while approaching her from behind.

"Yeah I wanna live here" She responds as she feels his hands wrap around her. "Get off me, you squeezing too tight. I'm just a bitch right?" She's trying to break loose and get away from the kisses that keep connecting with her neck.

"Baby my bad I was tripping. You know a nigga love you." He says then pauses to start sucking her neck.

24

"I'm under a lot of pressure right now baby. It seems like the more I try to get out the streets, the more they pull me in. Half of me wanna let that lil incident go because it don't mean shit to the bigger picture. I know who I am and where I'm going so that should be all that matters, right? Never mind that, that's irrelevant right. The fact of the matter is I shouldn't take out my frustration on those who love me the most, period. The situation is skeptical, but I shoulda never made you a suspect. So for that I apologize, do you forgive me?" While he's waiting for an answer he slides his hand down the front of her shorts.

"You just gone ignore me baby? You don't love me no more?" He has her pussy soaking wet now from playing with her clit. His other hand managed to slide under her shirt and start playing with her nipple. Once he heard her moan he knew he had her where he wanted.

"Say you still love me"

"I still love you." She whispered back to him.

"You forgive me baby?" He asks while he's slowly pulling down her shorts.

"Yeah I forgive you daddy."

"I still owe you for that performance right?" He asks while leaning her over the bottom of the bed.

"Umm-hmm." She mumbles. O-Dawg has her shorts and thong around her ankles by now.

He slides his pants down fast, in record breaking time. Soon as he was getting ready to slide his dick in he sees his name tattooed on her lower back. She gotta really love a nigga he starts thinking while he's rubbing and massaging her ass cheeks. He slides his dick in slowly, only half way. She takes a deep breath in and starts moaning.

"Baby you wet as a muthafucka, damn." He spreads her cheeks further apart and grips them while he slides the rest of his dick in.

"Fuck, yo pussy still hella tight." He says while he's long stroking her from the back. He's still holding her cheeks apart and going all the way in, then sliding almost all the way out, real slow.

"Umm, umm, fuck me daddy, aww fuck." She's moaning and talking at the same time.

"You want me to beat it up?" He asked her.

"Yeah! Oh, my, gosh! Beat it up, beat it up." She replies in a sexy moan that makes his dick even harder. He lets her cheeks go and watches them jiggle back into place.

"Spread yo legs farther." He instructs her. Then he puts his hands on the bottom of her back and starts speeding up.

"This is how you want it right!?"

"Ohh, ooohh." Is her only reply.

As he reaches full speed it started sounding like somebody was clapping. It made O-Dawg look down and enjoy seeing her fat ass slapping and slamming into him. This turned him on even more so he sped up ramming her.

"Aww daddy! I can't take it, I can't stand." She screamed while falling on the bed making his dick slide out. O-Dawg started laughing then said,

"Wow so big bad Tamia can't take the dick? With all that ass you should be tapping me out."

"Shut up you was going too fast and pushing me, you pushed me over nigga."

O-Dawg just stood back for a minute and enjoyed the view. Tamia laying halfway on the bed with her ass poking in the air and panties around her ankles. "Scoot up a lil so I can go in." She's laying fully on her stomach now with her legs spread. He slides himself in and hears her gasp for air. He starts getting into rhythm bouncing up and down on her ass. Their bodies are making clapping sounds that could be heard from the hallway. He starts sucking on her neck while bouncing than asks,

"Whose pussy is this?"

"Yours." She replied.

"No say it right."

"It's your pussy daddy!" She screams, then "I'm bout to cum nigga!" She yells then grips the covers.

O-Dawg sees something in his peripheral vision. His 1st instinct is to reach for his gun on the floor.

"Fuck niggaz done caught me slipping" he starts thinking while he's turning his head. He was surprised and felt relief at the same time at who he seen at the doorway. Jaleesa was standing there grabbing her titties as they made eye contact. This scenario put him over the edge and had him ready to nut.

"Keep yo face in the cover like that, I'm bout to nut."

He demanded her. After a few more bounces on her ass he pulls out and nuts all over her ass and back. The whole time he's staring at Jaleesa as he's jacking off the last few squirts he has left. When he finished he made a knocking gesture with his hand to tell Jaleesa to go knock on the door.

"You done baby or do you want me to keep going?" He asked Tamia.

"Naw we done, this ain't even our house yet." She replies then starts laughing.

A loud knocking sound comes from the front door.

"Shit that's the lady from downstairs coming to give us the tour and paperwork. Tamia said and then jumped up.

"So what? She can get it too. I'm sure she won't be mad or disappointed."

"Shut up nigga and go distract her while I try to find some towels. This is so embarrassing and nigga she won't like you, you aint even her type. You conceited as fuck, and don't get that bitch beat up while you tryna be funny."

"Whateva" He said then walked out the room.

"I see you found something else besides my smile to cheer you up." Jaleesa says sarcastically as soon as he entered the front room.

"Actually I didn't, that was for her. She had an attitude bout some shit so I had to solve the problem real quick."

"So that's how you solve all your problems, with sex?" She asks.

"Naw that's just one way. But look I see it all in your eyes that you're curious and wanna come fuck with a real nigga so what's up?" He asks getting straight to the point.

"So what, you want me to be wanna your lil play things?"

"Naw I want you to be whatever I need you to be. I don't have play things cause I don't play games. Every person you see around me plays a role whether it's small or big." He informs her.

"So what's her role and what would mine be?"

"Her role is none of your business, and nobody else's is her business. I don't know what I'll have you doing, but whatever it is, it will benefit the both of us."

Jaleesa pulls out her card from her purse and tries to hand it to him. "Here take my card and call me so we can finish this conversation."

"I'm not taking this card. You probably got 100 of those in yo office. Which means 10 of those will be given to some average niggaz. That's the point, I'm far from average. You remember my number, 503-991-4752. Call me later on today. Not tomorrow, or the day after, tryna play those games that females love to play. That's your first test, see if you know how to win and follow instructions." Jaleesa was a lil shocked because she was used to niggaz eating out of her palms.

"Okay Marshawn, I'll call yo cocky ass today." She replied.

"Oh yeah, that's not my name. I said that because we were having a business conversation, things are different now, call me O-Dawg." He instructed her.

Jaleesa's mind started trying to place that name that she knows she's heard numerous times.

"Why have I heard that name before?" She asked.

"Probably because you done heard so many lies and rumors. Most likely cause I run Portland, I'm sure that's why you heard it." He replied with a smirk that showed nothing but pure confidence.

"Ms. Jaleesa sorry for keeping you waiting I had to use the bathroom. We want to move in as soon as possible." Tamia said while entering the room.

CHAPTER 4

I don't like leaving niggas walking around half-dead

The Gutta squad was walking through the Lloyd center mall. All of the heads were present going shopping for the function on Friday and talking about their current situation with Mob Life. Butta was feeling himself and laughing at what he considered to be weakness being displayed from Mob Life. When he laughed it seemed like his whole body shook due to him being so fat.

Butta was 6'1, 300 hundred pounds, dark skinned with waves and was dressed in all black. His huge G.s medallion was bouncing off his stomach. All of the main members had the same chain. The G.s. initials were dripped in diamonds inside of a huge diamond circle.

"I'm telling you Pressha them niggas is pussies. Them off brand niggas is living off an old reputation, when the last time they caught a body? And O-Dawg I done lost all respect for." Butta said while walking through the mall with his squad.

"Gucci Ty, tell this nigga that they pussy."

"They pussy if you ask me." Gucci Ty replied while texting on his phone. He was the flyest one out the bunch and always wearing Gucci, hence the name. He's 6'3, medium build, light skin, with tattoos covering his whole body. He rocked a shortcut that had curls in it. He's often mistaken for just a pretty boy, but he's much more than that. He has G.S. Tattooed under his eye and is known to bust his gun.

"I'm telling you cuzz the nigga O-Dawg walking around half dead." Butta said to Pressha trying to convince him of how he felt.

Pressha who's 6'5 and lanky, with his dreads wrapped in a ponytail was taking everything about the situation into consideration. That was his biggest strength, being a calculated killer. "That's the problem, I don't like leaving niggas walking around half-dead. It's too risky cause at any moment they can come all the way back to life. Regardless of how you feel about them niggas we can't underestimate them. We can't deny the fact them niggas got bodies, no matter how much they done fell back recently. I know personally that O-Dawg aint no bitch, something ain't adding up."

"Man cuz, fuck O-Dawg and all them slob life niggas. When I see them niggas I'm airing them out on site, fuck the bullshit. I just got a handgun that holds 17 .357 rounds. I don't know what the fuck it's called but its got bark. I'm on one and that's on Crip" Said Pull-out who Butta's little brother.

Pull-out is the youngest out the bunch at only 17. Physically he's the opposite of his brother. He's skinny weighing only 160 pounds soaking wet. He's dark skinned with long straight back braids. He always fly due to his big brother being a factor in the dope game. But being fly or being the biggest D-boy was not his goal in life. Being known as the most vicious killer was, something his brother could never outshine or take credit for giving him.

"Man fuck those niggas cuz, let's sit down and order some food." Replied Half-dead. He had it on thick today. Making it appear he wasn't the slightest bit worried about Mob life or gave them any thought. When in fact he had been begging Butta to retaliate since they jumped him. To make matters worse Burnside was still fucking his baby mom.

As they were sitting down in the food court talking and looking for female to get at he spotted a red bone wearing a pink Valor sweat suit waiting in the McDonald's line.

"Ay cuzz look at that bad bitch right there in the pink." Everybody at that table started looking in her direction.

"That bitch got the fattest ass I've ever seen nigga." Dirty Dan blurted out. She was talking on her phone while waiting in line. When she turned her head while putting her hair in a ponytail they all got a glimpse of her face. Then she looked head on at the whole group and every one of them thought she was staring at him.

"Ahh cuzz that's the slob bitch Shanell. She fuck with Burnside but I ain't seen her in a minute. I'm bout to go knock that nigga bitch." Half-Dead said thinking back to how Burnside was rubbing on his baby mom's ass.

"Naw Nigga I'm at that bitch, what you ain't heard? You dark skin niggas is played out." Dirty Dan said to Half-Dead and making everybody laugh.

"Nigga you ain't even black you a muthafuckin albino! What real nigga you know got Sandy Brown hair?" Half-Dead shot back at Dirty Dan. He wasn't fazed though he's been getting called white boy his whole life and fighting.

His mother was white and his father was mixed, half black and half white. He had some type of skin disorder where he looked white and people thought he was until you heard him talk. He had a deep voice, was 6'0 tall and muscular. Over the years he's learned to master his swag and confidence level.

"Half-Dead you ol' knock off young LA fake teardrop having, crooked mo-hawk having ass nigga. I bet a stack I get that bitch number and fuck her before we go to Magic Monroe's." Dirty Dan replied making everybody at the table laughed even harder.

"Bet nigga" he glanced up to go talk to her and ran his hand over his clothes.

"How do I look haters?" He knew he was dipped wearing his Abercrombie and Fitch jeans with stitches in them, blue and white Gucci hoody, with matching Air Force 1's. He walked over to where she was standing in line and stood next to her staring. When Shanell finally sensed him staring at her she asked

"Can I help you or something?" He put his hand out to shake and replied,

"My name is Dirty Dan and I came over here to tell you that I think you're the most beautiful person I've ever seen." Shanell was kind of surprised for numerous reasons. First, she thought he was white until he started talking and she looked more closely at him. Second, she never had a man come over to shake her hand and tell her she's beautiful.

"My name is Shanell and thank you for the compliment. You don't look so bad yourself." She replied with a huge smile.

"Order number 39!" The cashier yelled out.

"That's me, hold on a second." When she returned holding her tray Dirty Dan said

"Here I'll take that for you beautiful and imma sit with you if you don't mind."

"Thank you, and no I don't mind." 25 minutes into their conversation Half-Dead came over and told Dirty Dan they was about to leave.

"Aight I'll be over there in a minute." Shanell watched him returned to his table then asked,

"Them your homies over there?" He turned his head their way then replied

"Yeah, why? You used to talk to one of them or something?"

"No but the last man I was in a relationship with used to have problems with them and I'm assuming you too." She said with disappointment in her voice while grabbing his Gutta squad chain.

"Who was your nigga?"

"You probably know him as Burnside." Dirty Dan sucked his teeth before he responded.

"Man, fuck Burnside. Our issue with him ain't got nothing to do with me and you."

"I know it doesn't but I don't want you to look at me weird. I was never involved with his street life, only reason I know is because the beef was over a female. I guess he was in the club cheating on me, feeling on one of those niggas baby moms ass. I was his woman so that part of the story defiantly got back to me. From the conversation we just had you seem like you got a good head on your shoulders. I'm not trying to act all good almighty but I'm tired of messing with niggas that's only concerned with the streets. You get money, that's cool but you're supposed to be in and out, but niggas don't understand that." Dirty Dan looked at her in a new light now. He thought she was a high-class gold-digger when he first saw her. But from their conversation he could tell she wanted more from life. Plus she was sexy as hell.

"What you know about getting in and out? You sound like you used to play in the game." He said while laughing.

"I know a whole lot, especially since my father and brothers are doing life in the Feds." She replied.

"Oh I'm sorry to hear that." "It's aight, anyways I gotta finish shopping and I know your friends are waiting on you. So do you want to swap numbers or are you not interested in me now?" Shanell asked.

"Hell yeah we gonna swap numbers, let me see your phone so I can call mines."

After the transaction was complete and they both stood to leave dirty Dan asked

"Do you think it's too soon to ask for a little hug?" Shanell started laughing,

"Yeah you can, but don't think you can grab my booty, yet."

"I wouldn't do that." He responded.

"I was just playing, I'm a sarcastic person." She said. While they were hugging he said

"Damn, you smell so good. What kind of perfume do you wear?"

"I'll tell you one day or maybe you'll just find out." She responded flirting a little bit.

"Call me." She said while walking away.

Dirty Dan got back to the table with it on thick.

"What I tell you niggas cuzz?"

"Ay cuzz that bitch is so thick, when you done just make sure you pass her up the ladder." Butta said.

"Ha-ha real funny fat boy." He shot back.

"Did she say anything about Burnside?" Pressha asked.

"Yeah she admitted they used to be together but she really didn't know too much about his street life."

"At least she was up front so we know she aint on no shiesty shit." I know she aint cuzz because I got at her. Ain't like she got at me on Facebook or something. I don't be seeing them together."

"I wish that bitch would, that way we could bury them together. They can have connected tombstones and whatever other romantic shit the cemetery got to offer." Pull-Out said jumping into the conversation.

"Butta, why this lil nigga always want to kill somebody?" Gucci Ty asked.

"I don't know, too much Saints Row and Grand Theft Auto." Butta answered making everybody laugh.

"Man fuck y'all niggas, I bet I dropped the most bodies next time we go to war."

"Ain't gone be no next time lil bro we too busy getting money. What I tell you bout that shit?" Butta chastise his lil brother.

"Whatever man let's shake. I gotta get to Ron Tha Don's house. We got some stripper bitches coming through." Pull-Out replied.

"Yeah c'mon. And tell that hot ass nigga the same thing." Butta said.

The next day Jersey Joe was riding with Burnside in Burnside's 650 BMW convertible. They were on their way to Unthank Park for Gotti's son's 4th birthday party.

"I'm telling you son these niggas out here is food. One call to my sex, money, murder niggas back home yo and it's a wrap. No disrespect to your man's but he going too soft on these niggas. Telling you son we can take over Portland and have it our way."

"Joe how we gone take over something we already control? You just don't understand how shit work out here blood. Far as O-Dawg, that's the most complex nigga you ever gone meet, trust me. This shit is chess to him, he play on a whole different level. Then he's got his big brother Jaxx who's the fucking puppet master. Nigga we ain't made it this far with this much money by accident. When the war pop off trust and believe we gone be left standing." Burnside schooled his cousin.

"Well what's up with that apology shit blood? Word to my mother I ain't never saying sorry to no man yo." Jersey Joe sounded mad just repeating it.

"Look nigga I'm not about to read between the lines for you. I just told you the nigga play on a whole 'nother level."

"Whatever son. Yo look at all these bitches out here in this fucking park! Hurry up and park son." Jersey Joe said excitedly.

Just a few blocks down Pull-out was riding shotgun in Ron's old-school Lexus.

"Ay cuzz you sure you wanna tear these slobs off? Yo brother gone flip the fuck out." Ron asked Pull-out. I'm bout to air these niggas out cuzz. Shit I'm doing my brother a favor, he just don't know it yet. That bitch bet not of been lying either they better be out here. If you scared of Butta than don't do shit, just chill and drive, I got this my nigga."

"Yeah they out here look." Ron said as he was passing the park.

"There go Burnside bitch ass getting out that beamer." Ron said.

"Swing around the block I'm about to let this thang go wild in public on Crip." Pull-out said while making sure his gun was off safety. After they drove back around the block Ron stopped in the middle of the street.

"Right here cuzz, watch this." Pull-out hopped out the car and walked around the back so Ron wouldn't hit him when he started shouting.

"Crip Life! Fuck Slobs!" Pull-out yelled at the top of his lungs while taking aim.

Boom! Boom! Boom! Pull-out started Firing while walking over to the basketball court. Boom! Boom! He saw somebody fall. Boca! Boca! Blat! Blat!

"Burnside I knew yo bitch ass wouldn't let me down." He said out loud to himself. The park was in pandemonium people running everywhere and falling. But he could see Burnside crouching behind a bench shooting back Boc Boc Boc! He seen a bald dark skinned nigga shooting at him now. Bap Bap Bap Bap! Ron starts shooting his deuce deuce out the window at the bald nigga. Boom! Boom! Boom! Boom! Pull-out switched his aim to the bald nigga. Blaatt Blaatt! He seen Boobie running through the field aiming an automatic at him.

"Oh shit cuzz! Get in the car!" Ron yelled. Bap Bap Bap! He responded with his .22. Boom Boom Boom!

"Fuck Mob Life nigga!" Pull-out yelled while shooting and retreating.

Boca Boca Boca Boca! Burnside was up and running now. Pull-out hopped in the car and yelled "Pull out! Pull out! Nigga hurry up!" the back window got shot out while he was pulling off.

"Oh shit!" they yelled. Pull-out stuck his hand out the window while the car was in motion. Boom Boom Boom! Scuurr! The tires were screeching while he turned the corner. They could still hear shooting. After they drove a few blocks Pull-out broke the silence.

"Ay cuzz we got on those slobs tops!"

"Nigga fuck you, you got my window shot out!" Ron replied trying to sound mad.

They drove a few more blocks in silence till they reached a red light. Then they both looked at each other and started laughing.

"We did get on them niggas, but yo brother is gonna be hella mad."

"I don't give a fuck! Nigga on Crip we hit like 3 people. Did you see O-Dawg's bitch ass dive for cover? He was holding a light skinned bitch and a kid. Bitch nigga ain't even bust back." Pull-out replied.

"Yeah I seen that hoe nigga cuzz. But fuck that who was that bald nigga? He was on us nigga!"

"I don't know cuzz, I think that's Burnside cuzzin from out of town. I been hearing lil shit about the nigga. Oh well, just another slob on the list."

"Fuck that nigga, you tryna go to thick ass Domoniq house? Bitch talking bout she love both of us, she might let us G her."

"Yeah cuzz lets go over there and lay low. And she stay in Troutdale, that's exactly what we need. If she on some square shit then we'll make her call her sexy ass cousin." Pull-out replied.

"Aight fuck it, let's go flav out there then." Ron responded while getting on the freeway.

THA LAST OF MY KIND

☙❧

LATER ON THAT NIGHT

☙❧

O-Dawg and Olay were arguing in the bedroom.

"Marshawn this shit is getting worse. I have stitches in my wrist now! How am I supposed to play in my tournament next month with my hand like this?" Olay was referring to the incident that happened at the park earlier. When the shooting started he pulled Olay and his baby cousin on the ground. She fell in glass that was shattered and it cut her wrist deep.

"It's better than a hole in the head right?" he responded,

"What I'm saying is it shouldn't have happened at all! We were at a kid's party for crying out loud. Gotti got shot in the arm, some old man in the leg, and I got my wrist cut!"

"I know baby I'm sorry. I'm going to handle it just give me some time." O-Dawg tried to calm her down.

"Handle it how? By going to kill more people? Then they retaliate and it never stops! All over stupid colors and drugs!" she yelled.

"So how do you want me to handle it? I don't even know who did it! You're confusing me!" he yelled back.

"I want you out of the streets! You're trying to be king of the northeast instead of my man. What happened to our plans?"

"Baby I haven't forgot our plans. I just need some more time. I can't just leave my niggas like this knowing it's bad right now."

"Them niggas are grown! What about what I need? You know what, when I leave to L.A next month if you ain't on that plane then don't even bother cause I'm moving on without you!"

"Without me? Yeah fucking right Olay. Don't get sent back to the hospital talking dumb like that. You got me fucked up, don't forget who been paying for all those tournaments and camp and shit" O-Dawg yelled back getting madder by the second.

"Oh, so now I owe you! Nigga don't forget who was with you when you were broke! Who gave you their whole check so you could buy yo first package? Or have you forgot?" she asked.

"Man what the fuck are we arguing about? Just go to L.A and I'll be down there when I'm done wrapping shit up down here. Then I'm gone push my music shit with spike, what's the issue?"

"No! I'm tired of wondering if you're going to make it home. There's nothing else here for you Marshawn. You promised me! I thought you never broke your word? Either you come with me or don't come at all." She folded her arms the way only a black woman can, to show her decision was final.

"Man I gotta go to Gotti house, check up on my nigga and make sure he straight. I'm gone spend the night over there, give you some time to cool off." He said well trying to kiss her before he left.

"Whatever! Bye." She responded while turning her head so he couldn't kiss her. At the same time that they were arguing Pull–out and Ron were at Domoniq's house in Troutdale smoking. Pull-out was coughing and wheezing.

"Damn Domo yo square ass brother be having some fire!" Pull-Out said while passing the blunt.

"Shut up don't be talking about my brother, especially while you smoking his shit." She responded laughing.

"Man fuck what y'all talking about I'm horny as shit." Ron said while sitting on a chair in the corner of the room.

"You are always horny" she said.

"Baby tell Ron to take his ass home so I can hit that." Pull-Out said while leaning over to kiss her on the cheek, they were sitting on the bed.

"Why I gotta leave? She love me more anyway nigga." Ron replied.

"Get the fuck outta here, I'm flyer than you and I look better." Pull-Out responded.

"Nigga what? I bet my dick bigger than yours!" he challenged Pull-Out.

"Domo, who dick bigger? And who look better?" Pull-Out asked her. She shrugged her shoulders.

"Don't act shy now, keep it real. You say you love us both, so be honest."

"I don't know, y'all are totally different. Pull-Out is sexy chocolate with braids, you like a thug DeAngelo. You stay fly and you got that bad boy persona that I love. Ronald, you light skinned with waves and sexy tattoos on yo body and face. You look like Young Byrd sexy ass. You more laid back an in control like you ain't got a problem in the world, that's sexy in itself. Plus you a go-getter that can dress his ass off."

Pull-Out started laughing hella hard.

"Ah cuzz! She called you bitch ass Young Byrd! All you gotta do now is get yo chain snatched!"

"Fuck you nigga, hell DeAngelo was on TV. butt ass naked talking bout 'how does it feel' knowing damn well niggas was watching that video too! Plus she ain't call you a go-getter. And my name Ron tha Don, not Ronald!" Ron shot back.

"Okay well who dick is bigger Domoniq?" Pull-Out asked.

"I don't know I haven't compared em." She responded.

"Domo, bring yo sexy ass over here." Ron demanded. She got off the bed to walk over to him, soon as she did Pull-Out smacked her on her fat ass.

"oww! Boy that hurt." She said.

Domoniq was older than them at 22. She was black and Mexican. She was built like a stallion. She had ass for days, big titties, hips and thighs. Her hair was long and her lips were juicy. She was 5'6 with no kids and lived by herself. She was wearing some booty shorts and a tank top with her hair in a ponytail. Once she stood in front of Ron she asked,

"What you want?"

"Grab this dick so you can remember how big it is then kick this clown out." He told her.

She put her hands in his pants playing with his dick for a few seconds.

"That shit big huh?"

"Yeah you know it is." She replied.

"Fuck that cuzz, Domo come here and feel this python." Pull-Out challenged.

When she turned around Ron slapped her on the ass. After a minute of feeling on Pull-Out's dick she said,

"I don't know I can't tell, they both big."

"Well who you want to stay and who to leave?" Pull-Out asked.

"Why anybody gotta leave? She love both of us. We both love her so fuck it." Ron said.

"So what you tryna say nigga I'm a hoe?" she asked with attitude.

"Never that, I'm just stating the facts. Ain't nothing wrong with it baby."

"Yeah Domo why you trippin?" Pull-Out added his two cents.

Ron stood up.

"Domo sit on the bed and tell me that you really want this dick to leave." She sat down with her arms folded, confused. Ron walked up and pulled his pants down.

"Grab this dick Domo." He instructed. She started fondling with it. He took his shirt off.

"Tell me you don't love this dick."

"I do love it, you know that." She responded

"What about me?" By this time Pull-out was standing up with his Dick out and his shirt off. She grabbed his

"I love yours too."

"Put it in your mouth Domo." Ron said.

"I can't believe I'm doing this she said before putting it halfway in her mouth. "Aww fuck, there you go baby." Ron said well putting his hand behind her head. She was sucking his dick and jacking off Pull-out at the same time.

Sluuurpp! Slurrpp! She started making sucking sounds.

"Hold up, let me get some head too." Pull-out said. She took one dick out her mouth and replaced it with the other. Now she was jacking off Ron and making sucking noises while she had Pull-out Dick down her throat. Sluurrpp, Sluuurpp. She got into a pattern where she would swap dicks every 10 seconds.

"Fuck, you got some fire head!" Pull-out said.

"Fuck that I'm trying to hit Ron get in the bed." Ron hopped into the bed naked while she was taking her shirt off standing up. Pull-out pulled her shorts down for her.

"Baby go ahead and sucked the homie off while I hit it from the back." Pull-out instructed her.

"Okay." She said while getting on the bed. He slapped her ass while she was getting on.

She crawled to the middle where Ron was laying and leaned over to suck his dick.

"Go hard in the paint, don't stop till you swallow." Ron said while holding his dick. She put it in her mouth and went to work. Pull-out crawled behind her.

"Spread your legs some more, open them thighs up." He said while grabbing her hips and putting his dick in.

"Ohhh." She yelped when he got all the way in. Ron grabbed both sides of her head with his hands.

"Take the dick baby, you can do it. This is what you want, you love us right?" He asked while guiding her head. She nodded her head yes the best she could. Pull-out started pounding hard. He had one hand on the top of her ass and with the other he was doing the dougie, making Ron laugh.

"You like this Gutta squad dick?" He asked while smacking her ass.

"Yes." She barely got out due to the dick in her mouth.

"You gone start letting us hit it like this on the regular now?" She nodded her head yes. He put both his hands on each side of her ass cheeks while he was pumping away.

"Fuck you got some wet ass pussy!" She was sucking Ron's skin off and throwing her ass at pull-out, staying in one pattern she was the happiest woman on earth she had plenty fantasies of this moment and was ready due to her porn collection. Her ass was bouncing all on his pelvis area making loud slapping sounds. At the same time it sounded like she was sucking on a long Popsicle.

"Aww shit, this is the life." Ron said while leaning all the way back enjoying the show. After a few more minutes pull-out popped off the bed and told her to come suck his dick. When she finally took Ron's out her mouth it made a loud popping sound.

"Okay, here I come." She said while crawling over to him seductively. She was on all fours and put the dick in her mouth with no hands. She was bobbing back and forth using nothing but her neck and twisting her face. Pull-out grabbed the back of her head and started pumping her mouth. She wiggled her ass higher in the air letting Ron know she was ready to get fucked. Ron didn't hesitate, he entered her immediately. Dominique was in complete bliss. She was getting hammered and pulled from the back and at the same time having her head pulled forward. She wouldn't trade this for the world, she already busted two nuts going on her third.

"Ahh shit I am bout to nut, swallow this shit." Pull-Out said he then grabbed her head and forcing his dick down her throat as he exploded in her mouth.

"Ahh cuzz!" He yelled while standing on his tippy toes. He pulled his dick out slowly while she was still slurping him.

"Hmm-hmm." She started moaning and put her ass down Ron was going to work on her from the back. Pull-out was rubbing his dick on the side of her face then asked,

"You done with this?"

"Hol-hol-hold on, give me a second." She replied moaning and stuttering. She could barely talk because she was getting pounded and having her ass smacked.

"Ron you ain't nut yet cuzz?"

"Naw but I'm bout to." He responded.

"Well here, nut in her mouth. That way I can hit that one more time." Pull-out suggested. Ron pulled out of her.

"Turn around so I can nut on those big ass titties."

"Hold up, let me get on the bed. I'm trying to get road from the back." Pulled out said while climbing on the bed.

"Come ride this meat reverse cowgirl." He demanded.

She lowered herself on his meat slowly inch by inch. Then she started bouncing up and down until they got into the rhythm.

"Got damn this ass fat." She started rocking back and forth riding him like a stallion. Ron came over right in front of her.

"What about me? I don't get no love?"

"Go ahead and leaned forward and take care of my nigga. I got this back here." Pulled out said while smacking both her ass cheeks and palming them. Dominiq leaned forward and put Ron Dick in her mouth. He palmed her head so he could pump her mouth and because she needed her hands for balance. Pull-out had her ass bouncing and rolling. Her ass was so fat it looked like waves were running through her cheeks every time she rocked back and forth.

Pull-out was running the show. He had her bouncing up and down, leaning back and forth every few minutes. She was screaming loud as she could with a dick in her mouth.

"Lean back I'm bout to nut." Ron said. She leaned back a lil bit. He nutted some in her mouth, then on her face. The whole time she was playing with both her titties.

"Move your hands, let them nipples get some." She did as told and he jacked off on her titties as well. All she did was smile and moan. This was an ultimate fantasy come true.

"Suck the nut off your own titties." She started licking it off. Ron started wiping his dick on the nut, then on her face and putting it in her mouth. She opened wide each time.

"You a freak Domo." Ron said.

Buzzzz! Buzzzz! Pull-outs phone was vibrating on the dresser for the umpteenth time.

"Let me answer this shit cuzz." He pulled his dick out and walked over to his phone.

"What's good?" He answered.

"Man I don't know who did that, I heard it was the Hoovers." He went silent.

"Aight fuck it, I had the drop so I made a move." Silence…

"He right here but he busy." Pull-out said looking at Ron sucking Dominiq from the side laying down. He started slowly stroking himself.

"Aight cuzz we'll be there… Ay break that shit up. My turn, cuzz hold the phone. Pull-out said while aiming the camera at them. Ron hopped off the bed and took the phone. Pull-out through up Gutta squad before he hopped in the bed.

"Lay on your stomach and put the pillow under it." He directed. She did what he said. Her ass was high in the air while laying down due to the pillow. Pull-out laid on her back while sliding his dick in. "Damn bitch you stay wet." After five minutes of him jumping up and down on her ass and her screaming he said

"Whose pussy is this?"

"Yours daddy" she yelled

"And who else's?"

"Ron's, Ron's pussy too!"

"That's right bitch and you bet not let anybody else hit it."

"I won't! I promise." She moaned. Pull-out pulled his dick out and started nutting on her ass and back

"Aww fuck! She got some fire nigga." He kept groaning and jacking off till all his nut was on her.

"Yo turn cuzz, we switching every 10 minutes."

၈၁၈

MEANWHILE AT GOTTI'S HOUSE

၈၁၈

Gotti was pacing the room with his arm in a sling. He was wearing some trailblazer basketball shorts and a bulletproof vest. His usually fresh braided cornrows were all fizzy and his egg shaped head was nodding up and down real fast like he had it all figured out. For some reason he looked skinnier than usual. Gotti is 175 pounds, 5'11 and dark skinned.

"Fuck that blood, it don't even matter who did it. Whoever I even feel like thinks it's funny, I'm killing em. O, I can't do that 33 strategies of war bullshit you be on. Them Niggas almost killed my son! They shot up a four year old birthday party nigga." Gotti said walking even faster picking up one of the remaining guns on the table then putting it back down. Burnside was sitting on the couch playing with his baby dreadlocks. The sides barely touched the bottom of his neck and the front could reach the middle of his nose if he pulled down on it, he had the tips dyed red.

He was light-skinned with tats covering every space on his body. The females told him he looked like gun-play but he would always get mad, and say gun-play looked like him if anything.

"Yes we definitely killing these niggas, right O?" Burnside asked. O-Dawg was busy texting Jaleesa back.

"You can see me tonight if you serious." He text her.

"Yeah, once we find out who did it they time will come. Right now the cops are on us, waiting to see what we do. Especially with Gotti getting hit and that old man." Jaleesa texted back

"I want to see you every night for the rest of my life." O-Dawg read it and smirked then replied

"Ain't been long enough for you to feel that way, and I ain't even fucked u yet."

Jersey Joe was standing up in the corner rubbing his long chain hair and beard. He looked like a Muslim from Philly. Bald head, thick beard, and serious all the time. But when he talked, you knew he didn't believe in no God.

"Blood you already know what imma say. Yo son, why we even sitting here talking bout da shit? Its personal now, kill me dead if I lying cause imma murder one of those crab niggas! They almost popped me B."

Boobie was sitting on the couch playing with a .357 deep in thought. He always looked sneaky and that's because he is. You never knew when he was gone flip out or be waiting in yo bushes. Boobie is 5'8, dark skinned with a low cut. He has bumps on his face that pro-active could cure but he liked the grimy look. His mouth was full of gold teeth, no diamonds. He has a lil gut on him but overall he's medium build. He's what you call a real gang banger. Red dickies, murder one gloves, old school drop tops, and only listens to west coast underground music.

"Man blood, these crabs are starting to really make me mad. Niggas actually served us. Ay I was busting that Mack though huh?" Boobie said.

"Yeah son you did yo thang with that fully, but I was out there looking like Wayne Perry." Jersey Joe commented.

"I'm glad you niggas had fun because I can barely feel my mutha-fuckin arm! Punk ass .22 went to work on me." Gotti jumped in angrily.

"Chill out really, you don't think I'm mad? But acting off emotion is the reason most the homies is up state. We gone fall back and keep getting our money. Let niggas think we pussy and they gone get over confident. We gone play the sucka to catch the sucka, feel me?" O-Dawg said.

"Nigga fuck all that 48 laws of power, Machiavelli type shit you on. I bet them niggas ain't never been shot, because if they did they wouldn't be writing no dumb shit like that." Gotti fumed.

"You obviously don't know who Machiavelli really is then, but that's irrelevant. Chill out and get some pussy." O-Dawg said while reading his text.

"You've fucked me mentally, I need you in my life. What time u comin? What you want to eat?"

"I want dirty rice and chicken. Ill b there in 1 hour." He texted back.

"Nigga I can't get no pussy! Traci trippin, she act like she don't even want me in the room." Gotti replied.

The whole room broke out laughing.

"Joe, I'm bout to give you 10 pounds of fire to ship to jersey. You say you can wholesale em for 8, 9 racks right? Just shoot me 60 racks when you done with em."

"Yo son that's nothing! When you want me on that?" Jersey Joe asked.

"Imma have you ship them in a couple days but let yo family sit on em till you get there. So I'd say two weeks at the max. I need you to do two important things for me then imma ship you out." O-Dawg informed him.

"What two important things? Let me get on them ASAP so we can get this money." Jersey Joe replied enthusiastically.

"You can't do em right now because what I need you to do is connected to the actions of somebody else. It's actually impossible to have you do the first one right now and the second one I'm still working on the details.

CHAPTER 5

*It's gone be some things you bout to see that's
gone make it hard to smile in the future.*

"Aww shit" O-Dawg was moaning in his sleep. He was having a dream he was getting some head. He felt himself waking up but was trying to fight it. His senses started kicking in, he thought he was smelling bacon.

"Aww" He was moaning again. He felt something touching him so he opened his eyes in panic. He slowly started takin it all in. It was all making sense now. Jaleesa was on her knees with his dick in her mouth. She had on a green thong and matching bra. Jaleesa felt him moving and started looking up from in between his legs.

"About time you woke up, I've been sucking yo dick for over 10 minutes." She said then put it back into her mouth. She made her ass poke in the air higher now that he was woke. She started making it clap and O-Dawg leaned up on his elbows to get a better view.

"You love making that ass clap, with yo freaky ass." He said then leaned back. After another 5 minutes of moaning and head grabbing he was ready to nut.

"Aww I'm bout to nut. Take all of it, aww swallow it." He said while forcing her head all the way down. He nutted deep down her throat then let her head go as he relaxed.

"Got damn, now that's how a real nigga is supposed to wake up." He said out loud to himself. Jaleesa still had his dick in her mouth 30 seconds after he busted. She finally swallowed it then started sucking real hard and slurping loud as she made her way to the head. Slowly she took it out her mouth and kissed the head.

"Okay, I'm officially in love with this dick. It's thick, long, smells good, and taste good. I was questioning my skills last night after I couldn't get you to bust." She told him. O-Dawg was laughing inside cause that's exactly why he jacked off in the shower.

"Is this for me?" He asked while grabbing the plate of food off the nightstand.

"Of course. I do it all, cook, clean, suck and fuck." She said while laughing, but was dead serious.

"Enjoy yo breakfast, I gotta finish getting dressed and ready for work. Are you staying here while I leave or coming with me?" She asked while getting out the bed.

Before he responded he grabbed her ass and started massaging it.

"Yeah I'm in love too."

"Don't start nothing we ain't got time for baby, I'm already wet from sucking yo dick." "Imma leave when you do. I got hella shit to do today. I need that list ASAP too." He reminded her.

"I know, and yo money is on the table. I gotta leave in 30 minutes." She said while slowly removing his hand.

"Eat yo breakfast." When she left the room he text his brother Jaxx

"I'm bout to come shower, B there N 45."

ॐ

HOURS LATER

ॐ

O-Dawg walked into his bedroom and threw the brown paper bag by the closet door. Olay was sitting in the bed Indian style watching TV. She had a pint of ice cream in her hand and her eyes never left the TV as O-Dawg made his entrance. She must still be mad he started thinking to himself. He walked over to the bed and tried to kiss her. She didn't move an inch when she stopped him dead in his tracks.

"I wish you would put those lips on me nigga." He was shocked at her demeanor he took a step back then replied.

"Fuck you mean I can't put my lips on you? You belong to me."

"Marshawn go do something with yourself I'm trying to watch millionaire." She said while waiving her hand to dismiss him. This made O-Dawg even madder and she knew it. He walked over to the TV and cut it off.

"There, now you can catch a re-run. We got shit to talk about." he said with anger in his voice.

"Oh now you want to talk? You shoulda came home last night when I told you to. The talking window has closed so ain't nothin we got to talk about." She shot back.

"Olay you know damn well if I woulda came home all we was gone do is argue and yell. A nigga dealing with way too much right now and I woulda fucked around and said some shit I couldn't take back. So I posted at Jaxx spot all night and was thinking."

"Oh yeah? So what did you come up with, with all that thinking going on?" She asked sarcastically.

"How much I love you and how much I never wanna lose you. And how I'm going to find a solution to all my problems ASAP."

"Well there's only one solution to our problem and that's you getting on that plane with me, period." She said while staring deep in his eyes.

"You're really pushing my buttons Olay. I'm really trying to work this out, but you know damn well I don't do ultimatums. So don't forget who the fuck you're talking to while you over there feeling yo self." He replied angrily.

"Well you and yo pride can live here alone and talk about how tough y'all are because y'all don't do ultimatums. But me imma be gone. I've already said what I gotta say. So if you don't like wh-"

That's as far as she got in her sentence cause O-Dawg had managed to knock her ice cream out her hand and grab her by the chin in less than 2 seconds. He held her chin tight and made her eyes connect with his.

"Don't ever disrespect me like that again, I've sent niggas to the next world for less than that. I don't know who the fuck you been talking to that got you all pumped up, but don't fuck around and get both y'all killed, real shit. You've been on some real disrespectful shit recently Olay. You wanna leave? Fine. But don't think you gone disrespect me in the process. You ain't been acting like a real bitch no more anyways! All you wanna do is play golf and argue so I won't be missing nothing." He said with pure anger and let her face go.

Those last words hurt Olay the most. She was still staring him in the eyes. She finally spoke,

"I knew I seen it in yo eyes, you're going back to your old self. All that anger in yo eyes, it's not cause of me. I've known you my whole life Marshawn, I feel you changing in my veins. You haven't touched me like that in years, but I'm not scared because I know you'd never kill me over something like this, but kill, yeah you're definitely going to kill real soon. You can't hide the truth from me, I know you better than you know yourself. I love you, but I'm not gone sit here and watch you self-destruct."

O-Dawg just stared at her face for what felt like forever, thinking. He finally replied,

"You don't love me or understand shit! If you did then you wouldn't be doing and saying the shit you are. Leave the keys on the nightstand when you leave, I'm gone." He started putting his clothes in two duffle bags he pulled out the closet. Deep inside he felt his heart split in half, the good side dying. When he got done packing he took 10 thousand out the bag and tossed it on the bed.

"That's 10 for you to get situated down there. I'm sure you got way more and your coach and his son, I'm sure won't mind helping you. Hell they probably gone convince you to move in I'm sure you gone end up sleeping in the sons bed. Don't think I don't know he's been trying to get you to date his son, only reason I ain't kill them niggas is cause you needed him to perfect yo game, but I'm sure it's gone be a whole lot of practicing now."

When he reached the door Olay's words stopped him. "It don't have to be this way, come with me."

"You right it don't have to be this way, you the one did it. Fuck you, golf and that plane. I hope it crash!" And then he walked out the door. Olay just sat there staring at the door as if he was about to walk back through at any time. When she finally realized he wasn't she laid back on the bed and started crying.

She was crying for herself, but mostly because she knew what Marshawn had just turned into. She felt guilty, she felt like she's the one that brought it out of him. Sure it was on the horizon, but she was the one who officially let it out. She felt she coulda did a better job to contain it, but let her emotions get the best of her. That last look he gave her, she saw nothing but pure evil. Then it quickly tried to hide itself, but she had seen it. Only if she really knew how bad it was about to get.

ⱭXɔ

HOURS LATER

ⱭXɔ

The parking lot to Magic Monroes was off the hook. It was expensive cars and women everywhere Dirty Dan turned his head. He was sitting in his Audi A5 taking it all in. Shanell was sitting next to him watching him stare at some female's ass who was wearing a skirt way too small.

"Damn nigga do you see something you like out there? Don't let me be the reason." She said to him sarcastically. Dirty Dan knew he was caught but lied anyways.

"What you talking about, I'm just peeping my surroundings and seeing who I know." "Yeah whatever. Why are we still sitting here when everybody's inside already?" She asked.

"I'm waiting til the right bouncer pop up. I don't know these other ones and they might not let me pay them off. We should be good in a minute, don't trip." He said lying through his teeth again. Ain't no way that anybody's going to be inside with a gun on 'em. What he was really waiting for was the right moment to make his entrance.

He wanted everyone to see him with Shanell, especially Burnside. It would be the ultimate high for him. Seeing his enemy apologize then seeing the same enemy's eyes as his bitch was hugged up on another enemy. He'd been waiting on Butta's text message for 15 minutes confirmation that Burnside was inside and it was about to go down. The whole Mob Life was in there except Burnside, something wasn't right. Maybe his bitch ass went against O-Dawg command he started thinking to himself. Then he has another thought.

"You know what Shanell? Since you asked imma tell you why I was really staring. It's because a niggas dick is hard. You've been giving me blue balls for weeks now. You come over and kiss a nigga then play with my meat, but won't let me hit. How you gone let me suck yo titties and play with that pussy a lil bit then shut me down like that? That's fucked up. You sitting there looking good as shit with those skin tight pants on showing those thick ass thighs. You got that shiny ass lip gloss on and those titties on display with that blouse. So I'm sitting here with the baddest bitch at the whole function but can't get nothing popping. So I'm looking at these other bitches deciding if I should be sitting next to them instead. Because it's starting to look like, you ain't really feeling me. If that's the case let me know before I get in here so I can do me." Damn why this nigga gotta pull this shit right now. Shit! I've worked way too hard to let this nigga walk away now. Fuck that I gotta make sure he leave the club with me tonight. She was thinking all this before she spoke.

"You right baby, I'm sorry. I have been misleading you, imma lead you the right way now. I'm bored just sitting here anyways." She readjusted herself in her seat and started unbuckling his belt.

"Lean yo seat back and you lucky yo car got tints on it." She told him.

Dirty Dan couldn't believe it he was thinking as he was leaning his seat back. That's all it took was a threat to fuck with another bitch? He was asking himself. Shit if I woulda knew that I woulda been played that card. Yeah this nigga Burnside gone be sick! Hell I might put a baby in this bitch before it's all said and done. His pants are all the way down to his ankles and his dick was in Shanell's mouth.

"Bout time she stop playing with a nigga." he thought to himself.

"Aww yeah, that's it." He was feeling good now and getting harder by the second, as he watched her head go up and down in his lap. Sluurpp! Sluurpp!

"Aww Fuck."

Sluurpp!

"Ay why you stop?" He asked as he opened his eyes.

"My curls keep falling over my face. Hold my hair like this and don't let it go." She instructed as she pulled her hair back into a ponytail. Then she was back to slurping on his dick. He leaned back with his hand in her hair and closed his eyes.

"That's right baby, suck daddy's dick. Aww shit, aww." He said then started moaning.

೨X೨

INSIDE THE CLUB

೨X೨

The dance floor was packed, the tables full and the bartender was busy. The building was almost full to the capacity tonight. Tonight was the wet tee-shirt contest, the twerk contest and the rap battle tournament. This function only happened once a year, so it's always cracking. But tonight was even more epic cause of the special guest that was performing tonight. Spike, whose music name is non-stop was back visiting his hometown he brought his main nigga Juelz Santana with him and Waka Flocka. The females were going crazy and doing anything to get to their dressing rooms.

The V.I.P section was where all the ballers were at. So that was exactly where Mob Life and Gutta squad were trying to outdo each other. While they all were ordering Rose bottles and getting at females O-Dawg was on the couch thinking. He was thinking about his earlier visit with Jaleesa when she brought him the list. She asked about the name Delroy aka Half-dead. She said she kinda knew that name but couldn't 100% place it. Then she got to asking why people's moms and other family members were on there. O-Dawg couldn't get the sense all the way down, but to him it seemed like she has some fear. O-Dawg always thinks the worse and sometimes overthinks situations. I'm just going to fall back and see how she starts acting he was thinking. But if she heard his name, then she shoulda heard the rest because all them niggas be together he said to himself.

"Now when I say Mob. Y'all say Life!" He was interrupted by Jersey Joe standing on the couch shouting with a bottle of vodka in his hand.

"MOB!"

"LIFE!" They chanted back.

"MOB!"

"LIFE!"

The gold diggers were going crazy and niggas was on one.

"When I say we got, y'all say money!"

"We got!"

"Money!"

"We got!"

"Money!" With that last chant Jersey Joe started giving everybody in sight 100 dollar bills.

"Ay blood is that Shanell that just walked in with bitch ass Dirty Dan?" Boobie leaned down to whisper in O-Dawgs ear. Before he could respond Jersey Joe made his way back over.

"Son tell me that ain't the same bitch I use to see Burnside playing house with when I first came down here. She just walked in with the crab nigga, word to motha!"

Now Gotti and the other Mob Life's were listening and taking it all in. A good percentage of the whole Mob was there. T-Soprano, Lil Kenny, Shooter, Squeeze, Faze, Mack Ken, Geno and Dute Fly.

Soprano spoke first, "O, you already know what time it is with me. I've been in retirement, but I got that thang in the car. These niggas on some disrespectful shit, it's whatever." Soprano was older than everybody there at 30. He was short and didn't weight more than 150. He's been on some music stuff the last couple years but was always ready to bust his gun. Especially since most people thought he was a sucka cause he was super fly and a rapper that was only 4 inches over 5 feet. They didn't know that back in his prime he was the main shooter.

"Naw its good T-Spoon, but I'll let you know if I need you." Replied O-Dawg.

"Fuck that let's get on those niggas." Dute and Faze said at the same time, the two hot heads of the group and they both where under 21.

"I'm bout to call Burnside." Gotti said.

"No! Nobody call him. Trust me, he'll see with his own eyes in due time." O-Dawg demanded.

"Watch this blood!" Jersey Joe said while walking over towards the Gutta squad group. "Here, I don't want y'all feeling left out. Cause believe it or not y'all feelings matter to me." Jersey Joe said while trying to hand Half-dead a 100 dollar bill. The whole Gutta squad stood up.

"You trying to be funny nigga?" Half-dead asked.

The Mob Life entourage started walking behind Joe. It seemed like everything in V.I.P got quiet, all eyes on them.

"Naw you right, my bad. Bitches first, where's my manners at? Here gold digger." He said while turning to try and give Shanell the 100 dollar bill. Everybody in the room started laughing. Dirty Dan spoke up.

"She don't need that lil money nigga she fuckin with a boss. It's funny that you got money in yo hand but no bitches in here want you!" Laughter again.

"You got me fucked up Joe, I ain't no gold digger nigga!" Shanell yelled in his face.

"Fuck all that extra shit Cuzz, where Burnside at anyways? Thought you was a man of yo word? Seems to me like it's about to be an issue." Butta said interrupting everybody.

"What you say bitch ass nigga?" Lil Kenny jumped in.

"Fall back lil bro. And Butta this ain't what you want my nigga." O-Dawg finally spoke up.

"Naw this exactly what I want nigga." Butta responded getting closer in O-Dawg's face.

"Shanell you outta pocket bitch. You a groupie bitch, fucking dick hopper." Fallon yelled. She was standing next to Boobie and taking her earrings out.

Fallon was Olays younger sister by two years. She was hands down the baddest bitch in the club. Her body was the complete opposite of her sisters. She was an Amazon. Fallon is 5'10", 36D titties and 24-40 inch hips and ass. Her hair is jet black and you can see her Japanese features better than Olays. Her body was the type that niggas would kill over and would pay anything to fuck with her.

"Butta, it's gone be some things you about to see that's gone make it hard for you to smile in the future." O-Dawg said while still standing toe to toe with Butta. "And Shanell, tell yo nigga to leave that chain alone cause it's not worth the heat. Shit, it probably ain't worth nothing." He said to Shanell while staring deep on her eyes.

"Fuck you say about my chain nigga?" Dirty Dan said while stepping closer to O-Dawg.

"Nigga fuck all this talking in subliminal messages. What's really on yo mind nigga? Cause we bout whatever! Unlike yo man Burnside, he still ain't here. Bitch nigga knew what time it was." Butta said while mugging him up and down. At that point security finally came in the room and everybody quickly returned to their places.

"Joe come here my nigga." O-Dawg said while walking towards a corner. When Joe walked over he immediately started talking.

"O, I already know what you gone say son. But we couldn't let those niggas disrespect us like that in front if the whole club, b."

"Naw its Gucci. It was actually perfect timing, especially when the opps came in here. Almost got outta hand though. Here take this and don't let nobody know what it says. This is yo piece to the puzzle, I need you to follow it exactly to the T." He said while pulling a piece of paper out his pocket and handing it to him. Jersey Joe read it, then reread it for 2 minutes.

When he looked up O-Dawg was smiling.

"I'm confused son, how imma do this when there ain't been no funeral? And the second part says "old man." Is there a specific old man? I'm lost b."

"You lost cause you thinking too much. Didn't I tell you I had two things for you to do? But they were connected to other actions? Just be ready when the time comes. Then go home and move those pounds and be back in 14 days exactly. Part one should happen in four days max. Do part two the next day, aight?"

"Aight I got you son. You's a weird nigga yo, but you smart as fuck. One question. How long you been planning this shit b?" Joe asked.

"Ever since I hoped out that window. Now go enjoy these bitches and don't call yo relative because I know you want to." O-Dawg turned and walked away leaving Joe confused, but he knows now that Joe 100% respects him. In less than a week he gone fear me he started thinking to himself like usual.

30 minutes had passed since the altercation happened and Shanell was still mad.

"Baby, cheer up... fuck them niggas. You don't owe them niggas shit." Dirty Dan said to her cause she was just sitting there looking mad not talking to nobody.

"That was embarrassing Daniel! Do you know how that made me feel? And look? Now everybody gone think I'm a gold digger and can't be trusted." She snapped back at him.

"Baby, only thing that matters is what we think about each other. I know what time it is. And believe me every nigga in here will still fuck with you. I guarantee it."

"Can we please just leave? Let's go to the house and talk about this. Plus I'm tipsy and you still owe me from what I did in the car." She said while whispering in his ear. His dick immediately got hard.

"Come on, we gone." He said while grabbing her hand and walking towards the door.

"Cuzz where you going?" Pull-out asked.

"To the house, I got shit to do. Tell Butta get at me tomorrow."

"Aight, c-safe Cuzz!" Dirty Dan wrapped his arm around Shanell's waist and said,

"I can't wait til we get home, I'm bout to fuck the shit out you." Then kissed her on the cheek. He knew the Mob niggas could see him and that made him feel so much better.

"Here baby, let me open the door for you." Dirty Dan said while opening the car door for her.

"Thank you." When he got in she looked at him and said,

"Now you wanna be a gentleman because you thought you was getting some pussy." Then she leaned back and folded her arms.

"What? Don't start that shit. Fuck you mad for again? Got damn Cuzz you be having way too many mood swings." He replied back to her while pulling out his car.

"What the fuck Cuzz! You see me pulling out!" He screamed out his window to the car that blocked him in.

"Nigga act like he couldn't wait 5 seconds, like he in a rush or sum-min." He said out loud.

"Actually he is in a rush." Shanell said.

"What? How the fuck you know he in a rush? Stop talking out yo ass."

"Bye bitch." She said while opening her door. Dirty Dan thought he heard her wrong. "What you say? What the fuck you doing?" He said while trying to grab her arm. But he missed and she got out.

"Dumb bitch." He said while turning around trying to open his door. It would only open a lil bit. Then he looked up and got the surprise of his life.

Burnside was standing there pointing a gun in his face. He had on a red Milwaukee Brewers hat pulled down to the front. Death was in his eyes, fear was in Dan's.

"What's up pussy? You thought you had my pussy huh? Dumb fuck, you shoulda let Half-dead get at her. You fucked up the plan, oh well y'all all dying anyways." Boom! Boom! Boom! He shot him three times in the face with a .45 handgun.

"I apologize." He said while laughing. Then he reached in the car and snatched off his Gutta Squad chain.

He heard the horn going off behind him.

"Come on!" Shanell was yelling. Burnside was staring at how Dirty Dan's body was slumped over awkward, his head touching the gear clutch. He ran and hopped in the passenger seat and Shanell pulled out the park-ing lot. Burnside put the chain on then asked

"Baby how I look?"

"Oh shit!" She responded.

"What?" He asked.

"When O-Dawg was arguing with Butta he told him it was gone be hard to smile in the future. Then he looked at me and said

'Tell yo nigga to leave that chain alone because it ain't worth the heat.' When he said it I was confused as fuck, everybody was. Everybody assumed he was talking about Dan, even Dan stepped up about his chain. He was telling me to tell you, to leave that chain after you killed him because it would be evidence we did it. How the fuck did he know you was gone take it?"

"Baby the nigga is complex as fuck, he sits in front of a chess board and plans this shit out, literally. Sometimes it's scary how he does that shit. He always tells me that you know you're on a master level when you can tell somebody to their face you're going to kill them and disguise it so they have no idea what you are taking about until it's too late. He's saying those people aren't worthy of battle. What I'm saying is, he told everybody from they click they're all about to die to their face. But at the same time he's threatening the whole club."

"I'm confused, how did he threaten the whole club?" She asked.

"He's making an example out of them crabs. When it's all said and done they are going to remember his words and understand the true meaning when those Gutta squad niggas are dead. Then everybody that heard it will instantly have fear of him, because now they understand what he did. Then at the same time he's proving to himself nobody is worthy of battle cause they didn't know at the time he was threatening them too. You get it?"

"What kinda shit is that nigga on? He taking this way to serious. So don't you think you should throw that chain out?" She asked.

"No." He replied.

"Baby he said not to keep it for a reason."

"I know, but he knows me too good. He only told you to tell me so I can remember that he knows me way too good." He broke it down to her.

"So basically he's threatening you too?" She asked.

"That's exactly what he did baby."

"I seen him in the corner talking to yo cousin then pass him a note and point to it. He looked like he was tryna be sneaky when he gave it to him."

"Naw, that's how he wants it. So people remember that part too. Trust me. He gave Joe his piece to the puzzle, that's not good for somebody."

"Why he don't tell us the whole plan?" She asked.

"Imagine if the whole Mob knew you was setting them crabs up. Sure everybody woulda acted, but that anger and surprise wouldn't be in their eyes. And a nigga like Pressha woulda picked up on that shit. Everything has to be perfect for the plan to work. Don't trip, all the homies will know by tonight." Burnsides phone went off, he had a text. He read it then let her read it. It said,

"I know she confused and at the same time has a clear understanding too! Tell her I love her and we're the last of our kind."

"Baby."

"Don't ask, he just knows. Plus you're a female, y'all ask questions." He interrupted her.

"He just threatened me too huh?" She asked.

"Now you're getting it."

"But why?"

"So you don't snitch in the future." He told her and she leaned back in her seat, taking it all in.

"Fuck him, I'll never snitch."

CHAPTER 6

Get the fuck out my house, don't call
me till you kill somebody

O-Dawg put his phone back in his pocket after textin Burnside

"C'mon ya'll grab whatever ya'll taking and lets shake" O-Dawg announced to the crew that was busy taking shots and talking to females.

"Leave? Fuck that its poppin in here what kinda shit you on I'm tryina see the twerk contest" lil Kenny responded confused at why he suggested something so stupid.

"Aint gone be no twerk contest I hope y'all parked round the corner like I told ya'll too. We got 5 minutes before we be stuck here all night. We gotta slide out the back right now." O-Dawg instructed while getting up and making sure he wasn't leaving anything.

"That's the point I'm tryna be stuck here all night and tomorrow, ya'll feel me?" he said while shaking Faze up and making everybody laugh.

"O why we going out the back on some sucka shit?" Dute Fly asked.

"Gotti, Boobie and Joe lets go. Let these gangstas stay here wasting time we aint got." O-Dawg said getting madder by the second.

"Fallon you need a ride home because you damn sho aint stayin here."

"Naw I'm riding with Boobie C'mon lets go I'm ready." She responded standing up and putting her purse on.

"Fuck blood I guess we leaving." Lil Kenny complained then stood up to grab a bottle.

"What's up ya'll coming with us or what?" Shooter asked the females that were in v.i.p. with them.

"Coming where?" one of the females asked.

"We got a suite at the Hilton let's take the party over there." Lil Kenny answered.

"We all can come right?"

"Hell yeah and call some more too." Dute said making everybody laugh.

"Ya'll c'mon and make sure ya aint leavin nuttin cause you won't be able to get back in." O-Dawg said.

"Yo Ron look at dem bitch niggaz getting ready to leave." Pull Out said.

"Yeah cuz they knew what time it was and they going out the back." Ron said.

"Yo Gotti." Pull Out yelled out. When he looked over Pull Out started rubbing his arm,

"How yo arm?" He yelled and was letting him know who did it. Gotti tried walking over but was stopped by O-Dawg who whispered in his ear and they both smirked.

"Fuck they smiling at cuz like they know summin we don't." Ron asked. Then Shooter flipped them off so they returned it and threw up Gutta Squad.

"Fuck dem pussy niggaz that's why they leaving early." Ron stated.

5 minutes later they struck up conversations with two females they used to go to school with.

"Nisha, is you and shay coming back to the spot with us?" Ron asked. Nisha is light skinned, thick with green eyes due to her being mixed. Ron has been trying to get at her for years.

"What's the spot and you bet not say the hotel." she responded.

"The spot is our apartment."

"What's to do there that we can't do here because you know I'm not one of your groupies Ronald." Pull Out started laughing hard on the couch and spilled some of his drink.

"Cuz she just called you by yo government! Did you see her face that shit was epic. Tell her what's at the spot Ronald." He said then busted out laughing again.

Shay who's dark skinned with big titties on a petite body interrupted his laughing spree. "I don't know why you're laughing MALCOM, what kinda name is Pull Out? And why don't you tell me what's at the spot."

"I almost threw this fuckin drink in yo face let me sit this down. 1st off don't ever disrespect me like that again I'm not Ron, ain't no nice guy shit with me. I treat bitches just like I do these slobs. 2nd off I stay pulling out money, pistols and if she bad ill pull this dick out." Pull Out checked her while making everybody laugh. Then he pulled money out of his pockets along with a knife from his hoody.

"I couldn't get my smack in here so I got this." he said making everybody laugh harder.

"Ok, I see the money and your knife pistol but where the rest at MR Pull Out." Shay challenged him making everybody stare at him.

"A nigga I know you ain't gone let her blast you like that." Half Dead said from across the room. Pull Out picked up his drink and started sipping real slow then responded

"That's the answer to yo question bout what's at the spot, This DICK." He yelled making everybody laugh again.

"C'mon here baby let me talk to you come closer." Pull Out said tapping the space between them.

"I can hear you just fine from here." she replied with an attitude.

"Shay bring yo sexy ass over here." He said with a lil force in his voice. She sucked her teeth then scooted over with her arms folded.

"Happy?" She asked.

He grabbed her around the waist and made her sit on his lap.

"Now I am, why you sitting here with an attitude when everybody smiling you to pretty for that." He asked her.

"Because I'm the only one got niggaz threating to throw drinks at her."

"How you expect me to react when you came at me like that? If you gone be my bitch you gone have to behave yoself in public." She screwed her face up then responded

"Who said anything bout being your bitch I barley even like you right now. I don't even know why I'm sitting on your lap."

"I'm the one who said it let's cut the crap and keep it real. You know you feeling me like I'm feeling you. A nigga been tryna fuck with you since high school so you know I got love for you, so you can sit here and be mad or you can let me make it up to you. You gone let me make it up to you baby?" He asked then started kissing her neck and cheek

"You don't got love for me no more?" He asked. Rashay shrugged her shoulders.

Pull Out grabbed her chin and turned her face so she was looking right in his eyes. Their noses was touching and they were both silent for seconds.

"No more games all that ends tonight." He told her then started kissing her. First she tried to fight it then she gave in and started tonguing him back.

"So that's what's at the spot Ronald some dick?" Nisha asked while they were looking at their friends kiss.

"It's a whole lot of shit there we can watch movies or just talk. It's whatever you wanna do I'm just tryna spend some time with you."

"Is that what you tell all yo bitches to get em over then seduce em?" She asked with a attitude.

"Enjoy the bottle of Rose you can have it." Ron answered then got up to walk away but she grabbed his arm pulling him back.

"Why you leaving?"

"I'm not bout to sit here and play these games with you. You not bout to waste my time with yo punk ass attitude and 21 questions. You must think I'm soft or summin cause I try to be respectful and laid back. I'll flip the fuck out in here but instead of doing all that imma go find a bitch tryna fuck with a real nigga. So take your hand off me and enjoy the Rose like I told you." He chastised her.

"I'm sorry I made you feel that way I just didn't want you thinking nothing ratchet bout me. Can you sit back down?" She said with all the attitude gone now. Just when he was getting ready to respond the v.i.p. door flew open smacking loud against the wall.

"A cuz ya'll niggaz better get outside right now." Smelly said out of breath from running up the stairs. Everybody from Gutta Squad hoped off the couches and were staring at him

"Fuck you talkin bout nigga go outside for what?" Butta asked while throwing a female off his lap.

"Yo boy Dirty Dan just got smoked in his car and the boyz got everything taped off."

"Is the bitch dead too?"

"On Rollin Crip aint no bitch out there cuz." Smelly replied. They all started running towards the door

"I told ya'll summin was funny with that bitch." Pull Out yelled while rushing outside.

When they made it to the parking lot they seen the police had everything blocked off. Everybody was standing around being nosey trying to figure out what happened.

"Here come this faggot ass pig." Gucci Ty said. Butta watched detective Pacman and his partner detective Canfield make their way over to him. Detective Pacman was white bald and had a huge nose. Canfield was black with dreadlocks and tried to act like he was hood. He was the worst type, a straight up house nigga. Canfield finally came face to face with the group. "How you doing Mr. Mcloud what's poppin with you?" He asked Butta.

"Cut the shit you know damn well what my name is. Tell me what happened to my nigga." Butta replied.

"We came over to ask ya'll the same questions. So why don't you help us do our jobs and tell us who ya'll beefing with. Did anything happen inside the club that would make someone kill em soon as he got to his car? Give it to me straight."

"Naw aint nothing happen and we aint beefing with nobody. Is he the only one in the car?"

"Was there supposed to be anybody else in the car?" Pacman jumped in and asked.

"I don't know I'm just asking." Butta answered.

"Were going to most likely rule this a robbery homicide since we have evidence pointing that way and ya'll aint beefing." Canfield said then smirked.

"Fuck you mean robbery?"

"Those chains ya'll wear to rep ya'll gang, well his is missing unless he wasn't wearing his. So he must of put up a fight and got shot in the neck and face unless he didn't have it." They all looked around at each other for a few seconds without saying a word but their faces told the story.

"Ummh that's what I thought if you boys wanna talk ya'll know how to get in contact." Canfield said then walked away with Pacman.

"Ya'll niggaz get to my spot." Butta spat angrily walking away.

ೱೲ

THE MARRIOT

ೱೲ

Burnside and Shanell were laying in the bed talking after they just got done showering. Burnside was leaning against the headboard with only his boxers on. Shanell had on her bra and panties and was laying on her stomach rubbing his neck.

"How many people really know what your name means?" She asked.

"Anybody that's smart enough to put what happened tonight together. It's simple he got burned from the side so it must of been Burnside." he responded laughing to himself.

"Bernard shut up I'm serious you act like I don't know the truth. This is me is that you? When we have kids I'm going to be the best mom ever. I just can't understand how a mother can burn her own son with an iron."

"Man fuck that crack head bitch blood why you even bring that bitch up."

"I don't know I was just looking at it and rubbing it so it made me think. But while we're on the subject I bet not hear bout another bitch knowing your secrets I know that much. You act like you faithful but I know you're not nigga. You think I forgot bout that lil stunt with Felicia in the club?" She said with major attitude in her voice.

Burnside was confused as hell.

"Were the fuck is this coming from didn't you just see me kill a nigga today and you sitting here coming at me like I'm a sucka."

"Bernard please you aint scaring nobody with that killer shit. You act like you ain't seen me stab niggaz or have you forgot bout when you was getting jumped in the club. The reason I brought it up is cause I'm sitting here thinking bout how I risked my freedom for you. I got to looking at yo scar and thinking why this all started. Cause you putting yo dick in another bitch's mouth, you just nasty for no reason. What don't I do for you sexually?" She asked.

"Got damn stay on one topic you went from my mom to stabbings to yo freedom. Then to getting my dick sucked now you wanna talk bout sex? You're weird. Freedom? Man you like doing that shit you get to role-play and dye yo hair and whatever. And who said I got my dick sucked?" He replied.

"Whatever nigga let me find out you giving my dick away and I promise imma shoot you. You can call my bluff if you want to." She said while gripping his dick.

"How you go from never hurting me to shooting me in less than a minute? You a crazy ass bitch you know that."

"Yeah I know you just make sure you know nigga." Shanell said then straddled him.

"I love you punk." Then she kissed him on the lips. Burnside put his hands behind his head and smiled.

"You just want some dick and you aint getting none."

"Yeah right I'll take this dick." She shot back.

"I'll die for my niggaz dawg." Rick Rosse's voice started rapping stay scheming from the phone on the dresser. Burnside reached over and grabbed it.

"What you want nigga." He answered.

"You a bad man ya heard." Jersey Joe yelled through the phone.

"What you talkin bout nigga?"

"A son don't try to play me yo! I like that, but my shit gone be way more live. The homies over here said what's poppin we at the Hilton on some wild shit. This nigga Dute got regular bitches turned into strippers no lie." Shanell took off her bra and started squeezing her titties together.

"Get off the phone." Burnside flipped her off.

"Yeah Dute stay on some ratchet shit, he bout to turn it into King of Diamonds. Nigga you thought the mob went soft huh?" Burnside asked.

"Son ya boy O-Dawg is a beast ya heard I fucks wit em. The nigga maps everything out yo. Matter fact where Shanell and don't say she ain't with you ya'll ain't slick." Joe demanded "Here take the phone." he said passing her the phone.

"Hello" she said with attitude.

"And just to think I was gone kill you. You can't keep the god in the dark like that." Joe said getting pumped up.

"Yeah I love you too were busy bye." She replied then handed the phone back.

"Blood what's up with that note O gave you? I know it's some triv and I want in." Burnside told him.

"Oh now you wanna be partners after you played me? You ain't shit son." Shanell kissed him on the lips before he could reply.

"Daddy hang up the phone." She whispered in his ear then started kissing his neck and worked her way down his chest.

"That's what O wanted plus yo hot ass wouldn't have went for it anyway. You'd smoke em in front of everybody." Shanell took his boxers off.

"Yeah son, I got some shit lined up ya heard?" Shanell now had his dick down her throat. Burnside watched her head go up and down as she started making slurping sounds and bobbing her head faster.

"Aww shit." He moaned. He could hear Joe talking but wasn't listening.

"Blood imma hit you tomorrow." He told Joe who started laughing then responded.

"I see what time it is I'm bout to get in summin wet myself. I'll see what's poppin tomorrow son." Burnside hung up.

"Take it out and lick it." She took it out and kissed the head then started licking on the sides with her tongue ring. She kissed everywhere after she licked it.

"Like that?" She asked then slowly put it back in her mouth inch by inch. Burnside leaned back and enjoyed the show.

"Take yo time till you swallow."

೧೦

BUTTA HOUSE

೧೦

The group was sitting in his basement deep in their own thoughts. Butta was pouring himself a shot of Hennessey. After he downed it he started pacing.

"How the fuck did we let this happen? How didn't we see this coming!?" Butta yelled his questions to his squad.

"They used that bitch to rock us to sleep cuz." Pull Out offered his opinion. "No shit Sherlock I'm talkin bout how the fuck they knew we was at the mall that day? At the right time." Butta chastised him.

"Shit I don't know and why the fuck you got an attitude with me nigga." Butta pointed at him then at Ron.

"Cause it's ya'll fault the homie is dead that's why! If ya'll didn't shoot that fuckin park up none of this shit woulda happened!" Butta yelled.

Pull Out jumped off the couch lighting fast and replied,

"Cuz you got me fucked up don't ever put the homies death on me like that. Big brother or not we can go there. Nigga they planted that bitch way before we did that shit. You the one fucked up by paying those niggaz to run in his spot in the ville." He yelled back with his pants pulled up and fists balled up.

"Who said they planted the bitch at that time how you know Burnside didn't knock her back just to get at us." Butta shot back but he knew he was stretching it he just couldn't admit he fucked up.

"That would be a big fuckin coincidence and you know it." Pull Out fired back. Butta walked to a corner and picked up two bags then threw them at Pull Outs feet.

"There go some pistols and a chopper nigga. Ya'll aint even pose to be here ya'll ain't earned ya chains yet but ya'll bout too. Pick up those guns, get the fuck out my house and don't call me till you kill somebody. I don't care how you do it or when you do it. You niggaz kill anybody that's associated with dem mob slobs now go handle ya'll business" Butta said dismissing them.

The two brothers stared at each other for a few seconds then Pull Out picked up one of the bags.

"Aight cuz, you got that c'mon Ron time to catch a couple bodies." Everybody watched them leave the room with murder written on their faces. Pressha was just sitting there shaking his head as they left.

"What's up pressha why you shaking yo head?" Butta asks.

"You just gave a bunch of guns to two hot heads that's why. They bout to have the city on fire, they bout to kill or get killed and that's if gangtas don't get em first. Then to top it off all the heat gone fall on us and you wrong for blaming the homies death on them." Pressha told him keeping it real.

"You don't think I know all of that cuz? We gotta fight fire with fire and those two niggaz is on fire. Plus it's bout time they earn their keep."

"So you basically using them as pawns." Gucci Ty asked

"If that's how you wanna word it then yeah. We done all been pawns before growing up in this game and we all knew if we made it across the board we could turn into any piece we wanted to." Butta responded. He looked around the room to see if anybody disagreed with him. He also wanted to see if anybody had fear in their eyes, there was none. He noticed Half Dead with his head down and hand in his hoody. Every time he did lift his head he saw water and anger in his eyes. Butta knew he was taking it the hardest because him and Dan were best friends.

"Half what's up my nigga why you over there quiet with yo head down." Butta asked.

"Aint nuttin to talk about I don't even understand why we here and not out lookin for those niggaz." Half don't forget those niggaz left out the back just on time. Them niggaz is laid up with some bitches somewhere. They probably aint gone show they faces for a few days cuz. You know how many snitches done talked to that house nigga Canfield by now?" Pressha said trying to calm him down.

"We gotta think this shit out and move calculated. We need to find out where them niggaz live at and what bitches they fuck with. Let Pull Out and his squad keep the pressure up while we do the plotting." Pressha spoke to the whole group giving his opinion.

"The best one to get is Boobie that nigga always trickin in the clubs and fuckin with rats. Plus he's O-Dawg's right hand man and next to take over." Gucci Ty said throwing his two cent in.

"Look cuz it's been a fucked up night let's take the night off to come up with different plans and we'll meet back tomorrow. We too mad to really think anyway." Butta said while pouring himself another shot. Everybody got up to leave shaking him up as they left. When everybody was gone he decided he was gone sleep down there for the night. He put in his favorite movie Scarface and plotted how he was gone take over Portland and be the next Tony Montana.

CHAPTER 7

I don't want this life no more my nigga. My hearts no longer in it and aint no future in it. These niggas gone make me kill them then what

It's been a few days since the murder of Dirty Dan. The main members of Mob life have been laying low but that didn't stop the rise in gang shootings. It was a domino effect once the first shooting happened they just kept going. In the last 4 days there have been 20 gang shootings but no murders. O-Dawg was in his condo sitting in the front room talking to Boobie. Boobie had just took his last hit of the blunt and passed it to him.

"O don't you think it's time to start giving these niggaz the business? All these back and forth clackings is making the town hot. Let's knock these crabs off and be done with it." Boobie complained.

He has personally been involved in 4 of those shootings, but 3 of those he was the target and had to shoot back to save his life.

"Boobie what are we doing my nigga? We hopped in this game cause we was starving and our stomachs were touching our backs, now our backs are touching Benz seats. We made it so why are we still here." O-Dawg kept hitting the blunt while waiting for Boobie to respond.

"You wrong and you know it blood. Yeah we hopped in this dope game to get rich but don't forget it's Denver Lanes over everything.

We had that when we had nothing, way before you got that 745. Without the blessing of the G homies this Mob shit wouldn't exist. They let us branch off long as we didn't forget our roots and it seem like you forgot! We got big and our money got long now you think we can just walk away? Nigga Notice got killed bout this! Turk got killed bout this and Stix is rolling in his grave if he can hear you. Yeah we chose this mob shit but this life, we was born into that and that's forever. So what are we doing? We're killing crabs and getting money. We got the both of best worlds what else is there to do? This bout Olay huh? Nigga fuck a Benz and a bitch this the mob till we die period!" Boobie yelled and snatched the blunt back.

"I don't want this life no more my nigga. My hearts no longer in it and ain't no future in it. These niggaz gone make me kill them then what? Some new click gone pop up and challenge us for the title. We gone be having this talk again then we gone have to kill them too. Naw fuck that I'm done blood I'm shaking to Atlanta with Spike. You know they only know his as non-stop? He done created a whole new life and getting money. I'm bout to push this music shit my nigga."

"Fuck you mean aint no future in this? Rappers get killed too nigga. Aint no future for niggaz like us life's a bitch then we die, simple as that, but while we here we gone get this money and hold it down. We in the middle of a war and you talkin bout leaving town?! If it was anybody else I would say you sound like a bitch." Boobie said with emphasis on the last part.

He knew this would make him feel like he was questioning his manhood.

"Naw nigga I sound smart just because I don't wanna stay here and die that make me a bitch? Because I'm tryina change my life!" O-Dawg replied raising his voice.

"This is yo life nigga!" Boobie yelled and jumped off the couch. O-Dawg jumped up and was about to yell back when Tamia walked into the room

"Marshawn it's 1:30 in the morning and yall yelling like we aint got neighbors. They will call security and yall smoking with guns in here and shit. Niggaz do the dumbest shit." She said then headed to the kitchen. They both sat back down.

"She always talkin shit blood." Boobie said.

"Don't think I can't hear you Devon." She replied from the kitchen. They looked at each other shaking their heads.

Tamia walked back in drinking from a bottle of water.

"I'm going to bed baby I'll see you when you get in." She said then kissed him on the lips. He grabbed her ass with one hand,

"Aight baby." he responded.

"Goodnight Boobie I'm sure I'll see you soon. Love yo pimple face ass." Then she took the blunt from him and headed back to the room. Soon as she hit the hallway she turned back around.

"And you better leave my baby alone."

"Fuck you beaner." Boobie responded while smiling.

"I'm half Dominican not Mexican dumb ass." She said then flipped him off before disappearing into the room.

"Look bro, I'm done. Simple as that. I don't know why you acting surprised you knew this was coming. I'm still the same nigga though whenever you need me I'll be here. Imma go holla at Jaxx in a few days and tell em I'm giving you the keys, and when I blow up with this rap shit you already know I'm funding the movement." O-Dawg broke it down trying to get him to see the picture.

"How you think Gotti and Burnside gone take it cause Burnside got that ego and I'm sure he was expecting the plug."

"Gotti don't want the headache or responsibility and Burnside gone have to accept it. Tell em you playing behind the scenes and he can have the streets. Either way we gucci we aint never had problems and won't have none now."

"You sure bout this my nigga?" Boobie asked one more time while getting up to leave.

"Yeah I'm done bro we'll meet up after I talk to Jaxx. Matter fact he wouldn't accept Burnside anyway because he always say he too hot."

"Aight blood I'll fuck with you tomorrow." Boobie said then stuck his hand out for their mafia handshake.

"Money over most."

"Loyalty over all." O-Dawg said finishing the creed.

Boobie opened the door and before he closed it O-Dawg said,

"It's always gone be Denver nigga." Boobie nodded his head and walked out.

ॐ

NEXT MORNING

ॐ

Boobie was laying in his bed watching Falon get dressed. He like everybody else that's laid eyes on her was amazed at her body. Since he is only 5"8 he's always been infatuated with amazons. He's never seen a female thicker or more put together than she is. Falon was looking in the mirror while putting her bra on. She seen Boobie staring at her ass so she started wiggling it. She knew that drove niggaz crazy because of the huge

83

butterfly she had tatted covering her ass. So anytime her cheeks started clapping it made the wings look like they were flapping.

"You keep doing that and imma bend you over that dresser." Boobie said while grabbing his dick. Falon looked over her shoulder and replied,

"Didn't you get enough last night." Boobie smirked.

"Nigga can't never get tired of runnin yo thick ass. If I didn't have business to take care of I'd fuck you for a few more hours."

Before she could respond her phone started vibrating. She seen it was a text from Jersey Joe

"Bizz 2 take care of. Need extra hours 2 get u". Good cause I gotta go home and shower anyways. Shit if Boobie bout to really take over than I'm done with you anyways she was thinking to herself then texted back "OK."

"Tell yo boyfriends you can't talk while you at a real niggaz house." Boobie said while getting out of the bed.

"Who said it was a nigga and you sound jealous to me." She shot back.

"Blood you must be out yo mind I'm just fuckin with you. I know what time it is just like you do. When we together than were together and when were not than were not. You aint my bitch and I aint yo nigga. So don't get it twisted you don't see no handcuffs or car seats in the back of my impala." He shot back sounding mad while looking through his closet. I guess I just fucked my plan up she started thinking.

"Well you're the one made it this way." She replied trying to check his temperature.

"Come on with that shit blood don't sit here and say I'm the one who did shit. I aint the one textin other bitches after I just fucked you."

"What if I told you, you sound dumb because it wasn't no nigga?"

"Falon shut the fuck up you starting to make me mad. On all my dead homies if you show me that wasn't a nigga. I'll move you in my spot right now and buy you a Benz." Falon just stood there staring at him with her face twisted up.

"That's what I thought. I aint got time for this shit a nigga got way too much going on and it's bout to get worse since O stepping down. So let's kill the baby mama drama and enjoy each other while we can."

"Whatever do you really think O retiring? That don't even sound right I don't know what my sis did but it worked." She asked him

"Yeah he done I can see it in his eyes that he tired of this shit I don't think It's all yo sis either. He seen the homie Spike make it so he really tryna push his music shit. Add that with Olay moving and all the drama out here, yeah he done." Falon was dressed now and leaning on the dresser.

"Do you ever think about retiring when you reach a certain amount of money and having kids?"

"Fuck no retire and do what be a high school basketball coach? Fuck outta here I'm only 24 and aint hit my prime yet. Far as kids go if it happens than it does. But I'm not asking god for none at night. I'm a hoodlum and a killer so it's more than likely imma get killed. So why plan on destroying some kid's life? Naw I'm good on the family guy shit."

Falon put her purse on and headed towards the door.

"You know I hate when yall be talkin bout dying. Aint nobody gone die so stop saying that shit." She said then walked out the room.

"Ask that nigga you was textin I'm sure his square ass want kids!" He yelled back at her laughing

"Fuck you." He heard her yell back before the door closed. He was sitting on the bed rolling a blunt thinking how things were about to change then broke out laughing.

"I can't believe this bitch talking bout kids and shit. Bitch lucky I aint slap her all the money she been getting from me shit." He stopped talking to hit the blunt a few times.

"Fuck bitches they all snakes anyway. I'm bout to get this money and blow half of it at the strip club let me go make sure this bitch locked my door."

കൈ

THE BURIAL

കൈ

Pull Out had just got done watching Dirty Dan's casket get dropped in the ground. Some lady was singing while most the females were crying. He looked around and saw all his niggaz there. He was mad though because he saw way more niggaz there that he knew for a fact Dan didn't fuck with. He saw his brother approaching him and got madder. He was still mad that Butta placed the blame on him that Dan was dead. This oh fake Biggie Smalls ass nigga thinks he fly in that suit talkin bout bust yo gun. I bet this nigga aint left the house yet he thought to himself.

"Sup lil nigga" Butta said when they came face to face.

"Sup big nigga." He replied back with sarcasm. Butta knew he still was mad at him but he knew Pull Out was most dangerous when he was mad. That's exactly how he wanted him, mad. But he knew he needed to kill the tension between them.

"Why you aint called me or been answering yo phone?" He asked.

"Aint nuttin to talk bout you said don't call you till somebody die and aint nobody dead. I aint had the time to talk I've been busy riding." Pull Out shot back.

"Well if you would answer than you would know that we got the 4-1-1-on some of them niggaz. But we'll talk about that later. Have you noticed you're the only nigga here aint wearing a suit?" Pull Out was well aware of the fact but just to humor himself he looked around then back at his own clothes. He had on some black true religion jeans and a white button up.

"Have you noticed I don't give a fuck cuz?"

"That's not the point nigga and yo gun is showing through yo shirt smart guy." Pull Out looked down at the bulge poking through his shirt. He looked back up and shrugged his shoulders.

"Why the fuck you bring that? You shoulda left it in the car. The homie family here and anybody that's looking can tell that you got a smack." Butta grilled him.

"Listen nigga I heard enough preaching at the funeral cuz. My smack goes with me everywhere nigga I don't care if it's the bathroom. Shit it was only 5 years ago that Unthank nigga Notchie got killed in the church. Fuck you talkin bout you should be happy I left my vest" Butta started biting his cheeks and gritting his teeth. He came over to squash the beef but now he was getting mad.

'Look lil nigga you need to watch how you talk to me. You get away with all that extra shit cause you fam but you crossing the line cuz."

"Naw nigga you crossed the line at yo house cuz. Telling me not to call you like I'm one of yo bitches and throwing shit. Then you gone blame his death on me you got me fucked up." Pull Out responded back releasing all his pinned up anger.

Butta knew he was in the wrong and much as he didn't want to had to apologize.

"Look bro my bad. We fam and life's too short to be beefing with each other. Dan would want us riding not acting like this." He said then stuck his hand out. Pull Out grabbed his hand and Butta pulled him in for a hug. Pull Out tried to break free but couldn't due to Butta's size.

"Aight nigga we coo let me go!" Butta let him go and started smirking.

"I aint with that fruity shit cuz. I know these fags can get married now but I aint with it." He said while adjusting his button up then he seen it again. He seen it the first time, when Butta grabbed him, then when he pulled away. Now he was looking at his brother but could see somebody standing by the street entrance. That was the thing about the cemetery on 60th and Fremont. There was an entrance were you could come from the street. This way was barley used because it was only necessary if the deceased was buried in the back. And Dan was buried in the back. The person only stood out because he was wearing all red. Pull Out kept staring trying to remember where he recognized that face from.

"Naw I'm trippin that can't be right" he thought to himself. Ron approached and put his hand on his shoulder breaking his thought process.

"What's good with ya'll niggaz?" He asked them. Then it hit him hard, the nigga from the park. That's when he heard it.

"How ya'll gone have a funeral without the east coast grim reaper!" He seen the man yell at the top of his lungs. Butta started turning around and Pull Out just watched Joe pull a gun from his waist.

BOOM BOOM BOOM he started shooting into the crowd closest to him. He seen Gucci Ty try to run and fall down on his face. Every female was yelling at the top of her lungs. BOOM BOOM Butta threw Pull Out on the ground while Joe kept shooting. BOOM BOOM BOOM BOOM Pull Out seen Gucci Ty snake crawling. Fuck the homie hit he yells in his mind. Joe starts walking towards Gucci Ty's direction. Pull Out broke free from Butta's grip and jumped up shooting BOCA BOCA BOCA BOCA.

"What's up cuz come get yo issue!" He yelled. Joe ducked down from the shots. He wasn't expecting anybody to have a gun on them. "Good thing I brought the 30 clips" he thought.

BOCA BOCA Pull Out kept shooting and making his way towards Gucci Ty.

"You was talkin that grim reaper shit what's up nigga!" Joe popped up from behind a tombstone. BOOM BOOM BOOM BOOM BOOM BOCA BOCA BOCA. Joe seen niggaz running towards the parking lot and knew his time was short.

"Fuck that it's gone take dem 5 minutes to reach their cars, I'm knocking this nigga off." He said out loud pumping his self up. He hopped up running to the side entrance. BOOM BOOM he started shooting backwards when he seen Pull Out chasing him. Pull Out dove to the ground. Pull Out waited until he seen Joe run out the entrance door and seen him turn left then disappear. He jumped up chasing him then stopped when he heard somebody yell "NO" real loud.

He turned around and seen Pressha running after him.

"It's a trap cuz."

"Man that bitch ass nigga is running." Pull Out yelled back mad that he'd been stopped. Pressha rushed and tackled him just as the shots went off BOOM BOOM BOOM Joe popped back around the wall shooting then ran off again.

"Fuck cuz!" Pull out yelled. They got up and ran over to where Gucci Ty was laying on the ground bleeding.

"Ty where you hit at?"

"Aww fuck my leg and back is on fire." He said while trying to get up.

"Stop moving nigga you gone make it worse the ambulance on the way. Pull Out get outta here cuz." Pressha said to the both of them.

"I'm gone cuz ya'll hit me when ya'll touch the hospital. Come on Ron we on one." He said then took off with Ron right behind him.

CHAPTER 8

Getting out this game is like coming out of a coma. Emotionally and mentally it's gone be the hardest thing you've ever did, to wake up. It's so hard to leave you gone wonder how it was so easy to get in, but when you was trying to get in it was hard and you wasn't even thinking of getting out, remember

Hours after the shooting Jersey Joe was sitting in his white expedition outside of Falon's house. After the shooting he switched cars and clothes and took Falon on a shopping spree at multiple locations. Falon had just got off the phone with Olay and she wanted Falon to help her pack her stuff. She was glad Olay called because now she had a legitimate excuse not to let Joe spend the night. Her pussy was sore from last night with Boobie and she was even more exhausted from shopping all day. She had just told Joe the change of plans and he was livid as expected.

"What the fuck you mean you gotta go to Olay's house? You aint gotta do shit. You aint have to go help her when you were begging me to buy you that fuckin Louis Vuitton purse. We done planned this whole day since last week now you gotta go help yo sis. Naw you got me fucked up son."

"Joe why you tripping you act like I knew she was gone call," She explained to him. Joe breathed in and out real loud signifying his frustration.

"Yo stop fuckin playing with me son you already know what the issue is. A nigga planned on going shopping and coming back to chill. Niggaz is starvin and you supposed to be half naked cooking me dinner right now. I'm tryina smoke, eat and get some pussy. Wake up and do it again before I touch the pavement. Yo I told you I'm bout to be heading back to Jersey this week so I aint got time to be playing games ya heard." Falon slapped herself on the forehead before responding.

"So what the fuck you want me to do Joe? Tell my sis I can't help her cause you want some food and pussy? Why don't you push the date back so you don't be pressed for time?"

"I don't give a fuck what you tell her but you need to say something. I bet if Boobie asked then you would without question so miss me with the fuckery. And I can't push it back because O the one set it for a certain reason."

"You got me highly fucked up, Boobie don't run shit I got going on. He aint my nigga so stop always bringing him up. And Marshawn is retiring and moving to Atlanta so I'm sure he won't care what you do." Joe screwed his face up before he replied

"What the fuck you talkin bout retire? Who told you that shit?" Falon realized she slipped up and told the business before it was supposed to be told.

"Nothing never mind."

"Never mind my ass let me know the real."

"Joe you can't say nothing because I'm not even supposed to know yet." She complained to him.

"Who told you this yo sis?" Falon looked down in her lap then answered,

"Yeah." Then she looked out the window.

"Yo you gotta wake up real early to fool the kid. I grew up in the projects around liars my whole life and you're fuckin lying. Look at me." She turned around to face him,

"What?"

"Who told you Falon?" Joe demanded. She sucked her teeth then responded,

"I don't know why he falling back, shit. All I know is he's going to Atlanta with the homie on some music shit. Damn, is you happy now asking all these fuckin questions?" Joe leaned back in his seat taking everything in he'd just heard. Just when I started having respect for em he go and do some ho shit.

Then he had an epiphany. Since he leaving I know he gone leave Burnside in charge. That's gone make me the 2nd most powerful nigga. Then imma bring my niggaz down here to take over. He was formulating his plans when he had a 2nd thought,

"So since he leaving that mean Burnside gone be in charge right?" He asked.

"Look Joe can we just drop the shit. When O feel like tellin ya'll I'm sure he gone answer all ya'll questions." She said trying to avoid his question

"Who told you all this and don't lie." She crossed her arms and leaned back staring at the roof. 10 seconds went by and she still hadn't answered him.

"It all makes since now son. That's why you've been acting funny towards a real nigga. So that's the nigga you been spending all yo time with huh? Yo, get the fuck out my car we aint got shit to talk bout. Grab all yo bags and from now on unless it's business don't call me. Fuckin gold-digger." Falon sat there in disbelief. She couldn't understand how she went from a shopping spree to being cut off. And Boobie was acting funny this morning too. I gotta at least keep this nigga until I get Boobie wrapped around my fingers. Why I even open my mouth. All this was going through her head before she responded,

"Joe why are you acting like this aint nobody tryna play you. I just found out about it yesterday so how can I been acting weird towards you? You gotta stop thinking everybody is against you baby. Only reason he even brought it up was to throw it in my face. On some let's enjoy my time while we can because I'm bout to be busy. You making it seem like it's a conspiracy or something. Them niggaz is best friends they talk in private just like you and Burnside do. You sitting here calling me out my name because you mad at 10 things at the same time. You hear me baby?" She said then started rubbing the side of his face.

"Yeah whatever son. Ain't it time for you to go help yo sis pack? I got shit to do." He said then started the car. This nigga is really tripping imma have to sweet talk him now. She was thinking

"Baby turn the car off so we can talk." Joe turned it off and leaned back.

"What is there to talk bout yo I'm listening."

"Why are you really mad? I know you're irritated about being put off but that's small. Talk to me baby what's really going on." She asked.

"You keep playing these back and forth games with a nigga. You know what I'm saying? When you with me you act like you really feeling a nigga. Then the next minute you with that nigga and don't wanna answer yo phone. So what's the point of keep wasting my time on you, Go fuck with son.

"So that's the problem. This nigga in love with me and he's jealous of Boobie. I should start really throwing this pussy on him. He is fine in a thugged out way, and he doesn't mind spending all that money on me. But Boobie money bout to grow 5x more and he love trickin. Imma have to play em both close and see who'll do more for me.

She had all these thoughts going through her head before she asked,

"So you tryina have a relationship or something? I'm confused on how you really feel. I thought we was just kickin it, you've never had a heart to heart with me." Joe looked at her then back up at the roof. I'm just gone tell this bitch how I feel. If she aint with it than fuck her.

"I'm saying yo, I got mad love for you."

"What's that supposed to mean you got mad love for me? Is that the east coast way of saying you love me?" She asked.

"Yo why you tryina make this shit hard son? Yeah I love you aight." He finally confessed to her.

Falon sat there in shock for a second. She was used to niggaz getting caught up in their feelings and paying dearly with their pockets. But those were mostly lame niggaz that just happened to have money. Joe was a killer and she knew it. She knew he had some feelings, but love she wasn't expecting that.

"I got love for you too. I don't know if I'm in love with you though. That's something that takes a while ya know?" Joe started the car again.

"Yeah I hear ya, I'll check for you another time yo."

"Can you at least help me take all these bags in the house? Please baby?" She asked.

"C'mon." He replied then opened the door. Bitch wants me to bring the bags in but don't want me to stay. Ain't that a bitch he thought while hopping out his truck.

෨ඏ

O-DAWG HOUSE IN BEAVERTON

ഇൻ

It had been weeks since he'd been home. Ever since he had that argument with Olay and packed some clothes. It felt kinda strange when he stepped into the front room. The house smelled like Olay, The only woman he loved 100%. He knew she was home because her black charger was parked outside. He had been preparing his speech for the last couple of days but still felt butterflies in his stomach. He felt ashamed for some of the things he said to her that day. He knew deep down in his heart that she was the only woman for him. He's known her practically his whole life. Ever since his mother started forcing him to go to church with her when he was 12 years old. That's where he first met her, at church. They know everything about each other and he knew she wasn't there for his money. She knew him when he was broke. He took a deep breath in before he stepped into the bedroom.

Olay was sitting on the bed deep in thought. He could tell she was packing because there were boxes and clothes on the floor,

"Baby." His voice snapped her out of her daze. She looked up and seemed sad but happy at the same time,

"HI." Was her response.

"Baby I'm sorry how have you been doing?" He asked.

"I'm ok I just found out like a hour ago so it's still processing" O-Dawg was confused and she could tell by the look on his face that he didn't know what she was talking about.

"You don't even know what I'm talking about huh?" He still had that confused and worried look on his face when he shook his head.

"They got yo twin this morning in Vegas." O-Dawg's face dropped to the floor and he closed his eyes for a moment.

His twins name was Lonnell and their not real twins either. In fact Lonnell was Olay's cousin but him and O-Dawg were related through marriage on a different side. The two looked and acted so much alike that people honestly mistook them for one another. Their only visible distinction was that O-Dawg wears glasses. Lonnell had been on the run for murder for over a year before this morning. Hearing this news really altered his mood and distracted him from the real purpose of being there,

"Vegas? What the fuck that dumb ass nigga go there for? They know his mom live there. Shit Vegas is mostly bitch niggaz that's banned from the town out there acting like pimps. I know one of those snitch ass niggaz called crime stoppers. Ho ass niggaz made sure they got that lil reward money," He said to her venting his frustration.

They stood there in silence for a few seconds. While their eyes were connected she could see the anger building in him. She knows him better than anybody and she could see all the anger he had pinned up trying to escape. Olay just sat there on the bed watching him and feeling helpless.

"Marshawn what were you saying sorry for? You looked like you had some things on your mind." She asked him to change the topic. He stopped pacing and just stared at her.

"You know you're the only person who has grey hairs in their 20s?" She was insecure when it came to her hair. She's tried to dye it jet-black but he wouldn't allow her. She started touching her hair subconsciously then responded,

"That's cause I've had to deal with you the last decade, you be stressing me out."

"Baby you only got a few grey hairs so cut the crap. The point I was making is you're the only person who can make it look so beautiful. You have something that every female would hate to have because it makes them look old but you can take the ugliest, the most unattractive thing and make it look so special. Every time I look at you, it's like I'm seeing you for the first time. You're so beautiful and loving. You don't deserve to be hurt and I'm sorry for hurting you. I do feel like you're in the wrong but I still shouldn't of said some of the shit that I said."

"Thank you, you always did know how to make me feel pretty even when I don't feel like it. You hurt me though, you really did. I know you said that airplane thing out of anger. But that stupid thing about my coaches son where did that come from? I could tell you were serious so don't try to downplay it."

"Baby I didn't come over to talk about all that. We get to bringing up reasons why certain things were said, all that's gone do is start another argument. I came over to tell you that I'm done. I've already told Boobie that he's in charge now. I've talked to Spike and told em I'm moving in with him ASAP. I'm bout to go see Jaxx and let em know what's up. No more murders, no drugs, no nothing, just making music and supporting your golf career. And whenever you're ready we can start our family." Olay just stared at him taking it all in. She went from being sad to happy in less than 10 minutes. She's been waiting for years to hear those words come out of his mouth.

DING-DONG DING-DONG The doorbell was going off. O-Dawg's hand touched his holster subconsciously to make sure his gun was there.

"You expecting somebody?" He asked,

"Yeah my sister is here to help me pack up all this stuff. You know don't nobody come over here unannounced. Only a few people know where we live so calm down."

"I am calm I was just making sure."

"Why yo hand go for your gun then if you're so calm?" she said with a smirk

"Because we always tell each other before hand when somebody's coming over, that's why"

'DING-DONG!'

"Well if you woulda been home then you would know." She shot back as he headed out the door. O-Dawg reached the front room and opened it so Falon could come in. She was texting on her phone when she walked in and didn't even look up

"About time bitch what were you doing?" She said thinking she was talking to Olay. O-Dawg just looked her up from head to toe. She was wearing silk pajama pants and a small white shirt that spelled something in red letters. Her hair was in a ponytail and she had on pink rabbit house shoes

"You know I done killed for less right?" He told her half joking. Falon looked up with a confused look on her face,

"My bad you know I didn't know that was you. Hold up what you doing here?" She asked confused.

"I just asked Olay the same thing about you. I pay the rent here, I can walk around ass naked if I want to." Falon wrapped her arms around him for a hug

"Where you been at? You have been MIA since that night. You act like you can't call me and check in." Damn this bitch smell good he was thinking when he replied, "I been out the way tryina stay off the radar."

"C'mon let me go cuss this tramp out." She said then let him go then took off towards the bedroom.

He followed behind her watching her ass jiggle the whole time. That's way too much ass for one bitch. I don't think she got no panties on either he thought to himself. Every time she switched it was like a bowl of Jell-O moving. He watched each cheek move up and down then wobble back to place. I think she be switching extra hard when she knows I'm behind her he was thinking as his dick was getting harder. Finally they reached the room,

"Why the hell you been calling me all day when Marshawn is right here?" Falon asked Olay as soon as she walked into the room.

"I didn't know he was gone pop up outta the blue. He just got here like 30 minutes ago." Olay responded.

"He tell you he's a retired man? This nigga actually walking away." O-Dawg looked at Falon trying to figure out how she knew already.

"Yeah my baby just told me." She replied then got off the bed to hug him with a huge smile on her face.

"Oh now I get a hug cause she here." Then she kissed him on the lips too. "And a kiss, does it get better when she leaves?" He asked.

"Maybe" Was her response.

O-Dawg sat on top of the dresser then asked Falon.

"How you know I was falling back?" She looked at him and smirked,

"That nigga Boobie stay pillow talkin. Ya'll probably been laying up all day talkin bout shit that aint supposed to be discussed. Coming over here wearing house shoes and shit."

"I don't lay up and you know that. I've actually been shopping all day, courtesy of ya boy Joe. Since you all in mine."

"All in yours? Shit you the one talkin bout me with yo lil playthings. Don't tell me Joe took you on a shopping spree."

"Ok I won't tell you then." She said back being sarcastic.

"Falon don't play games with dem niggaz. You know how niggaz get over some pussy, we don't need that. Do they both know?" He asked sounding stressed.

"Joe does but Boobie don't. Shit Boobie won't care anyways. It aint like either one thinks were in a relationship." O-Dawg started shaking his head,

"Well Joe did tell me that he loves me today." She said smiling. Olay busted out laughing.

"Olay stop fuckin laughing the shit aint funny."

"Falon you better fix this shit before it gets broke."

"You act like something gone happen cause she messing with both of them." Olay responded.

"When niggaz get to talkin that love shit it's a whole different story and you know it. Now if something happen and I gotta come back down here and kill everybody including yo sister, you gone feel some type of way." The sisters looked at him like he had two heads,

"Are you serious right now?" Falon asked.

"Do it look like I'm playing? Either get an understanding with both dem niggaz or cut one off."

"Ok Marshawn! Got damn!" she replied raising her voice.

"Do you still need me to help you cause if not I'm bout to shake?"

"Big guns and big whips/rich niggaz talking big shit/double cup, gold wrist" Rick Ross and jay-z started blasting through the room from O-Dawg's phone.

"Hello." He answered.

"Crab nigga funeral got shot up, Gucci Ty in the hospital." Somebody said over the phone clearly making their voice deeper than it naturally is,

"Nuff said." He responded then hung up.

"Ya'll heard about a shooting today?" he asked them.

"When I was watching the 5'clock news looking for Lonnell I seen something about a funeral getting shot up. Actually the cemetery on 60th and Fremont" Olay answered.

"I saw people talkin bout it on Facebook. What happened with Lonnell?" Falon asked.

"They caught him in Vegas." O-Dawg said and Falon started shaking her head.

"That nigga Joe was acting weird today and kept telling me to remember I was with him all day." O-Dawg had forgot he was the one who set the whole situation up. His mind had been so focused on the future that he forgot the plan. Then it hit him. 'This nigga still got one more thing to do' he started thinking.

"Falon stop talkin like that in front of Olay. Matter fact stop talkin period." O-Dawg instructed her while calling Joe. 'I gotta stop this nigga before shit get worse' he thought to himself.

Joe's phone was going straight to voicemail,

"Shit" He said out loud.

"Imma have him help me sis, my bad I forgot to call you." Olay said.

"Aight we'll I'm bout to go home and find something to do. It's only 8:30." Falon responded looking at her phone.

"C'mon imma walk you out cause we need to talk." O-Dawg told her then followed her out the room. He was mad at her and Jersey Joe. But as he was staring at her ass wobble he forgot all about being mad. 'Got damn' he was thinking. 'I would be fucking her too if I was those niggaz. How the fuck Olay aint got no ass and her sister an amazon?' He questioned himself. He felt himself getting hard again. 'Them pajamas are so tight I can damn near see her cheeks. She lucky she wifey sister or I'd fuck the shit out of her. I know she'd be popping that ass for me. She switching way too hard and she know I'm behind her.'

O-Dawg was so distracted by her ass that he didn't notice they were almost at the door. Falon stopped but he noticed too late and bumped into her ass. For a split second he felt how it would feel if he had her from the back. He felt how soft her ass was. He was hoping she didn't feel how hard his dick was but he doubted it. He regrouped then told her,

"My bad I was deep in thought." Falon had a lil smirk on her face but he caught it before it disappeared,

"Yeah I bet. What were you doing looking at the ground? Look I'm going to fix things before they get broke, as you like to say. Just don't be mad at me ok?"

"Yeah aight, just do what need to be done. Oh and don't be telling people I'm falling back."

"I got you and I love you. Give me a hug so I can leave." While they were hugging O-Dawg started thinking she held on a lil bit extra and tighter than usual. Naw I'm trippin that's just my dick head thinking the most he told himself.

"If you need me to do anything for you, you know I will with no hesitation." She told him.

"I know sis don't trip." When she walked out he couldn't help but to get one more look at her ass jiggle as she waked off the porch.

ᕤᕬ

SOMEWHERE IN SOUTHEAST

ᕤᕬ

Jersey Joe was sitting in a stolen Toyota Camry. He's been waiting in the parking lot to the Rockwood apartments for over an hour "Hail Mary nigga run with me/hail Mary nigga come quick see/what do we have here now!! /are you gonna ride or die na na..." Joe was listening to Tupac and rapping along his own custom version

"Imma killer and niggaz done already pushed me!" He was talking to himself and smoking weed at the same time.

"Meek Millz had that shit right nigga. Tupac back! I'm bout to turn up on these niggaz son." While Joe was pumping himself up he seen a older black man walk by the car,

"Yeah that's him." He turned the music off and took one last hit of the blunt before he put it out. He watched the man walk down some stairs towards the front doors of two apartments. He hopped out soon as he seen the man put the key inside the lock. When the door opened he rushed down the stairs and pushed him inside and on to the ground,

"What the fuck man!" The old man screamed.

Joe closed the door and just stood staring at him. He knew nobody else was in the house because he knocked on the door 3 different times. Joe pulled out his .45 handgun and pointed it at his head. The old man lifted his hands to block his face and said,

"Whatever you want you can have please don't kill me young blood! I aint gone play with you imma give it all up!"

"This aint no robbery son and you aint got shit that I want." Joe replied. The man had the most confused look on his face that Joe had ever seen.

"What's this about then young blood? I aint ran the streets in over 20 years."

"I know all that yo you're Bobby fisher aka 2 shot bob right?" The old man shook his head.

"Lie to me again bitch ass nigga! And Imma push yo shit back son." Joe walked closer and cocked the gun back.

"Yeah that's me but I ain't went by that name in forever. I gave that life up young blood what's the beef?" He responded with fear in his voice

"Your nephew is the beef" He watched Bobby's eyes get wide with fear and confusion. "Yeah Ron fisher aka "the party shooter". I got a message I want you to deliver" Relief swept across his face when he realized he wasn't going to die.

"I'll tell em anything you want you got my word young blood." Joe smiled like only a psychopath could.

"Tell em the east coast grim reaper came by. He knows me we just spoke briefly today. Anyway, he clapped up my mans 4 year old son's birthday party. He hit my mans and his uncle. So this is where you come into play ya heard?"

"I'm lost young blood what is it that you want me to do? I'm sorry he did that. Just don't kill me I'll do whatever you want, whatever."

"Yo if you ask me not to kill you one more time son, Imma push yo shit back. I'm not gone kill yo bitch ass, even though I want to. You lucky I don't call the shots or yo whole family will be dead son. The man who does call the shots sent me over here to tell you a message. Tell yo bitch ass nephew next time he shoots when family is around that the gloves come off. Imma personally kill everybody with yo last name ya heard? Starting with yo daughter that goes to Jefferson high school. Tell that nigga we believe in eye for eye."

"OK young blood just leave my baby girl out of this. I'll tell em everything you said." He responded in a pleading voice.

"I know." BOOM

"Aghhhh! C'mon man! Ahhh my leg!" Bobby started screaming at the top of his lungs and grabbing his leg. BOOM

"AGHHHH! ok ok." He screamed louder and grabbed his other leg that Joe just shot him in. Joe started laughing then said,

"I told you we believe in eye for eye. Well in yo case son, leg for leg. Yo if you go to the cops imma have my lil niggaz rape yo daughter before I slit her throat. Word to my mutha you bitch ass nigga. I heard you was a rat back in yo day." Joe stepped closer and shot him in the shoulder. BOOM!

"Ahhh! no more, no more" Bobby yelled.

"That last one was for them niggaz you told on you fuckin snitch." He spit in his face then walked out the door.

ೲ

BACK AT O-DAWGS HOUSE

ꙩꙍ

When O-Dawg walked back into the room Olay had on her mad face that she'd mastered over the years,

"What's wrong with you now girl?"

"How you gone threaten to kill my sister right in front of my face?" She asked.

"Cause she play for the team and she know the rules. Stop acting naive Olay you know damn well the drama that can cause, it starts off small then blows up later. I had to show her how serious the situation is. Death is as serious as it can ever get. It's gucci though she understands."

"I'm just glad you're done with all this stuff. Do you promise that you're done?" She asked him while staring at him looking for any signs of deceit. 'Am I really done? I can't believe I'm actually walking away alive and not in jail. Look how beautiful she is he thought to himself,'

"Yeah baby I promise." He finally answered.

"Did you kill somebody that night you walked outta here?"

"C'mon with that shit Olay you know not to ask me shit like that. Where the hell that come from?"

"Cause I seen that look in your eyes and I know you. I also know somebody got killed that night at the club."

"Naw I aint kill nobody Olay." He responded.

"I feel like it's my fault. If I woulda never made you mad than he would still be alive. I seen how mad you were but I still let you walk out the door. I knew somebody was gone die that night. I prayed to god it wasn't you."

"Baby aint nothing yo fault cause I aint kill nobody so stop thinking like that."

"Stop lying in my face Marshawn. You're playing your lil word games and you know it. Of course you didn't kill nobody but you know what I

105

mean. You gave the green light for it to happen and it's all because you were mad at me. What you think I don't know who got killed and what hood he from?" She asked him putting emphasis on 'you'. O-Dawg let out a deep breath.

"Olay he was going to die that night regardless. That date was chosen weeks before that argument, so take that shit off yo conscious."

O-Dawg walked over to the surround system and started scrolling through the I-pod.

"Baby come here." He told her.

"Why are you playing music when we need to be talking?"

"Bring yo ass over here Olay were done talkin about that." He demanded.

She got off the bed and walked over with an attitude. Before she could say anything he wrapped his arms around her waist,

"I love you and that's all that matters. Everything I said that was hurtful I didn't mean it baby. Let's just focus on the future aight?" Then he kissed her on the forehead and started whispering in her ear

"Listen" He told her.

R. Kelly's voice was filling up the room "Now I might say you can walk, but I don't mean it/and I might name call, but I don't mean it/I may pull silly stunts but it's just a front, I don't mean it/now I may holler at you, and I may tell you were through/but I don't mean it/may give you looks that can kill, but it's not fo'real/I don't mean it... Olay had her arms wrapped around his neck and they were slowly rocking back and forth.

"You know you're the only woman for me and I love you to death. You hear me?"

"I love you too Marshawn, you know that. You're only trying to be nice because you wanna have sex. You're trying to take my panties off." O-Dawg put his hands in her shorts and palmed her ass,

"You don't even have no panties on. But you are about to get dicked down, unless you telling me that pussy aint wet."

"Shut up." She replied.

"That's what I thought." He said then pulled her shorts down to her ankles and took them off. Then he pulled her shirt off and had her ass naked.

"You're beautiful, now turn around slowly." He instructed her.

Olay turned around and paused to look over her shoulder at him. He smacked her on the ass and she finished turning for him.

"I've missed you so much, it's been over a month." She told him. He grabbed her by the ass and started tongue kissing her,

"Get on the bed and bust it open." He demanded her. While she was getting on the bed he went and changed the song. While he took his clothes off he was staring at her laying on her back with her legs spread open.

"I got summin new for you." He told her and climbed on the bed.

"Tell me how this feel." He grabbed her foot and started kissing it from her ankle to her toes. Then he put the big toe in his mouth and started sucking on it. When he was done he started licking between the big toe and the long one. He repeated this process all the way until he reached the pinkie toe. He heard Olay moaning so he stopped to look at her. She was playing with her pussy and finger banging herself.

"Stop putting your fingers in yo pussy, you know don't nothing go in that hole but my dick. Suck yo fingers then rub on your clit till I'm done with this."

"Okay." She put her fingers in her mouth and started sucking on them.

O-Dawg grabbed her other foot and placed the big toe in his mouth,

"umm." He heard her start moaning. By the time he made it to her middle toe she was moaning out of control and rubbing her clit fast.

"Put it in now." She begged him.

"I still got summin I wanna try first." He responded then finished sucking her toes and licking in between them.

"Move yo hand now, I got this." He started licking and kissing between her thighs. Olay grabbed his head and tried to force his face on her pussy,

"Not yet." He told her and took her hands off him.

"Stop teasing me." She moaned. O-Dawg opened her lips up and stuck his tongue inside her pussy then pulled it out.

"umm-umm." She moaned. Why you do that? Put it back in. Eat it all, please." She begged him. His tongue found her clit then he started slowly licking on it. This drove Olay crazy

"Ohh that feels so good." He went to work on her clit while Maxwell's voice set the mood. 'I should be crying but I just can't let it show/I should be hoping but I can't stop thinking/All the things I shoulda said that I never said/All the things we shoulda done that we never did/All the things I shoulda given but I didn't... When Maxwell's voice started sounding like he was crying Olay started screaming.

"I'm bout to cum." He stopped eating her pussy soon as she said that. When he stopped she started going crazy grabbing his head trying to get him to finish.

"Why you do that? Come here! Stop playing with me." She was yelling at him.

"Put your legs up then put your arms under them so you can keep them up. I want that whole pussy opened up and so you can watch what I'm bout to do to you." He instructed her. "Yeah like that, now hold it there." He started sucking on her pussy making loud slurping sounds. After he was done sucking he stuck his tongue in her ass. Olay jumped at the surprise of feeling a tongue in her ass. He grabbed her legs.

"Put your arms back under yo legs." He told her while laughing.

"Yo freaky ass just put half yo tongue in my butt without warning and expect me not to jump." She replied.

"You want me to stop?" He asked.

"No." She answered then put her arms back in place to keep her legs balanced in the air. O-Dawg put his face back down between her legs. He started licking around the hole doing full circles in both directions. This was driving Olay crazy.

"ohh-ohh. That feels, that feels so good. mmm-hmm." She said in the middle of moaning. O-Dawg then put two fingers inside of her pussy and started fingering her.

Her pussy was soaking wet and making slushing sounds every time he pulled his fingers out and put them back in,

"I'm bout to cum Marshawn! Make me cum baby." When he heard her start screaming he stuck his tongue back in her ass as much as he could get in. He kept taking his tongue out then back in while still finger banging her.

"I'm cumming! ohh right now!" She yelled then fell back on her back. He held her legs and started attacking her pussy and clit with his tongue. He was licking and sucking like he was trying to swallow every drop that came out of her.

"ohh-ohh! Put it in baby, put it in!" She demanded him." She was grabbing his head trying to force him off her pussy. He finally came up for air and started licking his lips.

"You taste hella good it's been a minute since I tasted you. How you like getting yo ass ate?" He asked her.

"You are so nasty, what made you wanna do that?" He started laughing then responded.

"That nigga J-mafia called me yesterday from upstate. He said he read in one of those sex magazines that bitches loved getting they ass licked but most niggaz won't do it."

"Well I like how it feel."

"And you got the nerve to call me nasty? Fuck all this talkin you know what time it is." He said then layed on top of her and started kissing her neck.

"You know that's my spot." She moaned.

He made his way to her mouth and they started tonguing each other. He grabbed her legs and pulled them all the way back to her head.

"You ready to get pounded?" She nodded her head and he instantly guided his dick inside of her. She took a deep breath in. Once he had her legs positioned over his shoulders he started long stroking her real slow.

"Ohh, I love you baby" She whispered to him. He was too busy trying to get his dick all the way in to reply. He kept having to rock back and forth just to get it in inch by inch.

"Yo pussy stay tight, shit feel like a glove on my dick." He told her while still trying to get it all in.

"Ohh!"

"There we go, we in the game now." He sped it up now that he was all in. He was long dicking her at a fast pace now

"Hmm-hmm I can feel it in my stomach." Hearing this made him speed up and start only taking half out.

"You feel this dick?"

"Yes! Yes! I feel it baby. ohh I feel it!" She screamed.

He started pounding her faster. Clapping sounds were being made from his balls smacking her pussy every time he slammed back into her

"Whose pussy is this?"

"Yours! It's all yours baby"

"I missed this pussy, did you miss me fucking you?"

"Yes! I missed you baby! Every day"

"Was you playing with yo pussy thinking bout this dick?"

"Yes!" She yelled out "I'm cumming again! I love you! I love you! Ahhh ohh-ohh!" She yelled out then started moaning.

"Oh this shit feel fire." O-Dawg kept going faster and faster. Olay knew he was about to nut,

"Cum inside me baby." She said in a low sexy voice.

"Aww shit I'm bout to bust! Aghh fuck!" He yelled out releasing a monster load of nut inside her. He kept stroking her but was slowing down with each one. He finally took her legs off his shoulder and fell on top of her. Olay started rubbing her hand through his waves and playing with his ear.

"Marshawn?"

"What's good?" He answered.

"I love you."

"I love you too baby. That's only round one so don't think were done. We on a 5 minute break then I gotta hit it from the side." He told her.

"You a freak." she responded.

☙❧

NEXT DAY AT JAXX HOUSE

☙❧

O-Dawg was sitting on Jaxx couch waiting to hear his brother respond. He had just told him that he was done with the streets and wanted Boobie to replace him.

"O you can't keep playing tennis with this shit. A few months ago you was talkin bout falling back a lil and you was still undecided then. Then you get shot at and tried to play possum. Acting like shit was all good, then what you do? Kill the nigga Dan then shoot the funeral up. Now you talkin bout retiring again? Nigga ya'll at war. So tell me how the fuck that makes sense?" Jaxx said trying to grill his younger brother.

"Bro you act like the homies can't handle those niggaz or summin. It's not gone make no difference if I'm here or not. It's gone be the same results, them niggaz dead. You still gone be making money so what's the issue?"

"There is a difference and you know it nigga. If not, then why the fuck you been the leader? But let's say you're right about the killing part. Between Burnside and Boobie there would be too many shootings before those other niggaz are even dead. It'll take a year before they can say they've actually won and you know it. You know how many cases they might catch before a year? Then next thing you know the gang task is kicking down doors. Guess what they find? Dope! Kilos and guns, then you know what's next right? The feds come. Now niggaz is looking at football numbers across the country. You think they gone stay solid? I'm not from ya'll lil mafia click so they damn sho gone tell on me. Boobie, Burnside, Gotti and Joe all know about me. Probably they baby moms too or whoever those lil mob bitches are that ya'll keep in ya'll business. You want me to put my life on the line just to help something stay on top that you created?"

"So what the fuck is the difference if I stay then? If all my niggaz is snitches then why the fuck you dealing with us then?" O-Dawg replied raising his voice and getting mad.

"I'm not saying they snitches, I'm saying I don't know. Gotti is family, but he be on some family man shit. He's too in love with that bitch and that's dangerous. Boobie and Burnside are my lil niggaz, I'll give them the benefit of doubt. That jersey nigga? I don't know him and don't want to. I don't fuck with outta town niggaz period. 90% is snitches from back home or running from something. But the point is, is that we have an agreement. If anybody that's under you mentions my name than you take the blame. You tell the police their lying and you're the plug far as drugs go. I can only get indicted if you turn state, which I know will never happen. I'm confident Boobie and I can work something out in the future. So here's the deal, and keep in mind I'm doing this as a favor for you. I'm not loyal to no gang at all, including yours. You stay here long enough to finish this issue and I'll deal with Boobie exclusively." O-Dawg leaned back on the couch and started thinking.

"What exactly do you mean finish the issue?" he asked.

"I mean to the point where Gutta squad are no longer a factor. This will help you in the long run also. After ya'll, them niggaz move the most dope in the city. With them fully knocked off that means more customers for ya'll. Which means the more dope ya'll get from me, we all win. Kill Butta and Pressha and that will knock them off the totem pole. Then you can leave with yo niggaz having the best plug."

"What if Boobie get killed or go to jail once I'm out?" He asked Jaxx

"Then I'll at least give Burnside a chance." He replied.

"Aight Imma kill these bitch ass niggaz before the months over then I'm done for good."

"Aight." Jaxx responded while smiling.

"Naw fo'real bro, real shit. Only reason I'm doing this is because I love my niggaz and don't wanna leave them on stuck. I'm loyal, summin most these niggaz don't know nothing about." O-Dawg told him then headed to the door. Before he walked out Jaxx had one more jewel to drop on him.

"Getting out this game is like coming out of a coma. Emotionally and mentally it's gone be the hardest thing you've ever did, to wake up. It's so hard to leave, you gone wonder how it was so easy to get in. But when you was tryna get in, it was hard. and you wasn't even thinking of getting out, remember?" O-Dawg just nodded his head and walked out.

CHAPTER 9

I'd rather shoot myself in the face than stab my niggaz in the back

"When I wake up first thing on my mind is get this cake up." Meek Millz was blasting in the front room while Burnside and Jersey Joe was counting money.

"We gone get this money, we gone get this money."

"I can tell this nigga really from the streets he don't try too hard or nuttin it just come natural." Burnside said while putting a stack of money into the money counting machine.

"You heard what that nigga said? The early bird gets the worm first! Nigga we was on the curb first! On my mama that's real shit blood. We bout to see who get that million first nigga." Jersey Joe was weighing up dope on the table not responding to him. Burnside knew something was wrong because usually Joe is hyper and never stops talking.

"What's up blood why you all quiet and shit?" he asked him.

"Yo I'm trying to figure out how we gone see a milli with O retiring." Burnside dropped the pile of money he had in his hands.

"What the fuck you mean O is retiring? Where the fuck that come from?" he asked.

"That nigga bout to fall back son and move to Atlanta like real soon."

"He told you this?" Burnside asked while staring at him.

"Naw, Falon did son."

"Olay probably told her. Damn blood I wonder who he gone give the plug to?"

"It should be you son." Joe said trying to pump him up so he'll get mad when he tells him the news.

"Yeah it should be but long as it stays in the circle then I aint trippin Blood."

"Yo what the fuck you mean you aint trippin? Nigga you put the most work in so it gotta go to you."

"Shit it might, I think it would. I was just sayin if it didn't."

"Yo if it didn't then that means son is playing favoritism and that aint boo."

"I don't know bout taking it that far some niggaz just aint made for certain roles."

"But you are son, that's the point." Joe said trying to instigate and feed his ego.

"You sound like you know what's going through the niggaz head. We'll see when he makes his announcement it might not be true anyways." Burnside replied trying to defuse the situation, but deep down he was thinking about it.

"It's true son and Boobie got the plug word to mutha." He said while trying to read Burnsides reaction.

"And Olay told Falon all this shit?"

"Naw son Boobie was pillow talkin and bragging to the bitch. Then she slipped up and told me yo."

"Well then that's what it is blood." Burnside responded brushing the issue to the side. "Yo I know that's ya mans an all but son we gotta branch off. Do our own thing, build our own movement up son. It's obvious you aint appreciated son. Fuck you gone do? Sit around waiting ya whole life for another nigga to decide when you can and can't eat?"

"Joe, I'd rather shoot myself in the face than stab my niggaz in the back" Burnside stated with full commitment and pride.

"Yo the real question is: would they rather stab you in the back or shoot you in the face? Cause either way you're getting fucked, and that's exactly what's happening."

"So what the fuck you suggesting? Kill our niggaz and take over? Naw fuck that. Death before dishonor remember?" he asked Joe

"It can't be dishonor if niggaz aint honorable to you son. Yo I'm not sayin kill those niggaz just fall back and do our own thing."

"Joe you know damn well that would start a war. Either way this conversation is over. Don't matter if it's Boobie or Gotti we still gone eat the same."

"That's the point yo I'm tryna eat more." Joe informed him.

"Then take yo ass back to Jersey blood. You don't see us tryna go take over Jersey." "Ya'll niggaz too soft to take over Jersey son."

"Nigga you out yo mind blood all my niggaz got bodies and you know it. Bring 10 of yo niggaz and I bet you we'll send those niggaz back in black bags." Burnside said getting angry.

Shanell walked into the room carrying plates and set them on the table.

"How much is this?" Burnside asked.

"It's a half. I'm bout to finish the last half and call it a night. I'll do the other 3 keys tomorrow baby."

"Aight baby love you." He responded while she was walking back to the kitchen. I'm bout to fuck the shit out her tonight. All that ass in those shorts he was thinking while watching her ass wobble cheek by cheek. When she disappeared he looked at Joe,

"A blood I don't wanna hear no more of that dumb shit. Get money and be happy or go back to Jersey. You get to venting to the wrong person and it get back to O you gone be dead before you know it."

"I'm good son I'm not trippin at all. I just didn't want you getting stepped on. If you good son then I'm good. Just know I got you ya heard? Its levels to this shit. Not no favoritism and shit. Everybody know you earned that spot son. I keep forgetting ya'll get down different down here ya heard."

"Yeah whatever son, b, kid or whatever corny shit ya'll call each other. Just don't forget we started this shit so ya'll different. Matter fact put the homie Problem in, Millz got enough play. Put that Denver Lanes music on." Burnside said while rolling the blunt.

O Dawg was sitting on the edge of his bed talking to Spike. He had just informed him of the news that he would be staying in Portland longer. He was listening to Spike with the phone on speaker and counting some money Boobie had just sent him.

"I hear what you sayin blood but you gotta learn to put yoself first sometimes. I love the hood but sometimes it's fuck the homies. If a nigga fell off aint none of the homies gone let me and my family move in with them. That's why I moved down here so I can do me. Niggaz is selfish blood and you know that."

"Bro you talkin bout the whole hood. I'm talkin bout our branch off the niggaz I know are trill. If I just left these niggaz on stuck what kind of nigga would that make me? At the end of the night I'm the one gotta look myself in the mirror blood. I know for a fact that if I did that then I wouldn't be able to. That shit would eat at me blood. You know how big I am on that loyalty shit. It's only gone be a couple more weeks bro." He tried to convince Spike.

"It's bigger than that. I had you studio time lined up with Juelz and Waka. Them niggaz is hella busy but was doing it as a favor for me. Now I gotta call these Niggaz and see if I can reschedule. You putting my word on the line and wasting time."

"I know big homie my bad. Imma make that shit right though on the Mob."

O Dawg was reaching down to put the money on the ground that he had just counted. He seen something slightly move to the left behind him. His gun was lying next to his right foot. His heart started beating fast as he decided what to do. Go for the gun he told himself. Instead he slowly turned his head to look behind him. A move that could have been fatal in a do or die situation. He locked eyes with Olay. She was standing at the door with her arms crossed and anger in her eyes. She had her golf material on the ground next to her. Fuck I forgot she was coming back from practice early he thought. Spike was still preaching over the phone but O-Dawg couldn't understand nothing he was saying.

"Spike let me hit yo back Olay been standing behind me and you on speaker." Spike broke out laughing.

"You dumb ass nigga, you aint gone have to worry bout the crabz killing you now. Olay don't hurt him baby girl." He screamed the last part before O-Dawg hung up on him. He was speechless. He didn't plan on telling her the truth. He figured he could handle his business low-key without her knowing.

"You promised me Marshawn." she said in a low chilling voice. He got off the bed to go towards her.

"Baby listen." was all he got out before he was hit in the head. She had cocked back and threw her phone at him before he could take two steps. Smack! He was hit dead in the forehead.

"What the fuck!" O-Dawg yelled as he rushed and grabbed her around the neck. He slammed her into the wall hard and started yelling. "Fuck is wrong with you bitch hitting me with shit!" he didn't realize how hard he was choking her. O-Dawg started having flashbacks of watching his mother get slapped, choked and beat. Hearing her screams behind a closed door. He got even more heated and tightened his grip.

After a couple seconds he snapped back into reality and realized what he was doing. The look in her eyes broke his heart. He finally let her go and watched in sorrow as she struggled to catch her breath.

"Baby I'm so sorry, Are you okay?" he said as he grabbed her arm to help her stand all the way up. Olay snatched away from his grip lightning fast and stood straight up and screamed at him.

"Don't fucking touch me! Never again in your whole life! Don't call me baby either. Matter of fact get out!"

"Olay I'm sorry for choking you. You know in your heart I didn't mean that shit. I would never hit you and you know that. I just reacted without thinking when you hit me but I'm still wrong for it. Give me a chance to explain everything to you." He apologized and tried to persuade her.

"There's nothing to talk about nigga and not cause you put your hands on me. I shouldn't have hit you at all. We was done before that anyways. I heard your whole conversation so there's nothing to explain. You broke your word to me you lied. I despise a liar and you're a liar. You wanna put your homies needs before mines then go be with your homies we're done."

"Olay you know you don't mean that shit."

"Are you leaving the house or do you want me to leave? I don't even wanna look at you!" she replied. O-Dawg has too much pride to keep apologizing and to beg. He feels his anger rising for her disrespect.

"Okay you got that." he shot back and walked out the door. For the second time in months Olay laid in the bed crying wondering if she made the right decision

ைௐ

SOMEWHERE IN THE NORTHEAST

ைௐ

"Damn Cuz I can't believe them slobs really went to yo uncle's spot like that. Niggaz wanna touch family, we gone start tearing they peoples off. The East Coast grim reaper aint that bout a bitch." Pull Out said to Ron as they were driving around looking for somebody.

"We gone fall back on that family shit cuz especially since they know my cuddy go to Jeff. But we most def bout to really start servin them niggaz. True that was a lil kids party but them niggaz know that park is a hot spot cuz."

"Fuck them niggaz cuz we gone catch one of them slob niggaz tonight. Who that nigga in red right there?" he asked Ron and pointed out the window while slowing the car down. They both stared at the man real hard and carefully observed him. Ron sucked his teeth,

"Man that's some square nigga wearing the wrong color cuz."

"That's aight we almost at Texas T's anyways. We gone catch one of these dumb ass niggaz posting in front of the barbershop."

"We can off one of these niggaz cuz but I want one of them Mob slob niggaz. Them hoe ass niggaz be hiding cuz. But we gone catch 'em in traffic and knock 'em off. It's only a matter of time." Ron vented his frustration.

"Aint this bout a bitch. These off brand niggaz is always out here deep. Soon as we get on one this muthafucka turn into ghost town." Pull Out said while circling the block looking for anybody in the area.

"Imma give that nigga O-Dawg his credit though cuz. That nigga is sneaky and smart on some playing Puppet Master type shit. We aint never seen this nigga with a gun but he keep shooting at us. Remember how he smiled at us in the club? What did you say when he did that?" Ron said to him.

"I said the nigga smiling like he know summin that we don't." Pull Out said reluctantly not wanting to admit he got played.

"And we already know what that summin was. That shit makes me wonder what else he knows. Like how the fuck he know where my uncle lived at and that he was even my fam."

"I don't know how the nigga knew cuz. But I know one thing, when he show his face I'm airing that nigga out on Dan. Another thing, I know that's that slob nigga Wet right there in front the store." Pull Out said while pointing and getting animated,

"Let me park this shit right over here." He said while turning down a street that was around the corner from the store.

Wet was standing in front of J'S Market on 33rd and Killingworth.

"That's the bitch niggaz car parked in the lot too. He must be waiting on somebody or just wanna be seen." Said Pull Out.

"Well we see 'em alright, A cuz I heard this niggas a snitch." Ron responded.

"I heard that too, the good thing is dead niggaz can't snitch." Pull Out parked the car and left the engine running. Ron put on his Scream mask and looked at Pull Out,

"This muthafucka clean huh? It got this lil button you push and blood get to moving around the face. Yeah we bout to bring the Scream movie to the Northeast." Then grabbed his .357 off the ground. Pull Out cocked back his Tech 9.

"How Jadakiss say that shit? Wit the air holes is how the new techs came. Since that funeral shit I've been riding round with this." He says showing Ron

"we bout to eat this nigga up cuz."

"You aint gone put ya mask on?" Ron asked him "fuck that mask its damn near dark anyways."

They hopped out the car with their guns behind their backs and started walking. There that bitch nigga is still posted by the door. Come on we at this nigga cuz." Pull Out stepped up his pace after he told Ron. "Hold on nigga slow down we gotta make sure aint nobody in his car or the others."

"I don't give a fuck if his grandma in that car we on his ass." Pull Out said while crossing the street.

"His bitch ass is looking at us cuz play it coo" Ron said. Wet finally seen that one of them was wearing a mask.

"Look he going for the car cuz." Pull Out told Ron before yelling, "Yo Wet it's us blood!" Wet stopped before he opened the door and replied,

"Who dat blood?" that's all the time they needed to reach the parking lot.

"The crips nigga!" Pull Out yelled then brought the tech from behind his back. Blaaat Blaaat Blaat The fully automatic started spitting while he was running towards the car. Wet had opened the door and tried to reach for his gun before the first shot went off. He was hit in the back and laying on his stomach over the seat. The wild tech bullets had shattered the window on the driver door. Wet finally grabbed his .38 and turned around to shoot back. Ron was right there with his .357 pointed at his chest. Wet's eyes went huge knowing it was his time.

Booyow Booyow. He flew back into the driver's seat. His gun had fallen to the ground.

"A hold this." Pull Out said while walking past Ron and putting the tech against Wets chest. He held the trigger. Blaat Blaat Blaaaat Wets body was jumping and shaking from the close impact. Blood was pouring from his mouth. His body finally slumping over towards them. They both jumped back as Wet was hanging halfway out the car. When Wets diamond grill fell from his mouth and hit the concrete they took off running to the car.

ॐ

LATER THAT NIGHT

ॐ

The meeting was in full effect at Gotti's house. O-Dawg, Gotti, Boobie, Jersey Joe and Burnside were all sitting around discussing the future.

"Yo son my thing is why we didn't have a vote or summin to see who was gone take over. Yo obviously I aint from here ya heard? So I aint used to conducting business this type of way. So my bad if I offend anybody when I said that." Jersey Joe spoke up to eliminate the silence.

"It don't matter if we woulda voted or not. My brother already said Boobie is who he wants to deal with on that level. He said Burnside is his nigga but he do too much hot shit. Burnside you know you my left hand. But without me you know damn well you woulda been in jail my nigga. Out of the whole circle niggaz on the street fear you the most. That's because you'll kill a nigga wherever you catch 'em. That's you and aint nuttin wrong with that. But when everybody else livelihood is on the line that's when it becomes a problem. You see how much I had to fall back? Could you really do that?"

"I'm not trippin at all my nigga. As long as everything stay the same then I'm content. I love being in the streets too much to fall back anyways." Burnside said.

"And Gotti…"

"We don't even gotta go there blood, I ain't got time to be dealing with everybody's shit. I don't want that shit I'm gucci" Gotti cut in before O-Dawg could even get started.

"Aight since we got that out the way let's move on. As far as that snitch nigga getting smoked tonight that was senseless. The crabz is getting frustrated and since they can't get us they shooting at whoever. I guarantee that was the lil niggaz with shit to prove. We ain't getting down like that at all. Tell our lil niggaz to do what they do best. Air them niggaz out on sight. As for us we only getting at the main niggaz blood. We gone plan, watch and execute them crab ass niggaz mafia style. Ya'll catch 'em in traffic and wanna serve them then go ahead. Oh, Bleed bout to get out of jail in a few months and I recommend that he take my place at the table. He can be the 5th head. Just cause I'm moving don't mean I'm still not gone be here. A nigga just trying to blow up on this rap shit with Spike. When that happen ya'll already know I'm gone invest hella money into this Mob shit. More keys, guns and cars. The only difference is we gone be known around the country. So don't think I'm turning my back blood. I'm just tryina take us to another level that's all. In order to do that I gotta fall back and focus." O-Dawg stated then looked into their eyes one by one to see if they bought his speech.

They took it better than he expected. He felt he made Burnside see his point and all was well from his end. Joe just needed to understand this wasn't the east coast. But that's normal for anybody that moves anywhere. He'll come around O-Dawg was thinking to himself.

CHAPTER 10

You don't reward disloyalty with loyalty, that's why Caesar dead

Knock! Knock! Knock! Gucci Ty knocked on the door to the apartment in the villa. "Who is it?" A female yelled from behind the door. "Wait till the second time." He told Pull Out.

"Who is it?! You dumb ass niggaz is always playing." Gucci Ty stepped to the side. After he counted three seconds he said go. Pull Out took a step then kicked the door as hard as he could. It flew open hard and hit the female as she was making her way to it. Soon as she screamed Gucci Ty rushed in with his two .380's pointed followed by Ron and Pull Out.

"Go ahead and reach! I dare you to!" he said to the man sitting on the couch that was in mid-motion reaching for the gun on the table. He pulled his arm back,

"What ya'll niggaz want?" Shut yo bitch ass up, tryna act like you in control or summin. "Nigga I'll kill you and yo bitch," Gucci Ty checked him.

"Pull Out, is this the nigga cuz?" Gucci Ty asked him. "Yeah this the slob nigga Kapo and his bitch Shawnda, with her thick ass." Pull Out replied while looking her up and down. She was wearing jean shorts with a little shirt that didn't cover her belly ring. She was dark skinned and thick with long fake hair that she wore straight down with bangs.

"Pull Out can you please tell your homie that Kapo is not my man." She begged him.

"I don't know Shawnda, it sure do look like it. Its midnight and you over here lookin all sexy and shit. This bitch nigga wearing some shorts and a tank top. Ya'll got weed on the table and some more shit."

"You know I live in the Ville and I only be over here to get some weed then usually leave." She replied still trying to persuade him.

"Fuck all this reality T. V. shit cuz! This is a Mob dope house and they're in here. Where the money at lil nigga?" Gucci Ty broke up their conversation and pointed his gun back at Kapo.

"I don't know what the fuck you talkin bout. Ain't no money or dope here. This my aunty house nigga!"

Smack!

"Agghh! Fuck! Bitch ass nigga!" Kapo screamed and covered his face up after Ron hit him in the face with his pistol.

"Aight cuz, kill that bitch and smoke the slob then we'll shake the spot down and bounce." Gucci Ty instructed both of them.

"No! Please don't shoot me. I think there's money upstairs cause every time he goes up or down it involves money. Pull Out I swear to you he is not my nigga and I'm not dying for him."

"Check it out cuz and hurry up," Gucci Ty gave his approval. After they went upstairs he walked up on Kapo. Picked the gun up off the table and handed it to Ron.

"If you don't tell me where the dope at nigga I'mma do you real greazy cuz. You niggaz shot me in the back, so this is real personal. I promise you, you don't wanna make me mad cuz."

"Fuck you nigga! And Ron you know you a bitch. Nigga we used to beat yo ass at Beaumont everyday. You know you can't see me without that gun blood." Kapo replied while swelling his chest up and looking like he wasn't scared. They both looked at him like he was crazy.

၁၀

UPSTAIRS

၁၀

Shawnda was bending over looking inside the closet, she made sure she spread her legs wider then needed and bent over more than necessary. Pull Out was standing directly behind her enjoying the show. She finally threw out a small garbage bag next to his feet.

"I think it's more in here, hold on." She told him. He bent over to pick up the bag and started looking through the bills.

"These all 20's in here." He said to her then stood up.

"Well these should be the rest of them." She replied while coming out the closet with two more bags.

"Here." He grabbed them and opened them up. The first bag was all 50's and the other was all 100's.

"I did good right? I told you I don't care about that nigga." she stood smiling with her hands on her wide hips.

"Yeah good looking out baby girl. Why the fuck you in here? You think that bitch nigga care about you?"

"I already told you why and we don't fuck around like that so I'm sure he don't care about me. Now you in here mad at me but you the one who never call me. I gave you my number at the mall and you barely get at me."

"Well I'm here now, come here." She walked closer and he gripped her ass,

"What's up, show a nigga that you really don't care bout that nigga."

"Okay, but you gotta talk to yo homie downstairs though."

"I got you."

Pull Out lifted her shirt over her head and looked at her titties.

"Them muthafuckas look nice."

"They taste nice too." She replied then put one in her mouth and started sucking. His dick got rock hard as he stepped closer to her. He put his hand on her shoulder,

"We ain't got that much time let me get some head real quick.

"Shawnda dropped to her knees and pulled his pants down. She started licking the side before she put it in her mouth.

"Aww, suck this dick. I'm bout to face fuck you so I can hurry up and bust." She nodded her head while focusing on sucking his dick good. Slurp! Slurp! Pull Out grabbed the sides of her head and started pumping her face.

છૹ

DOWNSTAIRS

છૹ

"Tell me where the bricks at and we ain't gone smoke you." Gucci Ty told Kapo.

"I already told you nigga ain't no birds here! Somebody gave ya'll the wrong info." Kapo said trying to sound as convincing as he could.

"Fuck all this talking cuz." He put the gun on his kneecap and gave one more warning,

"They say getting shot in the knee is the worst, do you really wanna find out?" Gucci Ty asked.

"I already told you ain't--" Boom!

"Agghh! Agghh!" He was cut off by the gunshot and started screaming.

"Alright! Alright!" Bap!

"Agghh! I said alright!" Ron shot him in his other knee for talking shit to him earlier. Kapo fell on the ground still screaming.

"Where's it at nigga!? Imma shoot you in yo elbows next!" Gucci Ty yelled at him while standing over him.

"It's in the closet over there on the top shelf in the diaper bag!" Kapo yelled from the floor.

"Ron go get it cuz! Pull Out hurry the fuck up nigga! What the fuck you doing?" Ron went to the closet and started looking for it. "I'm coming cuz!" Pull Out yelled from upstairs.

Ron came over and sat the bag on the table and unzipped it.

"It's four bricks in here cuz, uncooked." They looked as Pull Out and Shawnda came walking down the stairs. Pull Out was still zipping up his pants and Shawnda was carrying the bags.

"What kinda backwards ass shit ya'll got going on? You up there getting some pussy while we on a mission cuz?" Gucci Ty asked,

"It's coo cuz, we got the money and she rocking with us, what's good down here?" Pull Out asked.

"This slob nigga finally came off the work. We got four birds and that money now so we good."

"Shawnda where some trash bags at?" Gucci Ty asked.

"They're in the kitchen under the sink I'll show you." She responded.

They walked into the kitchen and she got on her knees to find the bags.

"Here you go" She handed him a bag.

"Good looking grab one more for me." When she reached back in Gucci Ty put the gun to the back of her head. BOOM! Her body fell into the space under the sink where she was looking. Blood and brains flew on the lower drawers and ground. Gucci walked back into the front room and told Pull Out to put everything in the bag

"Why you kill the bitch cuz, I was gone take her with me?" Pull Out asked.

"You don't reward disloyalty with loyalty, that's why Julius Caesar's dead. That bitch a slob! You didn't notice when we didn't answer at the door she said ya'll dumb ass niggaz always playing! That means she always over here, you dumb fuck!"

"BapBapBap!" Ron shot Kapo in the face and head while he was still on the floor.

"Bitch ass nigga," Ron said then kicked him.

"Come on cuz we outta here." Gucci Ty said then opened the door. When they made it out and was headed to the car Gucci Ty looked at Pull Out,

"I can't wait to tell the homies about yo captain-save-a-hoe ass."

"Fuck you nigga that bitch thick as shit and she suck dick good." Ron broke out laughing. BocBocBocBoc! Gunshots started breaking out from nowhere,

"Aww fuck cuz I'm hit." yelled Pull Out then fell to the ground. Ron and Gucci Ty ducked behind the parked car in front of them.

Suwooop! "There them niggaz go by the basketball court." Ron told Gucci Ty while pulling his. 22 revolver out. Gucci Ty pulled his .380s out and started looking over the car.

"It's two of them niggaz crouching behind that black Impala."

"What ya'll crab niggaz doing by the homies house?!" One of the men yelled,

"Go ask his dead ass, slob!" Ron yelled back.

"Stop talking! You letting them know where we at." Gucci Ty chastised him.

"Nigga fuck Dirty Dan!" One of them yelled and ran across the street directly from his homie. When he started running Ron took his chance. BapBap! The back window shattered on the car the man ran to.

"They tryin to trap us in the middle of them," Ron said.

"Pull Out when we start shooting you gotta get up and make it to the car, it's only three cars down. Where you hit at?" Gucci Ty asked him.

"In my leg cuz but I'm good."

"Act like you bout to get up then drop back down hella fast, hurry up! Ron watch the nigga on yo side.

"Soon as Pull Out got half way up the shooting started. BocBoc! Gucci Ty had a clear shot now since the one with the red bandana on hopped up to get Pull Out.

Boom Boom Boom Boom! He started firing with both guns. He heard glass breaking then the man yelled,

"Agghh shit! Freedo I'm hit blood!" The other one tried to make it across the street to help his homie. Bap Bap Bap! -Click! Boca Boca! The man had to retreat and began shooting back over his shoulder while diving behind a car.

"One of you bitch ass crabz is empty!" Freedo yelled. They heard police sirens in the distance,

"I told you about them revolvers cuz!" Gucci Ty whispered to Ron.

"But yo man is over there leaking! You by yourself slob!" Ron yelled back to him.

"Here take this cuz! You and Pull Out get to the car while I hold this nigga off." Gucci Ty told Ron and handed him one of the guns.

"Budda where you hit at?" Freedo yelled to him.

"Side of the stomach blood but I'm gucci for now! Kill that crab nigga that popped me!" Budda yelled back. Freedo seen Ron helping Pull Out limp to the car. He knew it was a trick and wasn't falling for it again, he had his own. He took off his shoe and threw it at the car across the street hard as he could. When Gucci Ty heard the loud thump he naturally looked and aimed towards that direction. Boca Boca Boca! Freedo started shooting at him as soon as he showed his face.

"What you hiding for nigga? You ain't bout that life!" Freedo taunted him while running to a car closer to them without Gucci Ty seeing him. He seen Ron open the door for Pull Out and started shooting at them. Boca Boca Boca Boca! They dove in the car while Freedo ducked down,

"I got thirty shots in this. 40 cal, we can do this all night crab!" He waited a few seconds but didn't get a reply. He heard something moving in the opposite direction. He got up and seen Gucci Ty running towards their car.

Boca Boca Boca! He aimed at his back. "Fuck cuz!" Gucci Ty yelled while ducking behind a car. Pull Out opened the passenger door and leaned out shooting at the car Freedo was crouched behind. Booow Booow Booow!

"Come on cuz run to the car!" Pull Out yelled and started shooting again. Booyow Booyow! Gucci Ty started running to the car while Pull Out had Freedo pinned down. Budda was sitting up against the car watching everything transpire. He seen Freedo being shot at so Gucci Ty could escape,

"Aww!" He yelled as he fought through the pain while standing up. He leaned over the trunk of the car for balance and started shooting at Pull Out.

Boom Boom! The front windshield shattered into pieces and Pull Out stopped shooting. Boom Boom Boom! He kept shooting without really aiming. He watched Gucci Ty jump into the backseat and the car take off. Freedo ran to the middle of the street and tried to get his get-back.

Boca Boca Boca Boca! The police sirens were getting too close for comfort. Freedo ran over to Budda and helped him move fast as possible,

"Come on blood we gone make it to Shanay spot! Fight that shit nigga! Think about yo daughter blood!" He kept saying to Budda to keep him alive and fighting.

"Aww shit blood, it burn! I ain't going out by no crab!" Budda replied keeping himself pumped up.

"Just two more doors and we gucci."

"It was Pull Out and Ron," Budda said while Freedo started pounding on the door.

"Shanay! Hurry up and open the door! Budda got shot!" Shanay opened the door as the police were turning into the Ville.

"Hurry up and close the door!" Freedo yelled as soon as he got Budda inside.

"Oh my God what happened to him?" She asked soon as the door closed,

"What you think? Look go get some bleach so we can clean his hands. Then you gotta try and drive him to the hospital. If something happen just say he went to the store for some swishers and came back shot. He was a victim of crossfire! Hurry up!" Freedo instructed her.

O-Dawg was on the phone with Gotti and pacing the front room.

"Blood I'm telling you bout my money, niggaz is about to die in groups!" O Dawg said while Tamia was sitting on the couch watching him.

"Naw fuck that! Ain't no calming down nigga! Shootouts is one thing but it's a whole nother level when niggaz rob me. Then to top it off they killed Kapo! I'm about to turn it up! It's gone be a lot of slow singing and flower bringing for fucking with me!" Tamia had never seen him so mad and out of control. He usually held his anger in check and thought everything through.

"I got some big plans for these niggaz blood. What I need you to do is find out where Budda keep his shit at. Can you do that? You are supposed to be our intelligence man. Matter of fact find out where all them niggaz mamas live, cars they drive, favorite restaurant and anything else. Pay who-ever you got to, just make it happen. Because when I'm done putting this master plan together I want everything perfect. I'm bout to get on some real Napoleon shit now." He got quiet for a minute,

"I'm not blaming shit on you or nobody else. I'm simply telling you what time it is. I already had a mission for Falon but was still thinking bout it. But now I'm definitely calling her number. I'm letting Burnside off the chain and Boobie gettin back on his trip. I got summin for you too but I'm still workin on the details." O-Dawg picked up his .40 cal off the table then put it back down for the tenth time,

"I'll holla tomorrow." Then he hung up his phone.

O-Dawg grabbed the vase off the table and flung it at the wall. Tamia jumped when it shattered into pieces,

"Baby calm down it's going to be okay." She said trying to get him to calm down, "That's four bricks and forty thousand I gotta pay my brother back! Plus I gotta pay for the lil niggas funeral too. So if you ain't about to go to Vegas and sell some pussy for me then shut the fuck up!" he yelled at her. Tamia hopped off the couch instantly,

"Nigga what? You got me fucked up! I'm trying to help you out and be there for my nigga and you disrespect me? Make sure you clean that glass up before you go to bed, killer." she yelled back at him and rushed to the bedroom. Damn blood I was planning on hittin that too, he thought as he watched her walk away in her bra and panties.

"Yea walk away! Typical bitch, that's all yall do is walk away when shit get real." The door slammed loud. He knew he was wrong but didn't care because he was mad and Olay was a primary reason. O-Dawg started pacing and talking to himself,

"Niggaz ain't never satisfied till they dead, but that's okay because everybody from the dog to the kids is dying! I ain't never met a bunch of niggaz who wanna die so bad! Do these niggaz really think they can see me? I'm do or die O-Dawg! Pull Out, Ron, and Gucci Ty welcome to the hit list!"

"I'm on my worst behavior, muthafuckas never loved us!" His cell phone went off on the table blasting Drake. The caller ID said "Dute"

"what's mobbin? . . . Is the pigs still out there? . . . You know I'm mad right? . . . They arrested Budda? . . . Oh he should be good then . . . Yea I know that already, I know exactly who. . . What I wanna know is how the fuck they knew about that spot? We lucky they didn't hit the main ones. . . Fuck all that blood check the triv. I want every crab outta the Ville. All the lil crab stragglers that's living around, get them niggaz out. Them niggaz is feeding the other crabs info. Shoot up all they baby mama's houses, grand-mas, mama's, I don't give a fuck. . . I know you don't like doing the house thing but do what I said blood. We can't kill all of them because then the Ville will be on fire and we gone lose everything. Start applying pressure and they people is gone move and they bum asses is gone have to follow. . . Soon as they leave make 'em come right back! They gone have to earn those pension plans fucking with me. Call Shooter, Lil Kenny, Gatman and whoever else and make it happen a.s.a.p. When yall done I got some money for yall. When yall done we bout to tighten them muthafuckas up! I'm not taking no more loses or the homies is gone start losing they lives. . . I don't give a fuck if they official or not! If they ain't from Denver Lanes, Unthank Park, some type of blood or one of ya loyal Hoover homies then they got to go . . . Oh and any bitches that be having crabz over tell them this is they warning!" O-Dawg dropped his phone back on the table.

He started pacing and talking again,

"I gotta do this shit right and make sure these snitch niggaz can't tell on me. And make sure my crazy ass bitch don't stab me in my sleep for disrespecting her." Tamia interrupted him while walking back into the front room with a bottle in her hand. She walked directly up to him and said,

"Apologize nigga if you wanna have a happy home." He wrapped his arms around her waist and kissed her on the lips,

"I'm sorry baby for saying that, I shouldn't have took my stresses out on you."

"Don't ever compare me to that bitch again nigga. I ain't no traitor. I knew what you was and was gone be when I met you. Yeah I want you to stop being in the streets, but I damn sho ain't gone leave you cause you're not stopping when I want you to. That's not real love nigga so don't ever come at me wit that again." Tamia flashed on him. O-Dawg kissed her on the lips again,

"You right baby." he told her.

"I know I am, now take your shirt off and lay on the couch so I can give you a massage."

O-Dawg took off his shirt and laid on his stomach on the couch. Tamia climbed on his back and started rubbing oil into his skin

"You love me?" She asked him.

"Yeah I love you baby." He responded. Tamia took a deep breath in,

"Good cause I'm pregnant." She gave him the news and held her breath.

ⲟⳡⲟ

NEXT DAY

ഐ

Jersey Joe was riding around in his truck trying to call Falon for the third time and got sent to voicemail again. It had been a couple days since he last spoke to her. The last time was when he took her shopping and then she stood him up. They've exchanged a few texts but that was it. He decided to text her at that moment,

"What's good? U ain't got time 4 a real nigga no mo? U actin funny" He sent it. He figured he might as well pick up the dope that Boobie has for him at his house. Let me hit this nigga. He thought to himself then made the call,

"Yo son you at yo spot? I'm bout to come pick that package up. . . Aight I'll be there in a minute." he said then disconnected the call.

He checked his texts. No new ones. He resent Falons just in case she didn't get the last one for some reason,

"Let me call this lil nigga." he said out loud.

"Yo shooter? . . . It's the Grimm reaper ya heard? How many times I gotta tell you to save my number son . . . Anyways I'm coming through in 45 minutes with that new shit ya heard? So get ready." he hung up then checked his texts again. No new ones

"Fuck this bitch yo! She wanna play games with a god." he vented to himself out loud. 15 minutes later he pulled up at Boobies house,

"I'm outside son." he said into the phone and hung up.

Boobie answered the door wearing a red robe and red slippers. When they got inside Joe couldn't help himself,

"Yo son, who the fuck you think you is Ray J or somebody? Walking around in ya robe and shit like you got 10 bitches in here fighting over you." They both started laughing as they sat on the couch,

"Nigga I stay with bitches fighting over me blood on the set. Anyways you know it's time to turn up right?"

"Shit it's been time if you ask me. The crabs bout to start getting they shit blew off now son. O-Dawg called the grim reaper and told me it's time to start collecting souls son."

"Joe? If you don't get out my house with that mortal kombat shit blood." They started laughing again,

"This the work son?"

"Yea that's it blood"

"Aight son I'm gone, I gotta get this shit to shooter." Joe said then grabbed the bag off the table,

"Oh you going that way blood? Drop this money off over there at the money house for me then." Boobie asked him.

"Aight son I got you."

"Baby! Grab that backpack that's sitting in front of the closet." He yelled to his bedroom "Yo I can't wait to body one of them crabs son. That nigga O done took the lid off and I'm bout to jump on every crab I catch."

"Yea dat. That nigga hot about losing his money. Them niggaz is stupid blood, they was better off shooting him. O ain't no regular nigga, shit he ain't even a street nigga. It's hard to explain, that nigga belong behind a desk at a corporation. You know how we always hear about conspiracy theories but never know who pulled the strings? That's the type of shit he be on. He done read way too many books in jail. Plus watched the Godfather too many times." They started laughing at that last comment.

"Here you go," A female said from the hallway that was walking towards them. Joe looked in the direction of the voice. Falon was walking towards them wearing one of Boobies button-up shirts. Their eyes connected the whole time she was walking. Joe could see the guilt and surprise on her face. Right then he knew that she had got all his messages and was playing him. Boobie took the bag from her,

"Good looking baby." That bitch car ain't parked outside, he must of picked her up. He was thinking while staring at her,

"What's poppin Falon? Nigga ain't seen you in a minute." he said to her

"Hi Joe, I've just been staying out the way." Falon responded then headed back to the room.

Boobie and Joe both stared at her ass while she walked away. When the door shut Boobie looked at Joe,

"That bitch got some fire with her freaky ass. And she thick as a muthafucka."

"Yea son I see why you got that robe on. I'm bout to go take care of this business ya heard?" Joe responded trying to keep the emotion out his voice. Boobie walked him to the door,

"Aight blood get at me after the drop. If I don't answer then you know why." Boobie said while smirking

ॐ

HOURS LATER

ॐ

"Half dead I know you took that shit hard cuz but you gotta get ya swag back. You barley talk and damn sho don't smile. Matter-fact have you even got any pussy since then?" Ron said trying to get a smile outta him with that last comment. They were riding around trying to catch a enemy slippin,

"How Pull Out doing? It was just a flesh wound in the leg right?" Half dead asked not even attempting to answer one of the questions.

"Yea cuz cool. That nigga hot he had to stay in the house. All he wanna do is ride all day, like yo hot ass."

"Drive by the Texan and let's see if some slobs is out there. I heard Burnside and that Jersey nigga is always there. Worse case its just some straight Unthank niggaz there, we gone kill them too. Cause when shit hit the fan that's who O-Dawg bitch ass gone run behind. So we might as well start knocking these clowns off now." Half dead said then took his clip out of his 9mm to count how many shots he had

"14 in the clip and 1 in the head, somebody bout to die tonight my nigga."

Ron could tell by the look in his eyes there would be no alternative, they were on a mission. Half dead turned up the Nipsey Hussle song that was playing. By the time the 'Fly Crippin' song went off they were approaching the Texan bar. They were driving down Vancouver St. towards Fremont,

"Yea cuz, park right here and let's scope it out." Half dead said.

"There go Pablo, Lone heart, Cheese, DJ and that bitch ass nigga Gotti! We got one cuz!" Half dead got excited seeing Gotti and tried to open the door. Ron grabbed him,

"Cuz what the fuck is you doing? You can't get out here, you know damn well these niggaz be laying in the bushes and shit. Don't forget about the alley right behind these apartments we parked in front of." Ron said while grabbing his arm.

"You make it sound like these niggaz can't be served or summin cuz. So what's yo plan then? Cause somebody dying in the next 5 minutes!" Half dead replied angrily.

"I'mma bust a U-turn right here and you empty that clip through the parking lot and we getting the fuck outta here. I know you want Gotti cause he Mob Life but that's suicide right now. Lean out that window and hit whoever god don't protect!" Ron said then slowly hit a U-turn with the headlights out. Half dead rolled the window down then said,

"Get as close as you can cuz, this for Dan." When Ron was almost driving on the sidewalk Half dead made his move.

"This for Dirty Dan!" Boom Boom Boom Boom Boom! Half dead was leaning so far out the window that Ron had to hold his hoody with one hand and hold the wheel with the other.

Boom Boom! He watched the crowd break up and run in different directions. Boom Boom Boom! He seen a woman fall and start screaming and a man turn halfway then fall. Boom Boom! Ron sped up when he heard shots rang out from down the block. Boc Boc Ron yanked Half dead back in the car and drove full speed.

"Aight nigga we gone!" He drove up Vancouver and turned right on Going St. Before he finally slowed down.

"You hit a few of those slobs cuz!" Ron said excited with his heart still pumping fast, "Look cuz that's the bitch nigga DJ walking outta breath! Pull up on em!" Half dead demanded.

"Nigga you trippin we gotta get up outta here before the boyz get here."

"The niggaz walkin our direction! Fuck that I'm on em!"

"Aight nigga let me drive a lil closer. Yea that is him too." Soon as Ron finished his sentence Half dead jumped out the car while it was still moving. DJ's eyes got big when he realized what was transpiring. He turned to run but Half dead was almost to him. Boom! The first shot hit him in the thigh. He was still standing and trying to run. Boom! The second hit his leg and he went down hard.

"Ahhh shit!" he rolled over on his back to see if the shooter had left. Half dead was standing right over him with the gun aimed at his chest.

"Tell my nigga Dan I sent you.

"Click Click! He had ran out of bullets. "What the fuck!" Half dead ran to the car and leaned in,

"Give me yo gun!"

"Hell naw cuz get in the car!" Ron yelled while looking in the rear view mirror.

"The nigga ain't dead and I'm empty!"

"Fuck that get in the car!"

"Give me the muthafuckin gun cuz!" Half dead yelled at the top of his lungs. Ron passed him his. 38 revolver,

"Hurry up nigga!" He said while half dead turned around. DJ was trying to crawl away, "Naw bitch nigga" Half dead said and kicked him in the stomach

"Aghhh!" DJ moaned and turned over holding his stomach.

"Yo niggaz gone be there in a minute, I probably will too." Boom! Boom Boom! He shot him 3 times in the chest. Boom! Then in the face. When he seen DJ was dead he turned around and ran back to the car. Ron took off without saying a word

৩৩

1 HOUR LATER

৩৩

Jersey Joe looked at his phone sitting in his lap for the 10th time. It was going off again and he seen it was Boobie again.

"Stop calling me bitch nigga! You think you slick with that lil move you did today. I know damn well that bitch been told you she was fuckin with me son. Yall probably been over there reading and laughing at my messages! That's ok ya heard?" Joe yelled then grabbed the bottle of Patron off the seat for another drink,

"Ahh!" he breathed out loud satisfied the drink was burning his chest.

"Yo! The nigga Boobie think he better than the god! He stole the plug from my relative! He stealing my bitch son! Then he gone throw it in my face while trying to send me on an errand! I ain't no fuckin errand

Boy! The niggaz a snake!" He was still venting to himself then took another gulp from the bottle, "Where this bitch at son?" Joe's phone started ringing again.

"Why the fuck you keep calling me son! Yea I know you're a fuckin snake!" he said while declining the call.

After another 5 minutes of drinking and talking out loud, he finally seen Falons silver Lincoln MKH pull up and park. He looked at his watch,

"Bitch it's 11:15 at night you shoulda been home." Falon was so tired she didn't even notice his Escalade parked across the street. She was making her way to the front door when a loud sound made her jump. Beeeppp! Beeeppp! She turned and seen somebody was honking at her from a red truck.

"I know that ain't." She stopped talking when she seen Joe hop out the truck

"Falon! Come here yo, let me holla at you." he shouted from across the street.

Falon walked fast as she could and met him next to the truck.

"What the fuck is you doing here? Waiting outside my house on some stalker shit." She hissed at him. Joe gripped her ass with both hands,

"We need to talk, then I wanna go inside and hit that. He said then palmed her ass even tighter. Falon ripped his hands off her then replied,

"Nigga you're drunk! We ain't talking bout shit right now and don't touch me. How long you been sitting out here stalking me?" That infuriated him.

"So you saying I can't touch you nomore? You wasn't saying that when you was spending all my money bitch! You let that bitch ass nigga Boobie touch you but I can't? What you think he more gangsta then me?"

"Bitch!? Nigga you got me fucked up! You the one been blowing my phone up the last week. You the one in love, you the one popping up at Boobies house knowing I'm there. You the one in yo feelings sitting outside my house. That's what bitches do! And that's exactly what you are, a bitch ass nigga. And I bet you won't say that shit to Bobbie's face either!" She shot back at him. Soon as she finished her sentence Joe grabbed her by the neck and slammed her into the truck,

"Who the bitch now?" he tightened the grip on her neck and lifted her higher into the air. Falon was grabbing and scratching at his hands trying to get free.

"Bitch you disrespectful!" he banged her head against the window then finally let her go after he seen she wasn't fighting back no more.

She bent over wheezing and trying to catch her breath.

"Yo my bad, I'm drunk and a nigga spazzed out, you ok?" he asked after he realized what he did. After a few more seconds she finally caught her breath.

"Don't ever talk to me or touch me again! Nigga I should get you killed! But O told me this would happen so I'mma take half the blame. But the next time you put yo hands on me you better kill me or I'm telling Marshawn! Get the fuck from my house before I come out and shoot you!" Joe had never seen Falon so mad before. He realized he fucked up by choking her. The family was real protective over her, especially O-Dawg. Falon was like the lil sister of the Mob. Joe knew he had to play his cards right for now.

"Aight baby I'm gone. Just know the alcohol had me fucked up yo and a nigga really love you. Hopefully one day I can make it up to you."

"Yea whatever nigga!" she responded then walked away to her house.

CHAPTER 11

My mom always said the greatest trick the devil ever played was to convince the world he didn't exist

O-Dawg was sitting across from Jaleesa at the olive garden. He saw her mouth moving but didn't hear nothing she was saying. He had way too many problems he was dealing with in his head. Two of them concerned her and he was still trying to decide what he was going to do. "Are you going to answer my question?" She interrupted his thoughts, "I'm sitting here pouring out my heart to you and your not even listening? I asked you why have you been avoiding me, and acting like you don't care about me."

"Aint nobody been avoiding you baby, a nigga just been busy. You act like we don't talk everyday or summin" He replied,

"Yeah but you always sound distant and not fully into me." She complained.

"That's because I can't be fully into nuttin with all this shit going on around me. My lil nigga and his bitch just got killed and niggaz stole hella money from me. The homie just got killed in the hood and Gotti got shot.

What the fuck you want me to do, come play house with you? But since we asking questions, let's get down to the real issue. Why you ask me about a name that was on that list I gave you?" Jaleesa looked surprised that he even brought that up.

"I told you the name seemed familiar but I wasn't sure. Where is this coming from?" She asked,

"So you don't know the name for sure?"

"NO." O-Dawg could tell she was hiding something. She seemed like she was trying too hard to convince him and the look on her face was one of a liar. He just stared at her for a few seconds.

"Aight it's a dead issue then, I was just checking."

He pulled out his phone and typed a text,

"Everything been checking out?" He sent it then focused back on her,

"Well it seems to me that you still don't trust me even after I did that for you. What more can I do? I'm trying to get you to love me and prove to you that I'm loyal." Before he could reply his phone started vibrating, he looked at the screen. It showed a random number and the location was Ontario, Oregon. He knew it was somebody calling from Snake River. He put a finger up to Jaleesa and answered the call.
"Hello…."

"You have a prepaid call… you will not be charged for this call. This call is from 'Big Gee' he heard a deep voice say.

"Oh this my nigga"! Big gee was Aaron gee from Lincoln Park bloods-murda gang. Gee was really from San Diego were the gang came from and acted just like a California nigga.

"A inmate at the snake river corrections institution. This call may be monitored and recorded, to accept this call press 5." The female recording said. O-Dawg didn't hesitate to press 5

"What's mobbin big bro?" He answered the phone super excited.

"Keeping this shit mob life and murda gang. What's brackin blood? I heard it's been triv out there!" Gee responded.

"Shit I'm just at the olive garden with my bitch Jaleesa tryna dodge these snitches."

"Yeah dat! Look blood, you enjoy yo date I'll holla tomorrow. Just 3way that nigga Burnside for me then put the phone down."

"Aight blood hold on," O-Dawg replied then called Burnside, "Burnside? Hold up, I got gee on the line" He clicked over.

"Gee you there?"

"Yeah you call em blood...what's up with my nigga blood," O-Dawg heard Burnside yell. He put the phone on mute then placed it on the table,

"My bad baby. Anyways I need you to do me a favor," He told Jaleesa. She shook her head,

"Picture that, I knew it was a reason you wanted me to meet you."

"I need you to let me have that extra room in yo house,"

"For what? Never mind, I'm pretty sure I know why. So you want me to put my freedom on the line again. Yet I can barley get you to spend quality time with me? Are you serious?" She asked him with curiosity in her voice.

"Listen you knew what time it was when you started fuckin with me. If you gone fuck with me you gone have to wear a neck brace, simple as that."

"A neck brace?" She asked interrupting him.

"Yeah the shit the doctors give you when you break yo neck. That's exactly what you gone have to do if you call yoself fuckin with me. I expect you to do what I ask you, without me asking you. Go out your way, break yo neck for a nigga to show me how much you really love me. You know how I am, you either with me or against me. If you with me than act accordingly, if not then get the fuck out my face wasting our time." He laid down the law then looked at his phone.

147

He seen they were still talking and he had a message from Killah. He was responding to the text O-Dawg sent earlier,

"Everything gucci still want me to babysit?" O-Dawg thought hard before responding. He knew Killah was basically saying he didn't like what he was doing, and was wasting time. O-Dawg had him on this mission for over a month now,

"Yeah but even tighter now. It's more important now. I can't shake the feeling. You getting paid to sit haha." then he sent it.

One thing Jaxx always taught him was that a beautiful face told the ugliest lies.

"You're a conceited asshole you know that? And you're very demanding." She blurted out.

"Imma Scorpio" was his response.

"I don't know why I even like you, I can't stand you," she replied trying to hide her smile.

"That's easy, I'm the flyest nigga you know and I get money. I look good, my dick big and I take care of business. I'm the realest nigga breathing; God only makes niggaz like me every 20 years. The key word is 'like'. I came after Big Meech and honestly he might not make no more after me. I wouldn't be surprised if he ends the world after I die. Oh, and fucking with me you know yo future is way more brighter than your past. Another thing, you love me, not like." When he finished his speech he leaned over and kissed her on the lips.

"I bet you really believe everything that just came out your mouth?"

"And I bet if I reach my hand under the table and touch that pussy it's gone be wet." He then tried to put his hands in between her legs. She snapped them shut before he could reach her pussy,

"Stop, I can't stand yo ass" she said then started laughing

"Have everything but the computer out the room by the time I get there." He instructed her,

"Ok baby, whenever that's going to be." Jaleesa said then stuck her lips out faking a pout. He followed up by saying

"that's not all."

"I got summin else to tell you too. I'm only telling you this because you work where I live and it's gone be in yo face. Anyway, Tamia is pregnant she just told me a few days ago." Jaleesa's eyes got immediately watery then she put her face down. He knew she would be hurt but he felt like she had to accept it. She met him while he was with Tamia, so it wasn't like she came into the situation with blinders on

"C'mon with that crying shit, you know I don't like that," he told her while touching her hand. That was one of his weaknesses due to seeing his mom do it so much growing up. Jaleesa picked her face up and looked at him. Tears were running down her face rapidly,

"Well what the fuck do you want me to do, smile? I can't be mad because I knew what I was getting myself into. But that don't mean it still don't hurt. In the back of my mind I thought I could have you all to myself, guess not." She started choking up and had to dig some tissue out of her purse,

"I don't know what you want me to say."

"There aint nothing you can say. Can we leave now? You've accomplished your two goals for the day. Got me to let you store only god knows what and to make me feel like shit in the same conversation."

"You know damn well I don't want you to feel like that. That shit wasn't planned it just happened and I wanted to tell you before she started showing." He said trying to reason with her.

"Whatever fine I gotta get back to work," She raised her voice then gathered her belongings before leaving the table. O-Dawg left the money for the bill then looked at his phone. They were done talking. He exhaled real hard

"Bitches," he said to himself then got up from the table.

149

ॐ

"How yo leg doing cuz?" Pressha asked Pull Out. They were riding around talking after they just dropped off a package to a client. Pull Out looked at his leg before responding.

"It feel straight now cuz, I'm just waiting for the doctors to take all this fucking weird ass Band-Aid looking wrapping off. Those slob niggaz kinda put the kid outta action for a while:"

"You'll be aight lil nigga, its better there than the head. You could be like Kapo right now so just count yo blessings and be on point next time. It's good you outta commission for a while. You doing too much right now, feel me? I understand you tryna earn yo keep and yo name, but remember that anything the streets know, so do the boyz. Most of these niggaz low-key work for the gang task. Don't forget we in this for the money and nuttin else. Let them other Crips gangbang and look dumb hanging on Albina all day. When its war then it's on, no question. But after the war it's back to the money cuz. And if it's not about no money or blatant disrespect than it shouldn't even be no war. This shit with them Slob life niggaz is bout money and disrespect. We also grew up with dem niggaz so it's past bad history. Don't think I'm coming at you on some soft shit either, because you know I got the most bodies from the hood. But at the same time you see what we riding in. I dropped 80 racks for this new jaguar because I put my money before the bullshit. The only way to survive in this game is to outsmart everybody else. You also gotta know and respect your enemy too. You too arrogant lil nigga and that can cost you yo life. Let me ask you a question, what you think bout Boobie and O-Dawg?" Pressha asked him setting him up because he knew what the answer would be. Pull Out sucked his teeth then replied, "They're two bitch ass slob niggaz I can't wait to kill. Fuck you mean what do I think of them?"

Pressha looked over at him smirking,

"that's why I said your arrogance gone get you killed. Tell me why you said O-Dawg a bitch,"

"Cause he is a bitch. The nigga always in the house hiding like a hoe. That nigga aint shot nobody since the shit popped off. When the last time he shot somebody? All he do is pay Boobie and Burnside to do his dirty work. That's bitch shit. Anybody with money can do that. I don't respect that slob nigga, why should I?" Pull Out said getting animated.

"I aint killed nobody yet and neither has your brother. Does that make us bitches?"

"Cuz stop playing word games with me. The difference is you aint hiding and will kill, he won't." Pressha started laughing in his face.

"You got a lot to learn lil nigga. You don't think their lil niggaz think I'm hiding? Just how you see me, it's the same thing over there. That nigga sitting around plotting just like Butta and me is, trust me. Just how you think you're the hardest nigga in Portland. Just how you will kill at the drop of a dime. Just how you feel your untouchable. Guess what? Them niggaz feel the same way. It's a million niggaz in America right now that feels the same way!" Pressha yelled the last sentence to drive the point home.

"So what I'm supposed to feel like them niggaz are harder than me? If that's the case then I'm a bitch too. Am I supposed to feel they're untouch-able? We're supposed to feel we're the best, if not then why bother?"

"You're supposed to feel you're the best when you are the best. You become the best when you master the art of war. First you gone have to admit when somebody's smarter or harder than you. Then you figure out how you can defeat them. You have to know your strengths and weak-nesses as well as the enemy's. You can't become a man until you can admit where you need strength at, or where your enemy has an advantage. If you can't admit or recognize then how the fuck you gone fix it? Now as far as O-Dawg goes, we gone kill that nigga no doubt. But he aint got no bitch in him and he'll say the same about me. That's respect. I know he a killer, but he hella smart with it. He got money and know how to plan shit out. He has patience and doesn't put himself in harms way. But I also know his weakness too. His heart aint in this war, he been on some falling back shit for a while. That's dangerous when yo heart aint into it. That means he won't go full throttle or think things 100% through. He gone start looking at situations only half way. We also know that if we kill Boobie and Burnside then he's left with a bunch of bitch niggaz that will scatter. His reputation lives through them, everybody fears him because of them. Once we knock dem two of then everybody gone see the untouchable get touched."

"So why don't we just kill him first then?" Pull Out asked in all seriousness.

"Show me where he live so we can go get him then."

"That's the point, we don't know. But we do know once we hit his main niggaz he gone have to show his face. Until then we gone keep knocking his lil niggaz off and taking his money and dope."

"All I know is once my leg get right I'm on dem niggaz. I don't care if I see O-Dawg at the mall, I'm popping that nigga on sight and that's on Dan." Pressha shook his head because he knew he was dead serious.

ᘒᘒ

INSIDES OF BURNSIDES CAR

ᘒᘒ

"Yeah blood that's my nigga right there, the crackers gave my bro 37 years. If that nigga was out it would be bad for niggaz on bloods." Burnside said to Jersey Joe while he was driving He had just hung up with Gee a few moments ago.

"Yeah son sound like he a real nigga. Yo after we drop this brick off, swing me by the barber shop yo."

"Nigga why the fuck you always at the shop and you aint got no hair?" Burnside said then started laughing.

"Yo I gotta keep my beard fresh for these west coast bitches son." Joe started rubbing his hand through his beard after he spoke. "New drink, I talked to that nigga O yesterday and its green light. Any brand we catch we air em out, fuck the consequences. I got this Mexican named Crook that live out in Beaverton, he a Norteño. He told me he got a brand new batch of smacks in stock, assault rifles. I'm gone go meet blood in a couple days and buy everything."

"Yo make sure you bring those muthafuckas straight to my spot ya heard." Joe told him then turned the music up

"This my shit son and the nigga yo gotti is Damu. Yeah, cold blooded, I feel this shit yo." Joe said commenting on Yo gotti and J. Cole new song 'Cold Blooded'. They both leaned back and let the music suck them in while driving down the street.

☯

"I'm only telling you all this shit because I don't wanna have to go to your funeral. When Butta and me retire in 10 years you gone have to take the torch cuz. You not gone be able to if you dead or not smart enough, feel me?" Pressha asked Pull Out. Pull out was only half way listening due to him texting Shay back.

"Yeah I got you cuz." Pressha knew Pull out had heard too much for one day so he just shook his head and kept driving.

Five minutes later they came to a red light on Lombard st & MLK Ave.

"Damn we got caught at the light cuz, I hate this long ass light" Pressha said while hitting the steering wheel. Pull Out looked at him to see what he just hit. He was about to comment when a car caught his attention from outside the driver window. Red Chrysler 300c with black racing stripes and it's on rims. That looks like that jersey nigga! It is! And pressha got the window rolled down. Pull Out had these thoughts racing through his mind. That's Burnside car I've seen it on Facebook 100 times. After this last thought he made up his mind.

"Cuz lean yo seat back and hurry up. Don't look around either." He whispered to Pressha. Pressha was leaning back when he asked,

"The police right here?" Pull Out gripped his 9mm Beretta.

"Naw but they bout to be!"

Soon as the words left his mouth he leaned over with the gun aimed at the car

"Gutta squad!" He yelled. Boom!! Boom!! Boom!! Boom!!

"Cuz what the fuck!" Pressha screamed then leaned further down in the seat. Boom! Boom! Boom! Boom! Every car that was in distance was trying to get out of harms way. Cars were hitting each other, people were lying down on the seats and the passenger window where Joe was sitting exploded. Boom! Boom! Pull Out was hanging out the window trying to target they're heads but they were ducking down. The Chrysler finally started to drive off but Pull Out kept shooting at it. Boom! Boom! Boom! Boom! Boom! He was aiming at the back of the car now. Boom! Boom! Pressha grabbed him by his hoody and yanked him back into the car. Pressha drove off and screamed,

"What the fuck is you doing?" Pull Out was smiling

"That was Burnside."

ℭℬ

Detective Canfield and his partner Pacman were watching the crime scene specialist do their jobs.

"How many rounds did they find?" Canfield asked while stuffing the last of his doughnut into his mouth.

"15 so far and 3 cars got hit. Oh and 4 bullets hit that house over there." Packman responded then pointed across the street.

"I just got done talking to the manager of taco bell and they claim their cameras don't cover this area. Same thing with the gas station. We don't need that shit anyways we know who did this"

"We do?" Packman asked.

"And you white people swear ya'll so smart. It's those fucking mob life's and gutter squads. It's been them the last few months, ever since they tried to kill O-Dawg in the ville. This shits outta hand, they're fucking hitting innocent people's houses."

"Yeah typical black people shit." Packman smirked then continued,

"It's been 4 murders and countless shootings. Hell nine houses just got shot up in the Ville the same night of the double murder. What a disgrace to your race, the few that are civilized."

These two have been partners for 12 years and always trade racist jokes.

"Fuck you, they aint my race, these is some straight up niggas. What we need is a good informant. One that's high up in the food chain that can bring everybody down, both sides. I got the chief riding my dick for some convictions. It's time for the gloves to come off, don't you think partner?"

"Yes I do but who's going to be our snitch? Well they all end up snitches anyways." Packman asked then started laughing at his own statement

"Let's head back to the war room and figure everything out. Let these flunky's finish up here." Canfield replied then took one more look around.

ꙩꙩ

1 HOUR LATER

ꙩꙩ

"Pull Out what were you thinking?" Butta asked. Pull Out, Half dead, Gucci ty, Pressha and Ron were sitting in Butta's basement having their meeting.

"Tryna kill two slobs at the same time. Now if Burnside woulda got killed then ya'll would be on my dick right now. You said green light. That means whenever and wherever, so I did what I was supposed to do. You said don't call you till we kill somebody. You also said anybody that aint got their chain can't be at the meetings. Well me and my nigga got bodies and we here. So let's cut the crap and give us our chains." Pull Out said then leaned back in a cocky manner.

"He right cuz." Gucci Ty added.

"Whoever feels like Pull Out deserves his chain raise your hand." Butta stated to the room. They all lifted their hands one by one. Ron lifted his also.

"Ron if you don't put yo hand down cuz." Butta said making everybody laugh.

"Pull out I aint against you cuz and you know that. But you gotta be smarter, especially when you with me. The shit might be on camera and that car is in my name cuz."

"I feel you big homie, my bad. Now go get my chain and bring my grey poupon!" Everybody started laughing again.

"Whoever feel like Ron the self-proclaimed don should have a chain raise your hand." Butta said. Everybody raised their hands and Ron couldn't hide his smile. Butta walked over to the closet and pulled out a shopping

THA LAST OF MY KIND

bag. When he pulled the chains out both their eyes got wide. They've been waiting for this moment for years. As he held them in the air the diamonds were sparkling like crazy

"Here lil bro this yours." Pull out was so anxious that he snatched it unintentionally "Here Ron." Ron grabbed his chain nonchalant, trying to make it seem like it was no big deal, but he wasn't fooling anybody, they've all been through it.

"I would like to make an announcement." Everybody started staring at him to hear what he had to say.

"From now on this is a dictatorship and you niggaz are my peasants. From now on I expect ya'll to give me 10% of everything ya'll make every 1st of the month." Gucci Ty threw a pillow from the couch at him smacking him in the face. After that they all started throwing pillows at him, Pull out sat down laughing.

"Aight don't try to say I didn't try to unify the union when the slobs start taking over."

"A Ron I heard yo dumb ass thought you was outta bullets and had a fully loaded heat on yo waist." Pressha said out of nowhere.

"Gucci you aint shit for telling niggaz that," Ron shot back. The whole room busted out laughing.

"Yeah cuz these two niggaz is like dumb and dumber. I made cuz take the slob niggaz heat while I interrogated him and when its war time he act like he forgot he had it! That nigga just wanted to get the fuck outta there." The room started laughing even harder.

"Then to top it off, I send Pull out upstairs with the bitch to get the money and guess what he does? This nigga upstairs getting his dick sucked! Then he got the nerve to tell me she coming with us! So you know what I did."

"What you do cuz?" Pressha asked,

"I shot that slob bitch right in the back of her fucking head! This ol sucka ass nigga was ready to cry, talkin bout why you kill her man? I loved her!" Gucci Ty said making his voice sound like a girl on the last sentence. They all started laughing again.

"Hell naw! That nigga adding shit to the story! Stop lying Tyrone, you aint shit. Tell them niggaz how I had to save you, even while I was shot."

"Ohhhhhh!" They all said trying to instigate.

"Shut up before I kick you in the leg." That comment got them all laughing again. For the first time in months they were all smiling and forgot about the many obstacles they faced. They had no idea what lay ahead of them.

ᘓᕽᘒ

O-Dawg was out shopping with Tamia at the Washington square mall. They were taking a food break at panda express.

"You love spending my money you know that? Eight hundred dollars for some fucking heels. I know one thing, I better see you butt naked wearing them real soon." O-Dawg said complaining to her. Tamia started smiling

"Blah blah blah, you like spending money on me and you know it. If not me than who else? You're supposed to take care of your baby mom."

"Aint that a bitch? You must be confusing a real nigga with your Dominican side. We don't take care of baby moms, you gone be on section 8 fucking with me." Tamia broke out laughing.

"I love you papi."

"Aww hell naw! Don't start speaking that Spanish shit now. Only time that side comes out is when you want some money or some dick."

"What if I want both?" She asked.

"What if I wanna take yo ass back to Dominican Republic where you come from," he responded. Tamia flipped him off then started eating her orange chicken.

"You look very beautiful today baby. I like how you're wearing yo hair straight down for me today. That's my favorite, but you know that. Don't ever think I don't notice the lil things or appreciate everything you do, no matter how small." O-Dawg said and Tamia couldn't help smiling from ear to ear. She leaned across the table and kissed him on the lips,

"I enjoy doing everything for you, it makes me happy to please you." She replied.

"This my Wayne Perry flow, ya'll don't know nothing bout Wayne Perry though." O-Dawg's phone started playing Jay-Z's song 'Tom Ford'. He grabbed it off the table,

"What's mobbin?" He answered. "What!"... "What's thee damage." he asked then got quiet again. "Grazed in the face? Who exactly did it?" O-Dawg took his glasses off and dropped them on the table. "Who all at the hospital?"... "Tell Burnside to fall back and calm down"... "No, not tonight Gotti. I can hear Boobie instigating ass in the background, tell em shut the fuck up!" Tamia was staring at him and trying to figure out how she could help him. She watched his eyes turn glossy black and get smaller. He was gripping the phone so hard she was just waiting for it to break.

"I just got Falon on a mission so it's all gone come together in a minute. Tell Joe to come see me when he done getting stitched up." O-Dawg hung up and stared ahead deep in thought.

"Baby can I tell you something without you flipping out on me?" Tamia interrupted his thoughts. He looked at her deep in the eyes. Tamia could feel the evil that was trying to take over him. She looked him back in the eyes and couldn't help but to think he was losing his soul. The love that was just in his eyes minutes earlier was completely gone. He let out a deep breath then relied,

"Go ahead Tamia." She started playing with her fingers then said,

"I don't know how to say this and still sound like a woman that wants you out the streets, so I'm gone just say it.

I love you so much and don't want to lose you, that's my biggest fear. Every time you walk out the door I pray to god that you make it back alive. I'm tired of feeling that way, tired of wondering. I watch the news and my friends tell me shit too. There's no talking it out, no ignoring it. We're going to have a baby in 8 months Marshawn and I want you alive. I need for you to kill whoever you have to so this shit will end. I don't care how you do it, just do it. You go and do whatever you have to, to make sure you come home at night. Go kill Butta and them, then whoever you think gone take their place so we don't have to go through this anymore." O-Dawg couldn't believe what he was hearing. He thought she was going to preach to him to change or to move. He felt himself loving her more. He knew at that moment what he had to do.

"People don't understand that once I start I'm not going to stop. It seems like no matter how hard I try to step away, niggaz keep pulling me back in."

"Like what..." O-Dawg's phone started playing 'Like What' by problem. He opened his phone quickly cutting off Problem. He had a text message from Killah,

"We got a situation." it said. "WHAT?" He texted back. A few seconds passed then pictures came through of a silver Cadillac cts parked in front of a house that he was real familiar with. O-Dawg called Killah,

"Hello." He heard Killah's voice come through.

"Blood don't tell me what I'm looking at, is what I think it is." O-Dawg said with pure anger in his voice.

"You been having me out here for all this time for a reason, now you got yo answer." O-Dawg knew he was right but didn't want to believe it. Ever since the day she gave him the list with the addresses and she acted suspicious. O-Dawg has made Killah park by her house every day. He always went with his gut in every situation. He especially needed answers since he was about to start keeping drugs at her house.

"What you want me to do my nigga? I'll kill em both and they'll make the 10'clock news tonight! And the homies got served today too? Let me yank both of em blood on the mob," Killah tried to convince him.

O-Dawg went completely quiet for a full minute.

"Did you actually see the nigga?" He asked.

"Blood I seen the nigga walk in the house. You got pics of the license plate, it's official my nigga."

"Go home, mission complete." He whispered not believing what he had to do.

"What! Is you serious blood? Just go home? We got a free body!" Killah yelled through the phone not thinking he heard his boss right.

"My mom always said that the greatest trick the devil ever played was to convince the world he didn't exist. So we gone act like we don't exist till it's time to reveal our trick. Don't worry you gone get yo action for me making you babysit. Shake the spot and don't tell nobody what happened. I got summin real special for them."

☙❧

10 MINUTES EARLIER

☙❧

Gucci Ty was sitting outside her house debating if he should go knock. It's been awhile since he last seen her but he knew she was still hurt. She had walked into his house and caught him cheating on her with her friend. To make matters worse her friend ended up pregnant. This happened almost a year ago but he still always thought of her. He wonders if she knows he made the friend get an abortion.

"Fuck it cuz, its only one way to find out if she still love a nigga." He spoke out loud. He knocked on the door and waited a few seconds. No answer, he knocked again. It seemed like minutes had passed since his last knock. Fuck it she aint here I'm gone. He heard the locks being unlocked then the door finally opened. They just stared at each other for seconds without speaking. Seeing Jaleesa made him realize how much he truly missed her.

She was wearing some gold pajama pants and a small black t-shirt. Her hair was in a ponytail and she looked like she'd been crying recently.

"What are you doing here Tyrone?"

"I was in the neighborhood and have been thinking about you a lot lately, so I stopped bye."

"Hi, bye. Thanks for stopping by." She dismissed him and tried closing the door but he stopped it. He knew she would be upset and emotional about seeing him.

"Don't act like that baby, can't we just talk for 5 minutes? Then I'll leave you alone." She thought hard while staring at him.

"You got 5 minutes nigga, then stay the fuck out my life." She walked inside without looking to see if he was following. Once inside Gucci Ty stared looking around.

"Do I still gotta take my shoes off?"

"Normally yeah but you aint staying long. Actually you can stand by the door and talk." She told him while going to sit on the couch. He took his shoes off anyways then sat on the couch.

"Do you ever think about me?" He asked.

"That is not the way to start a conversation with me." The truth was she did. Since she's been with O-Dawg she barley has, but before that it was all the time. This nigga sitting here looking hella sexy with his muscle man shirt. He knows I used to love when he wore his shirts like that. He still got those curls too. Ol pretty boy gangsta, he looks even finer than when I last saw him. He still wears that Gucci guilty cologne I got him started on. You just had to fuck up, dumb ass nigga. She was thinking to herself.

"My bad, I was wondering because I always think about you. I know I was wrong and I'm sorry. If you knew how many times I started to call you then hung up. How many times a day I look at your pictures on Facebook or text you and don't send it. A nigga still love you and I want you to let me fix it. I know I fucked up but that don't mean we can't work things out." Gucci Ty said trying his best to convince her.

"You wait a year to come say you apologize? Now you wanna get back together? Ok Tyrone I forgive you, but we're never going to be in a relationship again."

"Why? You got a nigga or summin?" He asked,

"It's complicated but that's none of your business. You need to worry about staying alive and stop getting shot." Jaleesa shot back with an attitude.

When Gucci Ty got shot at the cemetery it was all over the news and social media. She was actually going to see how he was doing at the hospital. When she heard the names of the people responsible she felt torn. Her cousin and ex-boyfriend are from one side and her current love was their enemy. When she first met O-Dawg she had no idea he was the man whose name had come up countless times. She couldn't even fathom that was the same person, his looks didn't match the reputation.

"For some strange reason I expected for you to come see me. I felt some type of way when you didn't show up." He confessed to her.

"I thought about it. For what it's worth, I called Half dead and checked up on you."

"Yeah Half dead is really half dead now. The nigga don't smile and barley talk."

"I know, he pretty much done cut the whole family off. When we do talk on the phone it's like I'm talking to myself." She agreed.

"So who's this nigga that got you walking around looking all depressed and shit. You must really love him if you won't even think about giving us another chance."

"Don't worry about who he is and what I got going on. You wasn't worried when you had me walking around worse than this." She replied.

"I apologize Jaleesa."

"You said that already."

"I still love you and you look even more beautiful than the last time I saw you."

"Tyrone you don't love me. Your just feeling some type of way cause I'm in a relationship. You're used to getting your way, especially with bitches. Thank you for the compliment though." They just sat there for a minute without saying a word.

They were both thinking their own thoughts and didn't know what to say.

"Well, thank you for coming by and apologizing, it did give me some closure. I need to get to bed now I got work in the morning."

"It's only 6:30 you aint going to bed this early, unless you pregnant." Jaleesa stood up, "You know what I mean. I gotta shower and handle a few things then lay in the bed and catch my reality shows before I pass out. Your 5 minutes was up 20 minutes ago anyways." Before he opened the door he turned back around,

"Can I at least get a hug? Please…" Jaleesa gave in and gave him a hug. He wrapped his hands around her waist tight,

"I love you baby for real." He said in her ear.

"Don't say that." She replied but didn't let him go. He kissed her on the cheek. She tried to get free but he grabbed her tighter and found her lips. Jaleesa put up a small fight then gave up and kissed him back. He gripped her ass and kept tonguing her,

"I love you." He told her again when they stopped kissing and were staring at each other. He went back in for another kiss but she jumped out of his arms.

"No! Stop Tyrone we can't be doing this. I have a man that I'm in love with, just leave." She told him raising her voice and being shocked at her own actions. She still had feelings for him and just really realized it.

"Fuck that nigga you know you still love me."

"No I don't, now get out and leave me the fuck alone."

"Aight I'm gone, but just know I'm going to get you back. He obviously not doing summin right, cause if you was still my bitch you would never let another nigga in. I'll holla at you later, love you." Then he was out the door. Jaleesa sat on the couch confused. Do I still love him? Hell naw I don't. Then why didn't I give up his address when his name was on the list? That don't mean shit. It just mean I didn't wanna do no snake shit like he did. She was asking herself these questions and answering them in her head. What the fuck am I doing?

CHAPTER 12

We was like this before we got here. These clothes, cars, diamonds, that's only the top layer. We are who we are and who we're not, we'll never be

Everybody at the 24 hour fitness had a workout partner except Falon. It was definitely not by force because she turned down at least 10 requests. Falon was wearing some black skintight stretch pants and a small pink tank-top. Her 34-27-44 body was on full display for whoever wanted to see. Falon noticed a light skinned woman in the corner that had just set her bags down. She was real light skinned with long straight hair pulled back into a pony-tail. Falon could tell she was mixed with white by her hair and skin complexion. She wasn't thick but she wasn't skinny either. Her legs and thighs were border line skinny but her hips were wide. Falon moved to a better position so she could see her ass. Just as she figured

"Nice lil bubble butt" She said out loud. The woman had on some small red shorts and a white t-shirt. Falon approached her

"Hi do you want to be my partner for today? Everybody else is already taken and I could use some help." The woman eyed Falon up and down. Falon could tell she was amazed by her body

"Umm, sure. What's your name?" Falon could tell she was a square by the way she pronounced her words

"My name is Falon, what's yours?" The woman stuck her hand out,

"My name is Beverly but people call me Beth for short. Nice to meet you Falon" She then shook her hand and asked

"I've never seen you here before, did you just switch gyms?" Falon shook her head

"I just started today, one of my friends told me I was getting fat" Beth inspected her body again

"That's so far from the truth. You have an incredible body Falon"

"Thank you, it can't hurt to tone it up and stay healthy then." They started doing their warm up stretches and that's when Falon noticed that Beth might be a lil bi-curious. Beth was lying on her back and Falon was stretching her leg for her. Her leg was all the way back to the side of her head

"Oh that feels good "

Beth practically moaned

"You like that?" Falon asked her then switched to the other leg. When she pulled her leg back this time she leaned forward into her chest a little bit more than necessary "This feel good too?" Falon asked

"Yeah" Falon pulled both her legs back at the same time. Their faces were almost touching this time

"How does it feel now?"

"It feels good" She replied. Falon released her legs and acted like nothing happened, it was just stretching. Beth stretched her out and couldn't help but to get a few grabs in. Falon had that type of body, one that couldn't be ignored or resisted. They stretched and semi flirted with each other for another 5 minutes. They went to the dumb bells and found the lightest ones. Falon eventually struck up a conversation while working out

"So what do you do for a living?"

"I work in the customer service department for Microsoft. I answer questions if I can; if not then I send them to a technician. What do you do?" Beth answered then turned the question on her

"I'm a tele marker, well I just quit so now I'm enjoying vacation for a while." She replied making them both laugh.

"Do you have a man or kids?"

"No, no kids. Far as a relationship, now that's complicated. I'm single technically, but I'm on and off with this dude."

"You?"

"No kids yet and no man either. I do have a special interest in one man though, but he's all over the place. I'm only going on 22 so I'm not in no rush" Falon responded

"I'm 25 and about to start going to Portland State University next semester so I ain't got time either"

"What you be doing with your free time? You look like the type that stays in the house" They laughed

"Yeah, I actually do just that. I be wanting to go out sometimes but all my friends got kids or husbands or study in college"

"Well you're in luck cause I'm a club hopper and need a new sidekick that's down to get it in" They broke out laughing and then Falon stated.

"Seriously though, shoot me your number and we'll hook up and have fun"

"Ok I'll make sure you get it when we leave the gym." Beth replied smiling happy to have met somebody she could kick it with.

O-Dawg was sitting in his front room having a conversation with Bleed. Bleed had just got done doing 5 years in prison before he got out 2 days ago. He was dark skinned, 5'8 in height, skinny with braids and a high pitched voice, especially when he's excited. He went in 16 and got out 21, so he was still wild mentally

"So what you tryna do blood? Was you in there reading those business books I sent you?" O-Dawg asked. Bleed sucked his teeth

"Man blood fuck those books, all them weird ass words and shit. I'll just give my money to you and let you invest for me, fuck the extra shit. You know what I'm tryna do, get money and pop crabs"

"You just got out lil bro, maybe you should fall back for a while" O-Dawg told him knowing the whole time that Bleed would never go for that

"Blood you sound stupid. All those pictures I used to stare at with yall sitting on them Benzes with them bitches. Look at that watch you got on, look at this fuckin condo.

"Nigga, I'm out here, so just tell me what you need me to do. I just did too much time to be wasting time. Show me where those Gutta squad faggots is at, so I can let everybody know that 'the Goer' is back"

"You still pushing that weak ass handle?"

"Nigga my shit hot! Bleed da Goer! You mad you ain't come up with that shit" He responded raising his voice

"Lil bro things are different now. We real organized now and everybody got rules to follow. Even when shit looks random, it's not. You can't just wake up one day and decide to go serve the crabs. Cause then you'll be jeopardizing your freedom and that means jeopardizing the role you play. If you can't fulfill your role then, that means sumn' not getting done for the mob, which fucks the money up. We playing on a whole 'nother level bro and we all gotta follow order. A nigga see these cars and jewels but not the stress and discipline that come with it. Honestly, I wish I could get out this shit, but every time I try sumn new pop up. I ain't tryna get you involved in some shit I'm not 100% feeling anymore, feel me?"

"Blood I'm with it. Ain't nuttin else to do, what I'm supposed to do? Sign up for college and get financial aid? When I was in those cells, I used to ask myself crazy ass questions blood. Like are we doing what were supposed to be doing? Grandma used to always say everything was part of Gods plan. So if that's the case then God can't be mad at me right? All I know is I'm tryna get my money up blood" Bleed responded with his personal philosophy on life

"You know what I came up with recently my nigga? I was super high and you know how I am when I'm high blood. Nigga get to thinking that the aliens helped the Egyptians build the pyramids. What I came up with is this. We was like this before we got here. These clothes, cars, diamonds, that's only the top layer. We are who we are and who were not, we'll never be"

"Blood you sweat jay-z. I heard that nigga say that shit before in a song. You did add yo own lil twist to it though" Bleed blasted him

"Oh yeah, I was high listening to him when I came up with it" O-Dawg said making them both laugh. His phone started vibrating on the table

"What's hood?" He answered

"So how did it go?. . Good we need this inside connection. . . I know I owe you, I already asked what you want. . . Aight how much longer you bout to be working out?! Its 10 am right now, I'll be there at 1 o'clock" He disconnected the call

"Who dat blood?" Bleed asked

"Falon, she been officially rocking with the team the last few years"

"Ahh blood! Call that bitch back! I used to beat my meat to her pictures upstate. She always in the pictures making her ass poke out. Burnside sent me some with yall in the club and she had this lil ass skirt on, ass everywhere. What's up with her? I'm tryna fuck" Bleed said getting excited and his voice becoming high pitched

"Who don't wanna fuck? You ain't got enough money for her yet. She want Gucci pumps, Louie bags, scarfs and all that shit. That's before you even get to see her pussy. Trust me I know, that's lil sis" O-Dawg told Bleed trying to warn him

"Well shit, I know where I'm spending my first 10 thousand at!" They both busted out laughing

"What's up with Olay? She know Tamia live here with you?"

"Fuck that bitch blood. She got on some thinking she better than everybody else shit cause she turning pro. Bitch tried giving me an ultimatum, talking about leave the streets right now or else. I was kinda sick at first cause you know that's wifey, but bitches ain't shit at the end of the day. Matter fact I'm bout to go over there and make sure she gone. She bet not of took any of my money or I'll be sending you to Cali on a bad one" O-Dawg vented. Bleed sucked his teeth

"You would not kill her blood, cut the crap. I don't know who you think you're fooling"

"Whatever nigga, I'm bout to go over there now. I got some shit I want you to see later on today, Aight? Ima pick you up in a couple hours" They left O-Dawgs condo both deep in their own thoughts. Bleed wanted to know what it felt like to count a million dollars and fuck Falon.

O-Dawg was half hoping that Olay was already gone. The other half of him wanted to see and talk to her. No matter how much he tried to convince himself that he didn't need her, he knew he did. She was the one who calmed him down over the years. The one reason he had to live for and plan the future with. He knew that she was aware of this also, which made him even madder. When he pulled into the driveway his heart started beating fast. Olay's charger was parked outside. He started making his way through the house and didn't notice anything missing. When he made it to the bedroom he stopped at the sight of Olay. She was standing in front of the dresser drawer looking down with her back to him. He looked around and noticed some things missing. Shoes, bags, pictures and electronics, for some strange reason he felt his heart drop. Reality finally started to kick in; she was leaving

"I was just thinking how much I'm going to miss this place. All the happy times we shared here, all the memories" Olay said then turned around to face him.

O-Dawg still thought she was the most beautiful person God ever created. She was wearing some baggy grey sweat pants and a black t-shirt

"You look surprised like I didn't know you was behind me. I can feel you Marshawn, I can smell your scent from a mile away" Then she did it, she smiled that perfect smile that made him fall in love "Are you not going to say anything? As Much as your brain thinks I know you got a lot to say"

"Ain't nothing to say Olay, you done made your mind up already. I'm not about to get on my knees and beg you. All I wanna know is when you leaving and can I get a hug?" He replied dryly

"My plane leaves in the morning Marshawn. So that's really all you got to say?"

"I feel like with all the time we invested in each other, all the love and memories, that I at least deserve a hug" He said while smirking. Olay walked to him and they held each other tight without saying a word for several minutes. Finally Olay broke the silence

"I love you" O-Dawg waited 30 seconds before he responded

"No, you used to love me. You don't love me no more cause if you did then you wouldn't be leaving. But I do love you" He let her go out of his arms with that last statement. Olay was crying and it hurt him to the soul to see it. He felt the tears building up in his eyes and knew it was time to leave

"Goodbye baby" He then kissed her on the lips and turned to walk away

"Marshawn" He stopped walking but refused to turn around. He had too much pride to let anybody see him shed a tear

172

"I know why you won't turn around, but it's ok. Just know that I have to leave in order to really help you" She told him with pain in her voice.

He wiped his eyes with his sleeves and kept walking. He had never experienced pain like this and knew he would never let it happen again.

If only he knew the pain he was feeling, would be nothing compared to what was about to happen.

He thought by losing her he had lost the good part to his soul, but oh was he wrong. He hopped in his beamer and put jay-z on. When he found the song he turned it up to the max "I can't see em coming down my eyes/ so I gotta make this song cry" He rapped along, playing it four times before reaching Falons house. O-Dawg had been knocking on Falons door for a couple minutes. What the fuck this bitch doing he complained. After he knocked again louder he finally heard her yell from inside

"I'm coming nigga!" She opened the door holding a towel with one hand

"Bout damn time, shit!" O-Dawg spat angrily

"Nigga you said 1 o'clock, it's not even 12 o'clock yet. That's yo own fault!" She replied Falon turned around and headed back towards her room. She didn't have the towel wrapped around her tight in the back. It came loose and her whole ass was hanging out. O-Dawgs dick immediately got rock hard as he stared at her cheeks jiggle. He couldn't take his eyes off her butterfly tattoo that covered her ass and her lower back. Every time she took a step each wing wobbled by itself. She started walking faster when her towel was almost completely off. All this did was make her ass clap even more and he got harder. When she reached the end of the hallway she turned her head before walking into her room.

'Damn she caught me' he started thinking. He finally sat on the couch and realized he was stressed out

"Falon! I know you got some fire back there, bring that shit out!" He yelled out to her. This shit crazy blood. My bitch gone, Jaleesa a snake,

173

Spike starting to fall back. Niggaz done took my money, killed the homies, shot at me and sprayed Burnsides car, Shot Gotti, grazed Joe face, Shit at least they smoked that snitch nigga. Now Tamia pregnant, a nigga don't know what to do blood. O-Dawg sat there thinking and talking to himself for 5 minutes until Falon came out and sat some weed and swishers on the table. O-Dawgs dick got hard again at the sight of her. She was wearing some black boy shorts and a small red shirt.

Her long hair was still wet and was hanging straight down. She smelled like kiwi and watermelon due to the lotion she used and had on no socks. Even her feet are perfect he was thinking

"Why you got it so quiet in here? I'm bout to put my Beyoncé cd on" Falon said

"Hell naw blood I'm tired of that damn cd. I hear it everywhere, at home, the TV, even riding down the street. I just came over to get the wrap on the situation and find out what you charging, then I'm gone. Beyoncé can wait 10 minutes"

"What's the matter with you mar-mar? I could see it all over yo face when I answered the door. You haven't been coming out to the clubs with us or nothing. It seems like you've been distancing yourself from us. I know you don't trust nobody with your feelings but you can talk to me. I don't like seeing you like this, your usually so strong and hide your emotions good" Falon said while sitting down on the couch next to him

"Ain't nuttin wrong with me girl, just roll that weed up. So how's the situation looking?"

"It looks promising, I'm probably gone need a lil time though. But it will get done, have I ever let you down?"

"So what do you want? And don't say no fuckin Benz or nuttin outrageous. Shit I should make you do it off the strength" Falon licked the swisher shut then responded

"We'll talk about that in a minute after you tell me what's wrong with you" O-Dawg breathed in then out real loud to show he was frustrated. Falon lit the blunt then started puffing on it

"Here hit the blunt then talk to me"

"I ain't got time for this shit Falon" He replied then hit the blunt. He started smoking and neither one of them said a word for a few minutes

"Does it have to do with my sister leaving tomorrow" Falon blurted out. He passed her the blunt back

"Why the fuck do you care? You sitting here asking me all these questions and shit. Just tell me what you want so I can get the fuck outta here. You sitting here acting like you care, if the money wasn't involved you wouldn't even answer yo phone" Falon kept hitting the blunt and staring at him with contempt. She gave it back then blasted him

"Nigga you got me fucked up, you must be confusing me with one of those ratchet bitches you be fuckin. I ain't doing shit just for the money and you know it. Everything I do for you is because we grew up together and I love you. Nigga you acting like I wasn't there when you had those short nappy braids with the Sylvester glasses. So how you gone sit here and say some shit like that to me? If any bitch always had yo back than it's me. Name one time when I wasn't there for you. Name one foul thing I ever did. So don't take it out on me that my sister is doing some weird shit"

"Yall grew up in the same house right? Yall got the same blood in yall veins right?"

"So this is about her, wow"

"Some of it, it's an accumulation of things. It's way too much shit going on at one time. But far as yo sister go, I just left the spot and she was packing her shit. She wanted to hear what I had to say, I told her ain't nuttin to say and walked off" Falon finished the blunt then started rubbing his head

"You might as well keep going and get it all out" She told him

"Tamia just told me she pregnant"

"What?!" Falon yelled. He then stopped rubbing his head for a moment

"Yeah I know, I said the same thing. How am I supposed to bring a kid into this world and I don't even know if Ima die tonight"

"Don't talk like that Marshawn, ain't nobody bout to die" She said then started playing with his ear

"Kapo dead, DJ dead, Gotti shot, Joe got grazed, we got robbed, niggaz kicked Tamia door down, Shits been real. I'm tryna fall back and get this rap money but I can't until we finish these niggaz. The plug said he won't give it to Boobie unless Butta and Pressha dead. So I'm staying here out of the love for my niggaz. Then I just found out that one of my main bitches just had Gucci ty bitch ass at her house"

"What? Is she still alive?" Falon asked and was surprised at his last statement

"Yeah, for now. She don't know that I know. Then on top of all that, we tryna get money and stay off the snitches and cops radar.

This shit is stressful as fuck Falon; you have no idea" Falon kissed him on the cheek

"It's ok just know at the end of the day I got you. Ima come through for you don't trip"

"Back to that, now what do you want? I told you everything on my mind, now cut the crap"

"I want what I've been wanting since I was 13 years old"

"And what's that? Go ahead and say a pink Bentley so I can slap yo ass"

"Marshawn, how long are we going to play this game?"

"What game?" He asked her

"The one where you stare at my ass and act like you're not. The one where I don't notice you doing it, even though I'm making it jiggle a lil bit extra just for you. Unless you gone tell me I'm lying, can you put it on sumn you didn't enjoy that view of my ass you just got at the door?

My towel didn't fall; I made it unwrap just so you could see it. I've been giving you signs since I been 15 years old, when I got my ass. I want you to let me be yo bitch. I wanna be with you and only you and hold you down like my sister could never do. I'll cut off every nigga right now for you. That's what I want and you know that's what you want too"

"Falon that weed got you trippin" O-Dawg said trying to act like she was wrong. She reached in his pants and grabbed his dick

"Then why yo dick hard?" Then she stuck her tongue in his ear

"You know you like it, stop fronting. You might as well get comfortable because you ain't going nowhere" She whispered in his ear then let his dick go

"Let me be that real bitch in your life that you need. The one that's gone do whatever for you and understand this shit. You can tell me anything and not worry bout it leaving the house. You need somebody you can really talk to and unload all that weight you carrying. Let me prove myself to you, I'll do whatever you need me to do. I don't care if it's working in the strip club or setting somebody up. Long as I'm in your life than I'm contempt with that. I'm not gone stress you over other bitches or none of that lame shit. Cause I know in due time you gone realize ain't no other bitch realer than me" O-Dawg just sat there in shock. He always had a feeling he could fuck her if he really wanted. But he never imagined that she would come at him like this. He actually didn't know what to say. One side told him to go for it but the other was saying bitches ain't shit. He had enough female drama as it was. But he started thinking how she could really be an asset if he used her right. Falon got tired of waiting for him to respond. She sat in his lap straddling him and started kissing his neck.

He wanted to fight it but her lips and tongue were feeling too good to resist

"You know we can't do this, She yo sister" He said weakly

"Fuck her, she think she better than us anyways. Stop talking and enjoy what's about to happen" then she stuck her tongue in his mouth and made him kiss her. O-Dawg finally gave in and palmed her ass. Got damn its even softer than I thought and it feel way bigger. He was thinking. Falon stopped kissing him then said

"You've been wanting to do that for years huh? Don't think I don't feel that dick getting harder" She kissed him one more time then got off his lap.

When she stood up and took her shirt off he decided at that moment that he was gone fuck her and add her to the team. Then she took her shorts off and stood there ass naked. O-Dawgs dick was bulging through his jeans. Falon turned around slowly so he could get a good look at her hips and ass. She started bouncing her ass up and down making it clap

"Got damn" He said then grabbed a cheek

"Watch what the butterfly start doing" She started twerking and leaning forward. Her ass cheeks were spreading and clapping making the wings look like they were flapping. She bent all the way over and grabbed her ankles while still doing tricks with her ass. Her shaved pussy was right in his face and he couldn't take it any longer. He kicked off his shoes and pulled off his jeans within seconds. He took his gun out of his hoody and tossed it on the floor while taking his hoody off. When Falon turned around he wasn't wearing anything except his glasses and Milwaukee Brewers chain

"I thought you would see things my way" Falon said then got on her knees in between his legs. She placed a hand on each of his knees then lowered her head in his lap. Falon put the whole dick down her throat with no hands on the first take

"Aww shit" He moaned then leaned his head back in ecstasy. Falon started going to work. Bopping up and down on his dick fast as she could

"Got damn" He moaned. She slowed it down and started sucking it real slow and slurping loud. Sluurppp! sluurppp! O-Dawg sat there watching his dick disappear in her mouth then come back out. The whole time she was doing it her hands never left his knees

"You suck dick good as a muthafucka" He told her, she smiled with his dick still in her mouth then went back to work. She sped the pace up and was only taking it half way out her mouth now

"Aww, aww" He started letting out moans uncontrollably. He couldn't take it no more, he put his hands on the side of her face and started pumping. He was face fucking her and she started going faster, letting him know she could hang. Sluuuup! sluupppp! He leaned his head back again and kept pumping her face

"Aww, aww, aww! I'm bout to nut in yo mouth, swallow this shit!" Falon nodded her head and kept sucking. His hands made their way into her hair and he gripped it tight as he nutted

"Agghh! Fuck!" He roared and released a giant load into her mouth. Falon took half his dick out and gripped it with her teeth lightly while he was still shooting in her mouth. When she felt that he was done nuttin she stuffed his dick back down while swallowing his nut at the same time.

Then she started bopping up and down to make sure his dick was all the way hard. O-Dawg gripped the back of her head again and started guiding her

"Aww, let me hit that pussy now" She gave it one final suck and it felt like she was trying to peel his skin off

"Aww shit" He hissed. Falon stood up directly in front of him and he could see her ass jiggling from the front. He grabbed her thighs then made his way to her ass. He pulled her closer then she straddled him. Falon started kissing his neck then whispered

"It's yo pussy, you can have it whenever, wherever, and however you want it daddy" He grabbed her ass then lifted her up so she could put the dick in her. When she got the head in she wrapped her arms around his neck and slid down his pipe real slow

"Hmm-hmm" She started moaning while her face was buried in his neck

"Yea that pussy tight" He told her then palmed her ass tighter and started bouncing her up and down

"Oh, yo dick feel so good. Aww that's it, I love you" O-Dawg had her ass jumping up and down so fast it was making loud clapping sounds. Smack! He smacked her ass and then she started riding him faster

"Oh this feels so good! You like this pussy don't you? Hmm-hmm" Falon said then started moaning

"Let me hit it from the back" He demanded. Falon got off of him and put her face in the cushion and her ass in the air

"Got damn you thick as a muthafucka, scoot up some" He told her. After she scooted forward he gripped her cheeks and opened them up so he could slide in easier

"Hmm-hmm" She let out a moan as he entered her pussy. He let her ass go and watched her ass jiggle back into place

"I shoulda been fucking you" He told her then placed his hand on her lower back to help him control the rhythm. Her ass started bouncing against him making clapping sounds louder then he'd ever heard.

"Oh oh! It's yo pussy baby! I'm bout to cum"

Falon started screaming and throwing her ass back even harder

"Cum then bitch" He replied then smacked both of her cheeks

"Awww! I'm cumming!" clap! clap! Falon was throwing it back with all her force and it literally sounded like somebody was clapping their hands

"Oh yes, ohh yeesss" She started moaning again and slowed her pace down dramatically. O-Dawg knew she was done cumming when she stopped moving completely and she kept moaning real low.

He kept stroking her just to show her he could keep going if he wanted. Smack! He smacked her on the ass after a few more strokes

"Roll the rest of the weed up while I make this call" He told her while pulling his dick out then digging his phone out his pants. He found it then called the number he was looking for while Falon started rolling the blunt

"What's hood? Is everything in place?"

"Naw not yet, I should be leaving were I'm at in 30 minutes" Then he looked at Falon licking the blunt sealed and smiling at him seductively" Actually make that an hour and make sure everything official. If he try to leave early then make it happen. . . Aight yup" He hung up then watched Falon hit the blunt a few times

"You didn't even nut" She said while passing him the weed

"I did, you swallowed it. Don't trip I'm bout to really fuck the shit out you when I finish this blunt" He told her sounding extremely cocky. Falon got on her knees on the couch then kissed his dick

"So you gone take me up on my offer?" She asked

"We'll see" Was his reply then placed one hand on top of her head and pushed his dick in her mouth

"Aww, yea suck a real nigga dick" He watched her mouth slide up and down on his dick a few times before he leaned his head back and blew smoke in the air

"Keep sucking until I finish this blunt" Sluuurppp sluuurppp! This is the life. He was thinking while he hit the weed again.

MARCELLUS ALLEN

കൈ

HOURS LATER

കൈ

O-Dawg was sitting in his car with Bleed outside one of their enemy's houses

"How long you knew this bitch ass nigga lived here blood?"
Bleed asked

"I found out a couple months ago, I just been sitting on it waiting till
the right time. You know how I am, when I move everything is planned
and planned again"

"When you think he gone come out?"

"Real soon, the bitch called em 45 minutes ago. He ain't turning her
down, with his dumb ass. It's 7:43 right now" O-Dawg replied looking at
his watch.

A few minutes later they seen the front door open

"Here he come blood, put yo gloves on" He told Bleed. They watched
the dark skinned man with the singles in his hair walk towards his car

"A frog what's up with yo bitch ass!" They heard somebody yell and
looked down the street at two men walking Frogs direction. Frog was leaning in his car and acted like he didn't hear them. Then it happened so fast
they almost missed it. Boc boc! Frog hopped out the car, closed the door
then started shooting. He aimed in their direction then took off running
towards his house when he seen them duck behind a car

"Look at his bitch ass fumbling with the keys!" Bleed shouted. Finally
Frog got into the house and slammed the door. O-Dawg took the keys out
the ignition then said

"Well you know what they say, you can run but can't hide. C'mon lets go finish our breakfast" They watched the men walk up to the door and knock. When the door opened and the men walked in that's when they finally got out the car

"You be on some ol pinky and the brain ass shit, how you know he was gone do that?" Bleed asked as they walked into the house. Frog was on his knees facing the door and Faze was standing behind him pointing a 12 gauge at his head. The two men, who was Gotti and Dute fly turned their heads as they entered

"Didn't I tell you Faze, the bitch nigga ran right into you huh?" O-Dawg asked

"Yea blood, I almost popped his ass. The nigga ran right into the barrel" Faze responded

"Gotti grab that chair so we can put this crab in it. Bleed just asked me how did I know he was gone run in the house.

"Bleed? Did you read that 33 strategies of war book that I sent you? Number 13# says to know your enemy right? We all know he's a ho nigga that only busts his gun cause he be around a bunch of niggaz and bitches. When he by himself, he's a bitch so therefore, He damn sure wasn't gone clack it out with two niggaz. That leaves one option, to run his bitch ass back in the house. That's why I had Faze climb through the bathroom window"

"O-Dawg what did I do bro? I ain't got no beef with yall niggaz" Frog interrupted him begging for an answer. Smack! Faze hit him with the gauge in the back of his head

"Aghh cuz!"

"Shut yo crab ass up nigga! You don't get to ask no questions cause we in yo house. Ima smoke yo bitch ass you say one more word" Faze yelled at him. Gotti and Dute walked back into the room

"Here" Gotti said then put the chair right next to Frog

"Dute why the fuck you drinking this nigga orange juice blood?" O-Dawg asked. Dute stopped drinking out the large container with a smile on his face

"Why waste some good juice? Fuck this nigga he a dead man anyways" O-Dawg and Bleed shook their heads at his reply

"Get yo crab ass in the chair blood, I ain't even hit you that hard" Frog jumped up and got in the chair still holding his head

"Where his gun at?" O-Dawg asked

"I got it" Replied Gotti, O-Dawg looked Frog straight in the eyes

"Look nigga, this shit ain't personal with me blood. You just a casualty of war to me. Now my niggaz, they on you. I got the final say over yo life, so remember that while you answer my questions. We came here to get addresses and information. First off, don't think Rita gone tell the police or yo niggaz anything. Because she the one set you up" O-Dawg seen all the hope leave his eyes

"I need everybody's info that's from Gutta squad. Houses, cars, baby moms, lil sisters, anything you can think of. First time you lie to me, I'm walking out the door and you know what that means. First question, where Butta live?" Frog eyes showed genuine fear when he answered

"On my kids I ain't never been to his house" He knew he didn't know the answer to that question. Butta would never allow anybody outside the circle at his house

"Where does Pull Out live?"

"I don't know because he just moved. But I can call him and find out or whatever you want me to do. I swear to you I'm not lying" Frog was almost in tears because that was the second question he couldn't answer. After another 10 minutes of questions O-Dawg had got some info that he needed, but some he didn't

"So what yall think?" O-Dawg asked the room. When Bleed, Gotti and Dute said they believed him Faze blurted out

"Fuck that he lying blood! Let me kill this nigga, he a crab anyways"

"Please O-Dawg don't let him kill me, I told you everything I know"

"Yea I heard you did the same thing with the detectives too"

O-Dawg responded. He looked at Gotti

"No surrender, no retreat, no prisoners, and this Vietnam right?" That was a saying they used to say growing up before going on missions. That was how they pumped each other up and reminded each other that everybody was dying on that mission. Gotti just nodded his head "Give it to Bleed" O-Dawg finally said then watched him pass the 9 mm that Frog had shot earlier to Bleed. O-Dawg had come up with this plan days earlier to see if Bleed really was a killer or just a shooter

"Bleed, don't kill me my nigga! You know I got kids" Frog started begging.

"Bleed it's up to you if this nigga live or die blood. If you walk out the door then we gone follow you, if you shoot than we riding with you."

Once you take a man's life, ain't no going back my nigga. So I want you to really think is this situation worth killing him over. He ain't from Gutta squad, he just fuck with them. He a drop out 60's nigga. It's up to you" O-Dawg was lying through his teeth and hoping he made the right choice. If Bleed lowered his gun then Gotti was gone kill him on the spot. They created this whole scenario just for Bleed, killing somebody in a shooting and doing it while looking in their eyes were two totally different things. They couldn't have no weak links in the chain and O-Dawg tried to give him an out earlier at the house. Boc Boc Boc Bleed fired with no hesitation. All 3 shots hit Frog in the chest and knocked him out the chair

"Fuck this nigga and 60's, on me! I don't give a fuck about killing none of dem niggaz" Bleed said then threw the gun on the ground. He will never know how close he came to dying that day. If he would of waited 5 seconds then shot, Gotti would of still killed him. Just not in front of nobody. That was their plan, if he hesitated then he did it out of peer pressure...

"Dute make sure you take that bottle with you and yall retrace every step yall made, just to be safe, cause--" ... Booooyooowww! Everybody jumped as the loud gunshot cut O-Dawg off. They looked at Faze standing over Frogs body with smoke coming out the barrel

"I think he was still breathing blood. I had to make sure, yall know he a snitch" Faze lied, he just wanted to shoot Frog

"You stupid blood! Come on Bleed we gone. We gotta go take care of some shit. Dute what the fuck you laughing at? That's why I don't be fuckin with yall hot ass niggaz" O-Dawg said getting mad and walking towards the door. Boom! O-Dawg jumped and turned around. Dute had took his gun out and shot Frog too

"Fuckin clowns" He said then walked out with Bleed following behind him

ര

HOURS LATER

ര

Pull out was laying on the couch with his head in Shays lap. Ron was sitting on another couch talking to Nisha and rolling a blunt

"If my phone ring one more time cuz about Frog, I'm going to break this muthafucka" Pull out said to whoever was listening

"Is we gone ride for that nigga cuz?" Ron asked

"That nigga ain't from the squad" Pull out replied

"He a Crip though"

"Man fuck all that, I heard that nigga was a rat anyways" Ron sucked his teeth than replied.

"That was my nigga and I ain't never seen no paperwork. Niggaz in the town always tryna put a jacket on somebody"

"His paperwork was all over Facebook, I seen it. Yall don't need to be getting in trouble anyways. Baby you just got shot and finally started walking right. Every time I turn around yall names is poppin up in some bullshit" Shay jumped in their conversation

"I know one thing Ron, you need to slow yo ass down. Are you still spending the night with me?" Nisha added her two cent

"Why don't you just stay the night here?"

"Cause I ain't got no clothes over here. I wanna sleep in my own room tonight, Just pack a bag cause your coming" She demanded then looked at Pull out "And you're finally about to be grown in a few months, what you want for yo b-day?" Pull out busted out laughing then said

"Ask yo best friend" Shay slapped him on the side of his head

"I told yo nasty ass no, this nigga want a 3-some" Ron and Nisha started laughing now too

"Bitch you better give that nigga what he wants. It's 2014, Stop acting all square and shit" Nisha told her

"Bitch is you gone let another hoe suck Ron's dick?" Shay shot back

"Don't worry bout what I do with my dick, don't try and turn it around on me"

"Ron is you gone pass the weed or what cuz?" Pull out jumped in

"Oh, my bad" Ron started laughing then reached over and gave the blunt to Shay

"I wonder why niggaz killed that nigga anyways. That don't even make since, it didn't hurt us" Pull out said

"I don't know cuz, I'm starting to think some other niggaz did that shit. His own homies probably robbed em or sumn. Them slob life's wouldn't just go do that for no reason.

"Oh well, I guess in due time it'll all come out. Let me go get my shit cuz, I'm bout to go flav at they spot tonight" Ron said then got up to go to his room

"Nigga you act like you had a choice or sumn. You know if Nisha say jump then you gone ask how high. Shay staying her ass here tonight, so yall gone have the spot all to yall 'selves" Pull out replied while laughing and hitting the blunt

"Fuck you slob!" Ron yelled back as he was walking out the front room

"Ya mama a slob" He yelled back

"Shay I ain't playing bout my 3-some either cuz. Shit, if it will make you feel more comfortable you can invite Nisha to join" He smirked while waiting for one of them to reply, Shay smacked him on the head again.

๛

MEANWHILE AT FROG HOUSE

๛

"What the fuck do you think happened?" Detective Pacman asked his partner. They both were looking at his body lying in the awkward position that it was in

"I'm still trying to figure it out myself."

Two shots from a 9 mm outside and three in here from the same brand. The shooter didn't fire those two outside at him or there would be strikes in the house. He could of shot in the air but what would that do? Then a 12 gauge and a 40. cal was used, shit ain't adding up. We don't even have a witness or suspect. It's time to put our plan in motion sooner than later" Detective Canfield replied.

An officer walked into the house and walked into them

"Excuse me detectives, we found two bullet holes outside. One on the windshield of a truck and another hit the side of a house. Both of the owners said they weren't there last night. So they had to come from the shell casing we found outside"

"Thank you officer, we'll be out there to check it out" Canfield responded dismissing her. The female officer walked away smiling

"She got a nice ass on her huh?" Pacman said

"Yea for a white girl, I'll hurt her lil ass"

"You make it sound like you deal with black girls, when the last time you had one? Anyways, what's this shit all about? It seem like it just started out of nowhere" Pacman asked his partner

"I don't know but were definitely going to find out. It sound like he seen some people getting ready to make a move and started shooting. Somehow they got into the house, probably when he tried opening the door. Then after that. . ." He gestured towards Frogs body on the ground.

"Let's go outside and look at the bullet holes, make sure these idiots got it right" Pacman replied and walked towards the door.

ℰℐ

MIDNIGHT

ℰℐ

"Man blood I can't believe that bitch had that nigga over here. I thought she was loyal too" O-Dawg said to bleed. They were parked outside of her house

"So what we gone do, you want me to pop her?"

"We gone run through it and go from there. I gotta be able to read the bitch before making a decision. I still don't understand it blood"

"C'mon big bro, let's go find out" Bleed replied then got out the car to join Burnside and killah on the sidewalk. O-Dawg put on his killer face and jumped out the car. No words were spoken, he walked right past them and banged on the door

"Who the hell is it?" He heard Jaleesa yell

"It's me, hurry up and open the door" The door immediately opened up and she could tell something was wrong

"Are you ok? What's wrong? Why are you knocking so hard?" He didn't answer one question, he just walked inside then moved over so his team could come in. They all pulled guns out and started walking through the house. Jaleesa got petrified at the sight of them pulling out guns and searching her house

"Marshawn what's going on? What are they doing in my house" He just stared at her. She was wearing her black robe and had her hair wrapped up in a silk scarf. He was disappointed but he knew what had to be done

"Don't call me that, that ain't my name bitch. Sit the fuck on the couch and shut up, you fuckin snake!" Jaleesa's facial expression looked genuine when it showed confusion, shock and hurt

"Why are you talking to me like this? And I ain't never snaked you, what are you talking about"

"How much did you tell dem niggaz? What do they know? If you lie to me Jaleesa I'm going to kill you on everything I love"

"Baby what are you talking about? I have no idea what you're talking about! Can you please just tell me!" Smack! O-Dawg cocked back and slapped her. She hit the ground and started holding her face before she fully realized what happened. O-Dawg felt all the anger and frustration that had been bottled up start releasing itself. He grabbed her by the neck and lifted her off the ground and into the wall

"You think we'd be here off of gut feelings? Bitch I know your under-cover!" He hissed into her ear then let go of her. Jaleesa started crying and holding her neck

"What did you tell dem niggaz? I already know which one sent you. Now all I need for you to do is tell me what information did you give him? You sitting here crying and shit cause you know you wrong. If you tell me everything from scratch than I won't kill you, yo choice"

"kill me?! What the fuck are you talking about! Sent me where? And who did I tell? Marshawn I swear to you baby I don't know what you're talking about!" She was screaming while still crying. Smack! He slapped her again, she hit the wall then slid down.

O-Dawg watched her put her hands over her face and start crying even louder

"Jaleesa why you making this shit harder than it has to be? You think I like this shit? It's only gone get worse, trust me" With her hands still covering her face she responded

"I'm not gone say anything else cause you keep hitting me" Then started sobbing again. O-Dawg turned his head and seen everybody staring at him

"Yall ain't find nuttin?"

"Naw blood, here go her phone though" Replied Burnside. He took the phone and looked at it, the screen saver was a picture of them "So I guess Tamia getting pregnant was the turning point, right?" Jaleesa didn't reply she just kept on crying

"So you telling me that my nigga didn't see Gucci ty walk in yo house? Is that what you're telling me?" O-Dawg asked her. Jaleesa's hands shot from her face

"What? Yea he came over but didn't nothing happen. That's what you're mad about? Tyrone popping up randomly at my house." She answered with confusion still not understanding the situation

MARCELLUS ALLEN

"Don't try to downplay the situation, you know damn well he the enemy! What the fuck is my enemy doing at my bitch house? Right after he killed my lil homie! You stupid bitch, you blew yo cover the night you gave me the list!" O-Dawg said screaming and getting madder by the second.

Jaleesa put her hand to her mouth and breathed in real loud

"Oh my god, it's not what you think" O-Dawg pulled his gun from the holster but didn't aim it at her

"Now that you know you're busted, answer my fuckin question! What have you told that nigga! Bitch how much information have you gave up"

"Marshawn, I haven't told him anything and he doesn't even know you're my nigga" O-Dawg looked at Burnside

"Blood I'm bout to really kill this bitch, she think this a game"

"Fuck all this talkin, let me yank her" killah said with frustration in his voice

"Then why the fuck was he over here? Go ahead, I'm dying to hear this"

"I used to be in a relationship with him right before you, and he popped up trying to get back with me"

"What the fuck blood!" Bleed jumped in with his high pitched voice. O-Dawg looked at killah

"How long was he here?"

"Like 20 minutes" He answered

"Did it look random?"

"She answered the door and didn't let him in for a couple minutes. She looked like she had an attitude and I think she tried to close the door on him"

"Why you didn't tell me this at first?"

"I don't know blood. The homie just got smoked and he was over here, that's all that mattered" killah replied nonchalantly. O-Dawg looked at Burnside

192

"What you think?"

"Check her phone blood, let that be the truth" He responded

"Jaleesa, why you ain't tell me this?"

"Cause I knew you wouldn't talk to me no more. I didn't know you was the one they used to talk about until after you gave me the list. I'm sorry baby!" She yelled the last part

"Whose they?"

"Him and my cousin" She said then put her head down because she knew it was coming

"Who's yo cousin?" He said then held his breath because he didn't know what to expect and was anxious

"Half Dead" She mumbled

"Aww hell naw blood! This some love and hip-hop ass shit!" Bleed interrupted again. killah started laughing

"What's yo password?"

"Yo birthday" She answered

"How cute" Bleed said

"Shut yo dumb ass up blood" O-Dawg told him getting irritated

"Read the texts Burnside" He said then passed him the phone

"From Tyrone. Thanks for letting a nigga see you today. . . Her reply, you're welcome. . . When can I see you again? . . I told you I got a nigga. . . He probably broke, cut the crap. . . He actually ain't. . . Whatever, I'm gone knock you back. . .

Bye Tyrone. . . That's the end of the messages blood" Burnside said

"Look under Half dead or Delroy" O-Dawg instructed him

"Ain't shit in here but some family shit, the nigga sound depressed" Burnside reported

"He should, he's about to die. Aight blood, yall niggaz shake. Somebody take Bleed home for me. Jaleesa get yo ass up, you still outta pocket for lying to me and texting that nigga regardless"

Burnside gave him the phone and led the group out the house. When the door shut he turned his attention back to her

"Why you still on the floor, get up"

"Oh now I can get up? After you beat me up and had your goons run through my house? No that's ok I'd rather stay down here, I'm actually used to it" She replied full of sarcasm. He walked over to the couch and sat down

"None of this woulda happened if you wasn't keeping shit from me. You lied to me Jaleesa. I knew something wasn't right when you asked me about the list. I still gave you a chance to come clean and you lied in my face. Then this shit with Ty, that's crossing the line. What am I supposed to do? Act like it never happened and move on? I hate and can't afford to be around liars and people who keep shit from me"

"You don't have to do anything but leave and act like you never met me. You put your hands on me, you had niggaz run in my house with guns Marshawn! You've had fucking hitmen parked outside my house for months. What if I woulda got killed before I had the chance to explain? No! I can't do this no more. Just please leave and never call or talk to me again. I've been nothing but loyal to you and you come in here slapping me like a prostitute" She said then started crying again

"It's not that simple Jaleesa, you don't understand. You know too much for me to let you walk away. How you think that's gone look to my niggaz? We gone have to assume you're really giving info to yo cousin now. You gave me addresses baby! That makes you a co-conspirator. How I'm supposed to trust you not to snitch and you ain't my bitch?" He told her trying to reason with her

"So basically your saying if I leave you than one of your goonz will come kill me? What type of life is that Marshawn? If I stay than you're going to keep disrespecting me anytime you feel like it. So either way I'm dead, I'm being forced against my will" O-Dawg got up and walked to the door

"This is what we gone do. Your free to go, just don't ever let me hear bout you ever fuckin with that nigga again. Cause if so, that means you on his side and done told him whatever he wants to know. But don't worry bout it because you gone be attending his funeral real soon anyways. You ain't gotta worry bout me stalking you like he does. This is for the best anyways, because I never woulda been able to trust you again" Then he walked out the door and she laid on the ground crying all night.

ॐ

DAYS LATER

ॐ

Detective Canfield and his partner Pacman were two blocks away from their destination. They were speeding in their unmarked car where patrol cars had told them to come

"You had them place it in the trunk right?" Pacman asked

"Yea everything's a go and they found a 9mm under the seat. We got him right where we want his ass" Canfield answered him while driving through a red light

"You think we chose the right one?"

"Yea, he fit the criteria almost perfectly and if he don't work out, we can always find another, this is Portland

"They started laughing at his statement because they knew how true it was. They pulled into the parking lot of Javier's Mexican food on Lombard/Vancouver St. They saw a blue Monte Carlo parked and two police cars next to it. They got out their car and walked over to the officers

"So what do we got fellas?" Canfield asked

"We found a loaded handgun and what looks like a half of kilo of crack" Officer Murphy reported. Detective Pacman whistled at the news

"So it was cooked up huh? Where was the dope found at?"

"Yea it was cooked and after he gave us consent to search we found it in the trunk. The gun was under the seat with the handle sticking out in plain sight" Murphy responded while smirking. Pacman knocked on the car window to get the man's attention

"How you doing Mr. McKinney? You know you done fucked up right?"

"Fuck yall pigs! Yall planted that shit on me! I want my lawyer, fuck yall" The man said "I've heard that a thousand times, but the jury hasn't." "You're done, you're going to jail for life. The only choice is do we keep you or send you to the feds. C'mon partner let's get this piece of shit outta here" Pacman opened the door and they escorted him to their car. Then they went and grabbed the evidence bags from the officers "Thanks for locating this punk and catching him with this shit, we appreciate it. Anytime yall need anything or any back up, just call us first"

"I'm sure I'll be calling you soon then. Anything to lock these punk gang bangers up, yall can sign us up" Murphy responded while shaking both their hands. The detectives shook his partners hand next then got into their car. When they drove off to the precinct Canfield started putting their plan into motion

"I'm just curious Mr. Gang banger, why the hell did you give consent to search when you know you had dope and a gun on you. You know how much time you're looking at? Especially with the feds, the time is ran consecutive. Their theory is that you had the gun to protect your dope. I hate to say it to you brother, but you're fucked" He looked into the mirror to get a read on him in the backseat

"I'm not worried bout nothing you got to say you fuckin house nigga. You a straight up porch monkey, fuck you and yo confederate ass partner cuz" Canfield wasn't fazed by the insults at all. The goal was to always keep the suspect talking, and that's what he was doing

"So who do you think is gone raise your son while you're doing life? You know your baby mom ain't shit."

She probably gone be fucking with a blood, then yo son gone grow up one too. You think yo homies gone look out for you? You think they care about yo son? Your only real friend is dead and you know it"

"Keep my nigga name out yo mouth you fuckin race traitor. I already told you I want my lawyer cuz, conversation over. Yall planted that dope and you know it, I'll be out in a week" "Yea we did have it planted, so what? I got 4 cops saying you gave consent and they found it."

"Who do you think a white jury will believe, you or the people that protect them? You think about that while were driving. By the time we park and take you out the backseat the deal is off" Canfield said then turned the radio up to let his suspect weigh his options.

Ten minutes later they pulled into the parking garage of the Multnomah county justice center which was located downtown Portland. Canfield turned the car off and looked at him dead in the eyes

"Ok tough guy let's get you booked"

"How you gone say the deals off the table when you never put one on there. And don't say no stupid shit talking bout no snitchin either, cause that's out the window on Crip" The two detectives looked at each other then back at him

"That's exactly what we had in mind, tough guy. But it's a good deal though, it comes with no jail time at all. Would you like to hear it, or is it still out the window?" After a couple seconds they heard what they needed and hoped to hear

"What's the deal?"

"You tell us everything you know about whatever we decide to ask you. You become our informant and get everything you tell us recorded on wire. You do that, than you get a suspended sentence for the pistol you got caught with. Whatever happens in between now and the arrests that your directly involved in, we won't hold it against you" While he was thinking it over Pacman finally decided to speak

"Look Half dead, what my partner is trying to say is this. Whoever you shoot or kill before we make our arrests, we don't give a shit. Just don't go overboard with it, save some scumbags for us to convict. Wear the body wire at all the meetings you guys have. Get every single member to confess doing a crime, specifically a murder or selling large quantities of dope. Tie it all into what it is, an organized black gang that's lead by Butta."

"Talk about moving up rank and adding members. Especially get on wire this war that's been going on with Mob life. That's the deal, take it or leave it" Half dead leaned back in the seat and thought real hard for the first time in his life about snitching. The one image that kept popping up in his mind was Burnside getting his dick sucked by his baby mom Felicia. She claims she doesn't talk to him anymore but he knew she was lying."

That's the crazy thing about the game, it ALWAYS comes down to a woman.

The beef, the money and cars, the reason why most so called gang-stas would rather snitch than do their time. It always comes down to a woman and that's one fact of life that will never change. Wars had been started over them and one was about to end.

CHAPTER 13

If we have to die, fuck it, we die then

"Oh oh oh! Fuck me daddy! Harder, hit it harder!" Pressha sped up the pace and started hitting her from the back harder. He smacked her ass then he heard her start moaning

"You like when a real nigga hit it huh?" He asked her while smacking her other cheek

"Yes!"

"Do yo nigga hit it like this"

"No no!" She screamed back. He put his hands on her ass and gripped both her cheeks, then started pounding her

"Damn bitch yo pussy tight as a muthafucka. Ima have to start hitting it more often" She was throwing her ass back at him with everything she had. They had a steady rhythm going on and Pressha removed his hands to see if they would stay on beat. He was fucking her with no hands and she was on all fours concentrating on staying on rhythm

"Yea throw that ass back" She started making her ass clap while throwing it back. Clap clap clap the sound their bodies was making made his dick get even harder

"Aww shit!" Her phone started going off on the stand next to her head

"Fuck! I gotta answer it baby" She said half moaning then grabbed the phone before he could stop her

"Hi baby" She answered and put it on speaker then laid it on the bed

"What are you doing? Where you at?" Pressha opened her legs up more and started long stroking her real slow

"I'm at the mall shopping"

"You need to stop spending my money and get home. I need you to watch baby girl because I need to go handle some business"

"Hmm-hmm" She moaned low as she could

"Butta why you wait until I'm busy to call me with that bullshit? You ain't got nowhere to fucking go!" She yelled the last part on accident because she had her ass slapped

"Bitch get yo muthafuckin ass home right now! Who the fuck you talkin to?" Charlene didn't answer because her face was in the pillow to muffle the moans she was making

"You hear me bitch!?"

"Yes!" She yelled but not because of Butta.

Pressha had sped back up the pace and was hitting her spot. She was cumming and didn't know how to handle the situation

"Baby I'm cumming! Ok? I don't know why you treat me like this, I love you" Charlene yelled but was talking to Pressha

"Why are you talkin so loud?" Butta asked. Charlene couldn't respond, she was almost done cumming and it felt too good.

Pressha was giving her all the dick one inch at a time, real slow. She finally snapped out of her sexual bliss

"Because baby it's real loud in the mall and the reception is bad"
She lied

"Just get yo ass home" Butta demanded then hung up the phone

"You really enjoyed yourself huh?" She asked

"Fuck that nigga, I'm enjoying this pussy" Soon as the words left his
mouth his phone started ringing on the dresser across the room

"Fuck" He said then pulled his dick out to go answer the phone.

He knew that ringtone only belonged to one person. He leaned back
on the dresser watching Charlene get out the bed

"What's hood cuz?" He answered the phone

"Fo'real? How long ago was this?"

"Put him on speaker, I wanna hear his voice while you nut in my
mouth" She whispered in his ear while he gripped her ass. He put it on
speaker then placed it on the dresser

"So one of your bitches told you he was getting cuffed up? How long
ago did she say again?" Charlene dropped to her knees and grabbed his dick

"Yea she told me she was driving down Lombard and seen the whole
thing happen. So I've been sitting here tryna figure out why he ain't called
me" Pressha was making weird facial expressions trying not to moan from
the good head he was receiving. Charlene had one hand gripping his dick
and she was bopping her head fast as she could. Every time his dick popped
out her mouth it made a loud slurping sound. When she noticed him watching, she slowly deep throated all of his dick and stayed in that position

"They probably got him sitting in one of those holding cells for a couple hours. You know how dem pigs like to play games. Aww shit" Charlene
had started moving her neck back and forth a lil bit. Most of his dick was
still down her throat but she had took an inch out and was bobbing on it
back and forth

"Cuz where you at? What the hell you doing?"

"I'm at this bitch house and she just put my dick in her mouth" Charlene bit down on his dick a lil bit

"Oww, stop playing broad" Pressha raised his voice

"Aight, I'm waiting for my dumb ass baby mom to get here, then we gotta see what's up. We gotta see if his car still there then swing by his spot"

"Off top, when yo B.M. supposed to be there?"

"That bitch better be here pronto cuz, I told that bitch to get here now. You know when I tell a bitch to jump she better reach for the moon" Butta said then started laughing at his own line. Charlene had her hands on Presshas hips and was sucking him off with no hands

"Aight cuz let me finish this business with this bitch then Ima head to yo spot" When he hung up he leaned his head back and said

"Now who's enjoying themselves? You a freak, you know that?"

She didn't respond, she just kept on sucking and slurping. Sluuurrpp! sluurrpp!

"I'm bout to bust" She kept on sucking until she tasted his pre cum. She took his dick out and started jacking him off

"Aww here it come!" Charlene opened her mouth wide and let his nut shoot in her mouth and face. Then aimed his dick at her titties and chest

"Aww fuck" When he stopped nutting she licked around her lips to get all the cum that didn't make its way in her mouth

"You nasty as a muthafucka you know that?" Pressha asked. Charlene got up and grabbed a towel to wipe off with

"So when are we going to move forward with the plan? I'm sick of being around his fat ass" She asked

"When the time is right, probably a few more months"

"Are you doing this because you love me or cause of yo sister?" The question caught him off guard. Nobody ever brings up his sister because they know that would bring up the situation. Butta had been messing with his sister Unique behind his back. Pressha had told him numerous times to stop messing with her once he had got wind of the situation. He didn't want Butta talking to her for multiple reasons. One, he had a baby mom so he knew his sister would always just be pussy to him. Two, they were in the streets and he didn't want her getting caught up in none of their bullshit. Butta had gave his word that he wouldn't see her anymore so Pressha left it alone. Then one day Butta was caught slippin at a red light on 17th and Alberta St. Nobody knows who did it or what for. All he knows is a car pulled up and started shooting and now his sister is dead. The hood he was in is Blood territory but that doesn't help identify what gang did it. They've been beefing with too many people to narrow it down. What pissed him off the most is that Butta still lied about the situation to this day. When Pressha flipped out, Butta claimed she called asking for a ride. He knew that was a lie because she lived in the opposite direction. If he had cut her off like he claimed then he would have been the last person she called

"I started fuckin you cause of that. Then a nigga really started digging you and that's when I came up with the plan. Why you ask me that?" Charlene was putting her jeans on when she answered

"I was just wondering because that's a big thing to do. I wanted to make sure that you really loved me and want to spend the rest of your life with me"

"Yea I love you baby, now let's get over to yall house. You go ahead and leave, I'll check out and make sure nothing was left behind" He instructed her

"Ok daddy, I'll see you in a minute, love you" She responded then walked out the hotel room. Pressha sat on the bed and started thinking about everything that was going on. He knew he was wrong for fucking his best friend's girl but felt it was justified because of his sister. He felt that Butta had snaked him so now there wasn't no loyalty or rules. Then he started thinking about Half dead and what could be happening to him. He felt in his heart that Half dead was a stand up soldier so he wasn't worried about that. His thoughts finally landed on his sister and he started wondering what she would be doing right now.

It has been 3 years since her murder and he still felt no different about the whole situation. No matter how hard he tried to bury his feelings towards Butta, he couldn't do it

"The nigga could have at least kept it real about why they was together. His bitch ass tried to make it seem like it was her fault." He said out loud. Pressha grabbed all his belongings and left the room with evil in his heart

☙❧

BURNSIDE HOUSE

☙❧

"I told you blood, I had the plug on the burners" Burnside said to Jersey Joe who was picking up guns off the table and examining them

"Yo son, this a mp5 word to my mama. It hold thirty in the clip and got the switch to make it a fully. This me right here, ya heard?"

"You can have that shit blood, peep this. Nigga this a .45 with a drum on bloods. When I serve a nigga with this, they gone swear I had a space gun or sumn nigga!"

"Yo, what you gone do with that k son?" Joe asked referring to the AK-47 that was laying on the table

"I plan on putting that in one of the trap spots probably the ville. I got the banana clip and a hundred round drum. I got this for us though" Burnside reached to the side of the couch and picked up an AR-15 off the ground

"Yo! Let me see that son "Joe grabbed the assault rifle out of his hands

"This bitch hold thirty and got a scope with a flashlight, what else you holding out on son?"

"I got an M-16 and a Mack-11 that you ain't seen yet. The rest is just pistols. My plug said he bout to have a Mack-90 for me real soon. He said the clip hold 65 rounds and you put it in the side or the top of the gun, some shit like that. Oh, it hold the same bullets as the AK too, on bloods" Burnside informed him getting pumped up

"Yea son bring that muthafuck straight to my spot. Let's go paint the city red tonight blood" Joe announced

"Naw blood fall back, you done seen these choppaz and got too excited "

"Yo what the fuck you mean? I got 8 stiches in my face blood and yall niggaz been on that fall back shit! If O woulda been let me do me, I wouldn't of got grazed in my face! What type of fuckin operation is yall niggaz runnin son?"

"Joe lower yo voice blood, fo'real. Nigga ain't nobody been stopping you from doing shit. What you wanna do, go shoot Albina up? You wanna go serve Peninsula Park? That's for the lil niggaz with no responsibility" Burnside chastised him

"We need to shoot some shit up. You always talkin bout how yall organized and how O-Dawg is a chess player. If that's the case why we ain't killed them niggaz yet? It seems like we the ones doing all the runnin and duckin son. We need to be riding around looking for dem crab niggaz. Yo all we do is wait for O to send his commands through Boobie, what kinda shit is that son?"

"You sound stupid as shit blood you know that? We can ride when-ever we feel like it nigga. I got too much money to be shooting at lil niggaz on corners. All O do is get info on where these niggaz live or where they gone be at. Then pass it down and we take care of it, usually with a plan he came up with. That's what I do, get the main factors. If I see one of those crabs while I'm in traffic than I'm on em, other than that, it's planned. If you wanna take that choppa and go to work, than go do you. I'm bout to get this money and smoke those niggaz when the time is right. You don't think I'm mad bout getting my car shot up? The truth is we shoulda been on point and wasn't"

"Aight blood just make sure you ready when it's go time, ya heard? I'm bout to find out where dem niggaz live and then we going over there son" Joe replied finally giving in

"Why don't you go get some pussy or sumn? Call Falon or one of your bitches blood" What Burnside just said really hit a nerve with Joe

"Fuck Falon son, she a rat yo. First she had me and Boobie, now she fuckin on O-Dawg" Burnside stopped playing with the gun in his hand when he heard that

"Why you say she fuckin with O?" He asked

"The bitch told me she through with me and Boobie cause we ain't shit."

I swung past her spot and his beamer was posted outside son. I hit the bitch up later like, 'so you fuckin with O now?' She told me mind my business and she can fuck whoever she want. Bitches ain't shit yo"

"That nigga O don't give a shit about her, he probably fuckin her cause Olay just left him. Either way she ain't shit but most bitches ain't. A, I keep hearing that the lil nigga Pull out is going around saying he the one served us. I checked his Facebook status from that day, he was pretty much shootin subliminal shots. It's Gucci though, that lil nigga don't know he fuckin with some war veterans. We ain't doing no talkin, we gone catch em and blow his shit off"

"Yo I can't wait to I see one of those niggaz son. Kill em and let the grim reaper take em to wherever they going" Joe said getting pumped up at the thought of murder

"I thought you was the reaper?"

"That's the point son, Ima kill em then take em somewhere else, then kill em again!" He replied making them both laugh "On some real shit son, sumn need to happen to really make O mad so he can apply full pressure. Yo son, if he really wanted to, all those niggaz would be dead. That's word to my mama"

ৡৡ

THE LLOYD CENTER

ৡৡ

"How many 501 jeans you gone buy blood" Boobie asked Bleed. They were shopping at Macys inside the mall

"I'm bout to buy like two of every color, Shit that's only like 8 or 10 pants, that ain't shit. Blue, black, and these grey ones. Nigga that's 6, stop crying blood. You done buying all yo shit now you wanna rush me, ain't that a bitch"

"Naw you just taking forever and I'm hungry as fuck. Hurry up so we can go to footlocker" Boobie responded. When Bleed finally got done picking out his pants they made their way to the counter

"How you doing today?" Bleed asked the woman that was ringing up their merchandise. She was dark skinned with extension braids in. Her titties were big but he couldn't see how thick she really was

"Fine" She responded with a trace of attitude. When she finished bagging their clothes up Bleed took his receipt then grabbed a pen off the counter to write his number down

"Hit a real nigga when you ain't got an attitude and feel like smiling" He told her then left the receipt on the counter

207

"Sumn wrong with you blood you know that?" Boobie asked while laughing when they made it out the store

"Naw blood that bitch got potential, you just can't see it"

"Anyways, I heard bout that lil situation, how you holding up? You Gucci? I know it's a lot getting out a cell then knocking a nigga off the next week. I told O not to take you on that mission but you know how he is" Boobie said changing the topic

"I ain't trippin off that shit, I kinda don't like how he did it though. He used to send a nigga all those books on war and mind games. Then he use the shit against you and expect for you not to realize what he's doing. He tried to make it seem like it was my choice but that shit was a test blood" Bleed replied then sat down to read a text he just received

"Yea he do be doing that shit, but it be deeper than it seems. We really out here in war and can't nobody be suspect of freezing up or not being ready. It's fucked up you had to get out to this bullshit. You supposed to be on vacation somewhere"

"When I was getting ready to parole that's all I could think about my last month. Like please don't let my niggaz die, just hold on and we gone get it right. Nigga I'm from the mob, fuck everything else. I'm with whatever yall tryna do. I'm bout to push the line on all brand niggaz, on the set. A blood, on some real shit do you ever think about dying? Like in full detail?" Bleed asked

"Only when I'm super high. Real niggaz don't die, we just leave the earth physically. We the last of our kind Bleed, me and you, on some real shit. Ima do whatever to keep this mob shit alive, no matter who I gotta kill. I'm putting my life on the line every day I wake up, with no problem. But on some real shit, if we have to die, fuck it then, we die. What else is worth dying for more than family? To be real this shit don't even matter to me blood. Living, Dying, suburbs or the projects. I'm just along for the ride and I'm getting off wherever the reaper decides is my stop. That's why these bitch niggaz can't see me, because there scared to die and I'm not"

"I'm not scared either, I just wanna fuck Miley Cyrus before I die" Bleed shot back making them both laugh.

ᘓ᙭ᘓ

HOURS LATER

ᘓ᙭ᘓ

O-Dawg walked into his condo with Falon following right behind him. Soon as he walked in he saw Tamia sitting on the couch watching t. v.

"What's up baby?" He asked her

"Nothing just watching basketball wives and waiting for you to come home"

"Well don't stay up too late cause I gotta leave again. I just came to grab some money real quick and grab another burner I gotta go take care of some business with Falon

"When Tamia heard the name she finally looked in his direction and seen Falon standing there. They weren't enemies, but they definitely wasn't friends. Tamia didn't like her because she was Olay's sister and vise-versa

"What's up Tamia you're glowing and look beautiful" Falon told her

"Thank you" Tamia responded dryly

"I'm bout to go count the money up, post up and I'll be right back" He said then headed to the bedroom

"Aight babe" Falon replied then sat down at the table. O-Dawg was praying that Tamia didn't hear what she just said. No luck, Tamia jumped off the couch way too fast for a pregnant woman

"Bitch what the fuck you just say!? She yelled and tried to charge Falon. O-Dawg grabbed her before it was too late

"What the fuck is wrong with you? Sit yo ass down before you hurt the baby!"

"Nigga fuck you and this baby! Let me go! You heard what that bitch said? You fuckin her and bringing her into my house? Huh?" O-Dawg forced her down on the couch

"If you hurt my baby I promise you you're going to see another side you didn't know existed"

"Are you serious Marshawn? You really brought this ho into our house?"

"Ho? Bitch you got me fucked up. If you wasn't pregnant I'd beat yo ass bitch" Falon yelled back from across the room

"Let me go Marshawn" He stepped back but kept his eyes on her

"Are you fuckin this bitch, yes or no?" Tamia asked

"Wasn't he fuckin you while going home to my sister every night? Wake up bitch, he's a nigga. Ain't no nigga with that much money and power gone be fuckin on one bitch, including you. You sitting here worried bout the next bitch when you got everything you want"

"Falon, stop talkin" O-Dawg told her

"Naw she act like..."

"Bitch what the fuck I just say! Shut the fuck up before I slap the shit out you" Falon crossed her arms and didn't say another word

"Have you fucked her, yes or no?" Tamia asked again

"Yea but she know her role and where you stand?"

"Muthafucka!" She yelled and tried to jump off the couch swinging at him. He forced her back down

"I'm not playing Tamia, kill my baby and I kill you" He hissed at her

"Get her out of my house now!" O-Dawg took his keys from his pocket and threw them at Falon

"Go wait in the car" He instructed her. Falon got up and switched hard out the condo. Damn that ass be wobbling when she mad he thought to himself

"What the big sister pussy wasn't good enough"

"Tamia, that bitch don't mean shit to me. She's playing a major role and I can't afford to cut her off right now. She got the plug on the counterfeit money and she on some undercover shit for me right now. We on the way to meet the counterfeit nigga right now. You know how this shit go, fuck a bitch and she'll do whatever for you"

"Get the fuck out Marshawn; I don't want to even look at you right now. Get your money and go be with your amazon bitch! You let her disrespect your baby mom in front of you, in our home! I don't need you and neither does the baby. I'm tired of yo shit, this was the last straw" "Tamia on my dead dad if you ever threaten me with my baby ever again I'm going to beat the shit out you. You know how I feel about that shit! Keep fuckin with me about my seed and Ima kill yo whole family. You can dictate if you're my bitch, all day. But don't ever try to keep me away from my seed, you understand?" Tamia just sat there staring at him

"Do you understand!?" He yelled at the top of his lungs making her jump

"Yes!" She replied

"I'm sorry I can't be the nigga you want me to be, or the one I should. Just know that you're the only woman I love. I'm bout to grab my money and take care of my business. Obviously you don't want me here tonight so I won't come back. I'll check on you tomorrow and we can have a civilized conversation then, Aight?"

"Whatever just get yo money and leave" She replied while rolling her eyes. When O-Dawg made it out to the car Falon was texting on her phone

"What the fuck I tell you bout textin while you in my presence? It's an honor to be around me, so cherish every fuckin moment" He snapped at her soon as he closed the car door

"You wasn't even in here yet when I started textin"

"Shut the fuck up broad. That's yo problem, you talk too much, don't say shit" Falon put her phone inside her purse and pulled out some lip gloss

"I'm sorry daddy, I slipped up" She said

"Now you gone sit here in my face and lie? You know what the fuck you was doing when you said it"

"I was trying to be nice and respectful then she blew me off with an attitude. You need to be in there checking her, not me" O-Dawg grabbed her face hard as he could and made her face him

"Bitch what I just tell you bout yo mouth? Don't worry bout what I do with her, right now I'm checkin yo ass. Yo stupid ass got that dumb bitch talkin bout playing with my child. I should shoot both you bitches. Matter-fact once we done handling business I'm through with yo ass. We gone act like we never fucked and keep it strictly mafia" O-Dawg said then started the car. Falon was rubbing her face where he was gripping it. She finished putting on her lip gloss then said

"Daddy I'm sorry, please don't do that. Let me make it up to you, I'll do whatever you say. I'm sorry I shouldn't have said anything, I was outta pocket and will never do it again. Can you please just let me make it up to you?"

"Yea, you can start by shutting the fuck up. How about that?" He told her then pulled out his phone to start sending a text. Falon leaned over the seat on her knees

"I'm sorry daddy" She said then pulled his pants down. She kissed the head then started licking it. She slid it in her mouth half way then stopped. O-Dawg leaned his seat back then put his hand on top of her head to guide her down.

Falon swallowed the whole dick then left it down her throat for a few seconds

"Aww shit, go head and go to work, stop playing with it" Falon started bopping up and down on his dick and trying to suck the skin off. She took it out then spitted on the head and then slid it back in her mouth. Falon took it out again then started licking his balls. When she licked every inch she put them both in her mouth and started sucking on them real slow. O-Dawg just sat there staring at her suck his dick like their relationship depended on it

"Put it back in yo mouth" She did as told and started jacking him off while sucking it at the same time. O-Dawg leaned his seat back up

"Keep sucking while I drive. Matter-fact don't stop till we get to where we going"

"Aww! Shit you sucking this dick good. I might let you make it up. Aww shit! You gone have to learn how to control yo mouth. You hear me?" She nodded her head and then got back to sucking. O-Dawg pulled out the parking lot and was doing his best to drive under the circumstances.

ଔ

1 HOUR LATER

ଔ

Butta and pressha were sitting in Butta's black Yukon parked outside Half dead's house on 11th and Prescott St.

"The nigga car here so he can't be in jail. Why the fuck he ain't call nobody" Butta asked

"Maybe one of his bitches picked his car up for him and parked it. His phone still going straight to voicemail, so I don't know what the fuck going on. But we bout to find out" Pressha answered then hopped out the truck. He walked up to the front door and started knocking real hard

"This nigga bet not be in here" Butta said standing right behind him

"Half dead! Open up the door cuz!" Knock! Knock! Knock!

After another minute of knocking the door finally opened and there was half dead. He looked like he had just woke up and was wearing a tank-top and basketball shorts

"What's up cuz, why yall banging like the police?" He asked them. They both walked past him into the house and checked out the surroundings nonchalantly. Half dead went and sat on the couch and started rubbing his head

"I got a headache cuz, what yall niggaz want?"

"One of my bitches told me they seen you getting cuffed up. You never called and you wasn't in custody according to the website, so we came through to see what's up" Butta told him. That statement hit Half dead right in the gut. He had already been drinking and trying to sleep off the fact he was now a rat. The last thing he expected was to see his two homies at his house bringing up the fact he had been arrested

"Yea cuz I was at Javier's getting some food. Next thing I know gang task is runnin up on me talkin bout I was wanted for questioning. They forced me out the car and threw me in one of theirs while they searched the whip. They found my nine and tried to say I gave consent to search when the detectives got there. I told em go ahead and book me but I'll be out in an hour with a lawsuit. I was on the phone with my baby mom and she heard the whole thing. I told em I wasn't gone call her from jail, so it was gone look real strange when she told my lawyer and the jury the same story as me. Then the detectives looked through my call log and started cussing the task out. They let me go but kept the burner and that was it." He lied to them.

Half dead couldn't believe how good his story just added up. But when you're a snitch and you're trying to keep it a secret so you don't lose your life, you'll do and say anything at any given moment

"Why you ain't call us though cuz?" Pressha asked even though he fully believed the story

"Yall know how I am cuz, I've been on some solo shit. If it ain't about riding then I'm posted in the house, doing me. I woulda told yall at the next meeting but I didn't feel like it was that important to call yall right away. So yall came way over here to ask me why I didn't call? What the fuck yall think happened? Matter-fact cuz, what is yall tryna imply?" Half dead asked getting aggressive. Now that he had broken it down to them they started feeling stupid for coming over there

"We ain't implying nuttin nigga, we just tryna figure out where you was at. You need to get off that lone desperado shit and start coming around more" Butta said

"Man cuz I'm going back to sleep. Yall niggaz lock the door when yall leave" Half dead replied then walked to his bedroom

ര൯ഠ

DAYS LATER

ര൯ഠ

"Blood we gotta stop and get some more swishers" Bleed told Boobie. They were driving down MLK Blvd. after just leaving the studio

"Ima stop at the quick trip then we'll grab a couple. You need to learn how to roll and stop fuckin up the blunts"

"Fuck you nigga, a guess who hit me last night. That bitch with the attitude from Macys. She talkin bout she usually don't act like that but her boss was on her head that day"

"Blood stop fuckin lying all the time, you got a new story everyday" Boobie responded

"You got me fucked up on mob life blood gang nigga. That bitch was on my dick nigga, on me!"

"Let me see the text messages then nigga" Bleed sucked his teeth

"We was talkin not textin nigga" Boobie started laughing while he pulled into the Quick trip parking lot

"Blood all you do is text all day. Matter-fact, text her right now and tell her I need a friend"

"Naw nigga I ain't bout to tell her shit for you"

"That's what I thought, just be on point cause you know the crabs be over here" Boobie reminded him

"There go some posted over there on the side of the gas station, look they shootin dice" Bleed informed him while they hopped out the car. They went inside and told the man behind the counter that they needed two swishers

"Hold on blood I'm bout to get some Doritos and a pop" Bleed said

"Grab me a Pepsi too blood" Soon as they walked outside they seen a short dark skinned man wearing a Seattle mariners hat standing by the door

"Slob ass niggaz know what time it is with me cuz" He said when they walked past him "What you say nigga?" Bleed said when he turned back around

"You heard me cuz, homies been getting smoked and yall slobs over here in the hood" Bleed instantly took off on him with a jab to the chin. When he stumbled back Bleed rushed and threw a haymaker but the man ducked and grabbed him. They were both holding on to each other trying to get the other to fall. They both slammed into the wall hard and kept trying to trip each other.

Boobie walked up and hit the man in the head with his gun. Smack smack smack! He fell and Bleed kicked him in the stomach

"Bitch ass crab!"

"C'mon blood!" Boobie said then then started walking towards the car.

Boom Boom boom! Somebody started shooting from across the street. Booyow Booyow! Boobie returned fire with his 45 revolver. Boom Boom The man shot back and crouched behind a car parked in the street. Bleed finally got his pistol out and was ducking behind a car. Boc Boc Boc another man started shooting from the side of the gas station. He caught them off guard because they were focused on the original shooter. Boc Boc! He kept shooting and shattered the glass on the car Bleed was ducking behind

"What that Kirby Crip like?" The man taunted them

"How we gone do this blood?" Bleed asked. Boobie pulled his other .45 revolver from out his pants

"Member if we got to die, then fuck it we die?" Boobie said then came up shooting with both guns at the second shooter. Booyow Booyow Booyow! Boc Boc! The first shooter started shooting again now, Boom Boom! But bleed sent him back behind the car. Boca Boca Boca Boca! Booyow Booyow! Boc Boc Boc! The second shooter shot back, then finally got back against the wall of the gas station. They all heard sirens coming at a rapid pace. It came at no surprise since the police station was only 3 blocks away. The man that started the fight jumped up and tried running into the store. Boca Boca! Bleed shot him in the back and in the leg; He stumbled into the store and fell. Once they realized the two shooters had run off when they heard the sirens, they ran towards Boobies car

"I fuckin hate crabs blood!" Bleed yelled in his high pitched voice as he jumped into the car

ɢ

HOURS LATER

ɢ

"I don't care about that fuckin movie cuz; I got shit to do" Pull out said to the group. Him, Ron, Nisha and Shay were sitting on the couches in the front room

"Baby I wanna go see About last night" Shay whined to him

"Then go see it, ain't nobody stopping you from going with them. I'm bout to go record this song I've been writing"

"You act like you're a real rapper and that's a real studio. You got an I-mac and a microphone, you can record when we get back" That statement got under Pull outs skin for some reason

"I'm done talkin cuz, C-safe Ron" Pull out said then walked to his room and locked the door"

"That was a good way to get what you want" Nisha said sarcastically to Shay

"Fuck him he always complaining and shit. Like it's his way or the highway. I'm not bout to sit here and be bored while he records all night"

"C'mon lets shake then cause the movie start in 30 minutes" Ron said then checked his watch

"Bye! I'm leaving with them" Shay yelled then left the house with them. Pull out didn't hear a word she said. He had his headphones on and the beat blasting loud in his ear. After rapping to himself a few times he was ready to record. He hit a few clicks on the mouse then stepped up close to the mic. The hook played twice in his ear then he started spitting

"Blue light on sight now that's automatic/Lean over the homie seat and bust when I catch em in traffic/That nigga from outta town, I'm gunning em down/And with those stiches in yo face I know it's hard to smile/ Fly crippin and I'm flossy, .45 an off em/Send em back to the east coast in a red coffin/Burn a slob from the side fuck Burnside/He a bitch deep inside cuz I seen it in his eyes/Can't wait to catch you, Smith n Wesson gone wet you/The .45 sneeze tell the slobs go and bless you/And ya leader is a bitch, that means ya hoods fake/Hit the ground and didn't spray a round when it went down at unthank/You niggaz dumb he playing puppet master with you ho's/Gotcha risking ya life for some dope and a pair of clothes/And his cousin got shot but he ain't bust a round/Hiding in the house scared to show his face in the town/. . . Pull out listened to the verse a few more times then started working on the second verse.

His plan was to put the song on the internet and embarrass the mob life gang. He knew within 24 hours of putting it out there that everybody in Portland was gone be talking about the song. He was hoping that the pressure would force O-Dawg to show his face. There was nobody he wanted to kill more in the world than him. He knew that by killing him he would gain the most stripes and revenge Dan's murder. He wanted nothing more in life than to kill O-Dawg then Burnside. But what he didn't realize was the negative effects the song would have. He wasn't even 18 years old yet and didn't understand the consequences that the internet could have. Especially when telling the truth about real life street wars.

MARCELLUS ALLEN

ⲟⲝⲟ

MOVIE THEATER

ⲟⲝⲟ

Burnside finally found a parking spot in the crowded parking lot. He was with Felicia at the Cinemax theaters across the street from the Lloyd center

"This muthafucka is packed blood" Burnside said while turning the car off and putting his gun in his jeans

"I know right, it seems like everybody wanna see a movie tonight" Felicia responded

"I like this new charger you got baby, but you know having it red gone make it stand out" "I don't care, that's the point. I ain't hiding and care less who see me. Now c'mon lets go see this movie you've been sweating me about" Burnside replied then hopped out the car. After they made it half way through the parking lot he couldn't take it any longer. He had been watching her ass bounce and jiggle the whole time through the velour sweat pants she was wearing. He grabbed her arm

"C'mon I left sumn in the car" He told her. When they made it back to the car he wrapped his hands around her waist

"You not wearing any panties huh?" He asked then gripped her ass

"You told me not to ever wear any when I'm with you, remember?" He opened the door

"I'm bout to show you why, with yo thick ass" He turned her around then bent her over the seat, then pulled her sweats down to her ankles

"Baby we're outside in a parking lot" She said half way complaining. Burnside slid his dick in her pussy after rubbing it against the lips a few times to get it wet

220

"Hmm" She moaned. He put his hands on her hips and started pounding her

"Ohh ohh!"

"Yea Ima teach you bout not wearing panties around a gangsta" He said then smacked her ass. Smack!

"Oh yes, teach me daddy!" She said then started throwing her ass back. He palmed her ass tighter and took over control of the rhythm. She gave up throwing it back and just put her head down and enjoyed the feeling. Clap clap! Her ass was bouncing on his dick and he was staring at it jiggle out of control. He put one leg into the car and opened one of her cheeks to get a better feeling

"I'm bout to cum baby, oh-oh! Right now!" She yelled and started Cumming. Burnside couldn't hold it in any longer either. He sped up the pace and started ramming her harder

"This my pussy, bitch. Aww shit! You got some fire" A few more strokes then he was nutting all inside of her. He slowed the pace down and kept long stroking her until he was done squirting

"Grab some napkins out the glove box and wipe yourself off. I'm bout to go get our tickets" He told her while wiping his dick off on her ass. When Burnside was waiting in the line inside the complex something told him to look around.

What he saw made his heart start beating fast out of his chest. He saw Ron with two females standing in the line buying food

"I should get on this nigga blood" He said out loud. He watched the group walk down the hallway towards the movies. I bet that bitch ass nigga going to the same movie as me. He thought to himself. When he turned around from buying the tickets Felicia was standing right there in his space. Burnside was so caught up thinking about Ron that he forgot all about her. So when he turned around and she was standing in his face he got scared inside for a second

"What the fuck I tell you bout sneaking up on me? Ima shoot yo dumb ass one day"

"Then you won't be able to hit this pussy no more" She responded then kissed him on the lips. He thought about telling her that he seen Ron then changed his mind. He knew she would start acting paranoid and irritating him. When they made it into the theater he scanned the rows as best as he could, looking for Ron. He seen him sitting in the section all the way on the right end. He grabbed Felicia's arm and guided her to the left section

"C'mon let's sit over here it's less packed" He instructed her. He watched Ron out the corner of his eyes the whole time he was walking. . . Ron couldn't believe who he saw walking into the movies like he didn't have a care in the world. Ron waited until Burnside sat down then pulled out his phone. He debated on calling Butta then changed his mind

"He just gone tell me this ain't the right place or time" Then he thought about Pressha then came to the same conclusion as he did with Butta. He knew he couldn't call Half dead because he was almost certain that the female he saw with Burnside is his baby mom Felicia

"Let me hit this nigga" When Pull out didn't answer he got irritated

"Answer yo phone cuz!"

"Shay call yo nigga"

"I'm not calling that nigga, you call em" She shot back

"Do what the fuck I told you!" He hissed at her

"Why you talking to her like that?" Nisha jumped in

"You shut the fuck up and watch the movie, it's too much going on right now to hear yo mouth" He checked her. Nisha knew something was wrong for him to talk to her like that for no reason

"He not answering his phone" Shay informed him, with an attitude.

Ron positioned himself so he could see Burnside a little bit. He noticed only one head in the row and knew exactly what that meant "Yea I definitely can't call Half dead "

"You know I love you right" Felicia asked him in his ear

"No you don't cause if you did, you would do what I've been asking you to do" He shot back at her

"I already told you why I don't wanna do that. It has nothing to do with him at all, I give two fucks about him. I don't want to have to look in my sons eyes when he ask me how his dad died. I can't go through that Burnside, but don't try an act like I don't love you when you know I do. Besides that there's nothing I won't do for you"

"So how you gone feel if he end up killing me? What you gone say then?"

"Yall not bout to kill each other so stop even talking like that. Fuck him he don't mean nothing to me baby" Burnside stopped looking at her and focused on the movie while looking mad. In all actuality he didn't care about her, not even a lil bit. All she was to him was a light skinned female that had long hair and a fat ass. Also the fact that she was his enemy's baby mom gave him a little extra incentive

"Baby don't be like that" She pleaded with him. She moved his dreads away from his ear and stuck her tongue in it

"You know I love you daddy, just give me some time to sort things out" Burnside kept ignoring her and stared at the screen

"So you think you can ignore me?" She asked then grabbed his dick through his pants

"You know he can't ignore me no matter how hard you try" She pulled his pants down when he didn't respond. She gripped his dick with one hand then started licking around the head

"I said I was sorry" Then she started licking down the sides of his meat before sticking it in her mouth. After she slurped on it a few times she pulled it out

"You still mad at me?" Burnside didn't reply he just grabbed the back of her head and forced her back down

"Agghh!" He moaned then leaned his head back. When he turned his head to the right he got a glimpse of Ron trying to look over his way. When Ron immediately looked away and tried to pretend he was just looking around, Burnside knew what he had to do.

When the movie was over Ron gripped his gun just in case Burnside accidently ran into him. Everybody was standing up and moving at the same time and that made him nervous

"C'mon yall let's shake" He told them. He pulled out his phone and called Pull out again while they were leaving

"Fuck, this punk ass nigga still ain't answering" He complained then shoved the phone back in his pocket. When they finally made it outside without incident Ron stopped the females from walking

"Yall post right here while I get the car" Ron made sure he walked out the theater in the first group so he knew Burnside wasn't in the parking lot yet. He pulled out his .38 revolver soon as he stepped away from the girls

"Ron what are you doing?" Nisha yelled to him. Ron's plan was to find the most flamboyant cars that he could and check for any signs that it belonged to Burnside. He started crouching while he was walking to make himself less visible. When he came to a green Benz he thought he hit the jackpot. First he checked the license plate to see if it spelled anything gang related. He looked inside to see if the drivers set was leaned back or any blunt roaches that he could see. When he determined that this was too time consuming he decided to wait in a spot where he could see the entrance to the movies. He looked that way and seen the girls still standing in the same place. That's when he spotted a red Lexus across the lot

"that's the niggaz car cuz" He said out loud. Soon as he started making his way towards the car he heard the girls start shouting

"Ron run! He's behind you" He instantly ducked and started running behind a parked car. Boom! He heard what he felt was the loudest gunshot he'd ever heard. He knew he would of been dead if he hadn't moved in that second. Boom! Boom! bullets started hitting the car

"You thought you had me huh? You crab ass nigga! You shoulda known I was too sneaky by the way I did ya boy Dan!" Burnside yelled at him. Ron could tell he was only a few cars down crouching. He ran to the next car and tried to get Burnside in his line of sight. People started running wild in the lot and Ron pointed his gun at the nearest group

"Agghh! Don't shoot!" A female screamed. Boom! Boom! Boom! Ron heard the shots ring out and shatters a car window

"You a rookie with yo crab ass! It's a big difference when a nigga got a gun huh? I ain't Wet, lil nigga!" Burnside shouted being cocky. Ron seen him start walking his direction and started firing. Boca! Boca! Boca! Burnside ducked behind a car.

They heard police sirens that sounded real close

"Ima catch yo bitch ass on the rebound, I just wanted to show you that I can't be fucked with!" Burnside yelled. When Ron didn't hear or see anything after a couple seconds he got up and started running to his car. Boom! Boom! Boom! Boom! Ron dove on the ground and rolled next to a car

"Fuck! Bitch ass nigga" He said to himself

"Tell yo big homies to train you better!" He heard Burnside yell. Burnside ran to the other end of the parking lot and jumped in his car that was waiting by the entrance.

CHAPTER 14

Never put yo faith in man, cause man will fail you every time. Only put yo faith in God and never expect man to do what only God can do

"I just started fuckin with this nigga in Alabama and he told me he'll shoot me 30 racks per a brick. I'm probably gone take two down there just to see how shit goes" O-Dawg told Jaxx. They were sitting in Jaxx front room talking after completing their usual drug transaction.

"You don't know what you wanna do, lil nigga. I thought you was retiring and going to be a rapper with Spike down in Atlanta" Jaxx replied sarcastically while twisting a blunt

"That ain't changed at all, I'm just tryna stack some extra bread while I'm still in the game. The crabs been hiding and making it harder to kill they faggot asses. On some real shit bro, I can't believe them niggaz ain't been dead. These niggaz is low-key hanging with us"

"I mean what the fuck you expected them to do lie down and die?" I expected for my goons to been wiped them niggaz out. I'm bout to get more hands on with the situation real soon though. Tell you the truth, I kinda think most of the homies want this beef to play out long as possible. They know once the crabs is dead that I'm out the game. I've already had a few of the homies tell me they think shit gone get fucked up when I leave. But I don't think so, I got faith in my niggaz blood" O-Dawg stated then grabbed the blunt from his brother

"Yea that's always been yo biggest weakness. Putting yo faith in these niggaz, I don't understand how you still ain't woke the fuck up. Since you got all this faith then answer these questions. Where was these niggaz at when you was flat out broke? Remember you didn't have anywhere to stay so you was sleeping on my couch? But you had faith in them then, right? Where was these niggaz at when yo so called favorite cousin snitched on you? Why he ain't get killed so you can get out? Then you just sat here and told me that you think yo niggaz is half ass riding. You told them to kill those niggaz ASAP right? Now when you told them that, you had faith they was gone follow yo orders right? All them niggaz is around for money and don't ever forget that shit. Niggaz fuck with you because you control their present living arrangements and their future. You think cause they do what you say that their loyal? Let yo ass go broke and see how far a demand goes with them niggaz. How you gone put faith in something that's only around for self-interest? That's not faith, that's called he who has the gold, makes the mold" O-Dawg let out a deep breath

"So you telling me Boobie and Burnside are around for money too? You act like nobody was around before this money started coming in. Plus every reason you just named is the reason why we started our own shit in the first place" O-Dawg shot back

"Nigga please, you started that shit for power and you know it. Power to decide who can be a member, power to decide who dies and when. Most important, Power to choose who gets paid and who stays broke. I taught you this game so don't ever think you can go over my head. Shit, you own yo whole hood and yo click. Both sides depend on you for their well-being, quiet as it's kept. Nigga that's called power and everybody wants it. So don't think for a second that shits gone be the same. When power steps down, another power steps up! That's called a power struggle, watch how many of those niggaz you got faith in start beefing with each other. Listen lil nigga, cause I'm only gone tell you this once in yo whole life. Never put yo faith in man, cause man will fail you every time. Only put yo faith in GOD and never expect a man to do what only GOD can do. Only GOD will never fail you, no matter what" Jaxx pointed his finger at him during the last sentence

"It's time for me to shake blood. You always getting on that don't trust nobody shit. If that's the case, what's the point of even having a team? What's the point of friends? You act like it's impossible for niggaz to love you and vise-versa" O-Dawg said getting frustrated

"That's yo second biggest problem, you control everybody with love. Love is for GOD and close family members. You're surrounded by niggaz, and with niggaz the only thing that prevails is fear. Them niggaz don't gotta love you, just like you. When you add that with fear, you give yourself the highest percentage to succeed. Niggaz used to fear you, now they just respect you. Trust me lil bro, it's a huge difference"

"They respect me because they got some fear of me"

"No! Niggaz fear what you created, and that's yo click. But trust me, if they could find a way to kill you and get away with it, they would. That goes for friends and enemies nigga" Jaxx clarified

"Anyways moving on. Have you heard the song the lil crab nigga Pull out made? Nigga called it 'when it's time to pull out'. My phone started blowing up as soon as it got dropped" O-Dawg asked. Jaxx started coughing from the weed

"Yea I heard that shit, that nigga dry snitchin if you ask me. He placing niggaz at scenes of crimes and everything. But on some real shit, he was on yall niggaz. That nigga made you out to be a straight bitch, you gone drop a track on em?" Jaxx busted out laughing

"Fuck I look like? Where they do that at? All he did was put himself on my kill list. That lil nigga a problem though, Ima get em knocked off before it's too late"

"It's already too late lil bro, you just don't see it yet. He been riding hard and that song is gone make niggaz start really thinking and second guessing you" O-Dawg got up to leave

"I ain't worried about it bro, niggaz know what time it is with me. They memories ain't that bad"

ꙮ

1 HOUR LATER

ꙮ

"Yall hear this bitch crab ass nigga yo!? Son just started riding a few months ago ya heard? Now the nigga think he king Tut! Word to my mama Ima murder this nigga!" Jersey Joe vented to the whole room. He was in "the ville" kicking it with the young members of Mob Life inside one of their apartments. Gatman had Pull outs diss song blasting out of his lap top that was sitting on the table

"That nigga a bitch on the Mob! Nigga busted his gun a few times and act like he really with the shit" Dute fly joined in

"He was real disrespectful towards O-Dawg blood, he got my nigga fucked up " Added Shooter

"That nigga bout to get turnt up huh?" Asked Dute

"I doubt it son, it's gone take for somebody in his close circle to get smoked before son start blasting his pistol. I be telling that nigga all the time, like yo, you gotta start fuckin with the lil homies more. You gotta start letting niggaz see yo face and getting it in. Yo I be feeling like he think he better than everybody else. But at the same time, when you that high up on the pole, you gotta distance yourself a lil bit" Joe stated

"Shit I don't care if he don't ever show his face, that nigga made sure I had money on my books upstate. Niggaz make it seem like he don't fuck with niggaz or sumn. I was just with em the other day." Said Gatman. He had just came home from prison after serving 3 years for a shooting

"Anyways yo, we need to be focused on this bitch ass nigga Pull out. What do yall know bout this crab? What bitches he fuck with?" Joe asked changing the subject

"I saw this bitch named Shays Facebook the other day. She had a couple pictures all hugged up on his bitch ass. One of my bitches is coo with her so Ima try to get some info out her" Gatman said

"A blood what's up with that shit that happened at the movies" Shooter asked

"Burnside caught the crab nigga Ron at the movies with some bitches and aired em out ya heard? Son said the lil nigga actually tried to creep on him but didn't know he was falling into a trap. Son said if the bitches didn't start screaming at the last second then that nigga would be food ya heard?" Joe said giving them the story.

"Burnside be on niggaz, on the set. He should've called me that would've been an easy body" Dute said

"A joe, was it hard to smile when you got those stiches in?" Gatman asked making everybody laugh. Joe didn't find it funny at all. Now that the stiches were gone he had a long scar going from his earlobe to his chin

"I wouldn't know lil nigga, because real killers don't smile. Ain't nuttin to smile about son, when you got demons and niggaz souls inside of you" He shot back with anger in his voice. He was mostly mad at the text he just received after he just tried to call Falon. He read it again "Stop callin' I Don't fuck wit u no more"

He responded "U probably got Boobie dick n yo ass"

She had just texted back "Lol R U jealous?"

"Yo fuck bitches son" He said out loud on accident

"That's how I feel too, bitches ain't shit. Matter-fact let's call some rats over here" Dute said then pulled out his phone.

ඬ෦ඔ

FALON HOUSE

ඬ෦ඔ

"Bitch ass nigga why would I want you when I got the boss" Falon said after texting Jersey Joe back and tossing her phone on the bed

"Talkin bout I'm probably sucking Boobies dick, this nigga a clown She grabbed her weed off the headboard and started rolling a blunt

"What the fuck!" She yelled then grabbed her phone, she thought Joe was texting again. She seen who it was calling and answered it

"You close? . . . Aight here I come"

She replied then got off the bed to walk to the front door. When she opened the door Beth walked in looking stressed out. She had her hair down and was wearing some black pajama pants and a tank-top. Falon gave her a hug then said

"Sit down while I get some wine then you can tell me all about it. I hope you don't mind what I'm wearing, I just got out the shower. Shit I usually walk around like this anyways, this the only place a bitch can feel comfortable" Falon said commenting on her pink bra and panties she was wearing

"Girl that don't bother me I walk around my house naked" Beth replied while sitting down on the couch

"We need to be at yo place then" Falon said while walking away. When she heard Beth laugh she turned around a lil bit and seen her staring at her ass. Falon came back into the front room with two glasses and a bottle of wine. She sat on the same couch as Beth and poured both of them glasses

"Yo square ass smoke" She asked then grabbed the blunt of the table

"Uhh, not really. Every now and then when I'm really stressing"

"Well you're stressin so you're bout to get high with me. Get tipsy off this wine and cry on my shoulder if you want to"

"You think your funny, no I'm done crying now. I've cried the last 3 days, I'm past that phase. I swear niggaz ain't shit!" Beth vented then started sipping her wine. Falon started coughing from the weed then agreed with her

"You got that right"

"I mean what the fuck more can I do? What do they want from us? I'm square, I don't party, I never cheated and I've only had sex with 3 people my whole life"

"Here girl, you need this" Falon passed her the blunt while laughing

"Wow you only fucked 3 niggaz? So is this nigga in the streets?" Beth started coughing real hard and couldn't talk for seconds

"No he work at the bank. And he's a piece of shit cheater!" Falon busted out laughing in her face

"What!?" Beth asked

"You sound white as shit! Then you got the nerve to be crying over a banker! Can bankers fuck and eat pussy good?"

"He's pretty good with his dick but he doesn't really eat pussy. We was together for 3 years and he's probably ate me out like 4 or 5 times" Beth confessed

"Aww hell naw! That's the problem right there, I wish a nigga would. What you need is a thug in yo life that know how to lay pipe and eat pussy good!" Beth almost spit out her wine

"I'm scared of street niggaz they're crazy. Is your man in the streets?"

"Now that's a long story. I'm not in a 100% committed relationship. I love my nigga and don't let any other nigga get this pussy, but were not officially together"

"How the hell does that work?" Beth asked

"It's kind of complicated. Basically I'm loyal to him and trying to convince him that I'm the only bitch that he needs. He a street nigga so he definitely ain't faithful and he got his main bitch pregnant right now"

"And you're fine with that arrangement?" Beth asked

"I'm content right now because I came in as a side bitch. But over time I'm gone be the only bitch" Falon broke it down to her

"That's why I'm just bout to stop fucking with niggaz for a while. I'm going to just focus on my career and whatever happens just happens" Falon took a couple sips of wine

"You know what you really need?" She asked

"No but I'm sure you're going to tell me and I'm sure it's going to be crazy"

"You need a massage, a full body one"

"Yea I really do, I ain't had one in years. I'm going to schedule me one real soon"

"Bitch you bet not pay all that money for sumn I can do for free"

"You don't know how to give a real massage"

"C'mon Ima show yo ass. Grab the glasses and yo square ass follow me" Falon instructed her while grabbing the bottle and some weed off the table and walking to her bedroom. When they got in her room Falon stated scrolling through her I-pod to find some music

"This is a big ass bed, what's this? King size?" Beth asked while flopping on it

"Naw it's a California king, you know bosses gotta do boss shit. Lay on yo stomach while I get the massaging oil" Falon told her then started playing Ushers confession album. When Falon came back from the bathroom Beth was laying down with her face in the pillows. Falon dimmed the lights then brought over another glass of wine to Beth

"Here, kill this shit, it's gone make everything feel better" Beth grabbed the glass

"I'm already a lil tipsy" then drank the whole glass and passed it back to her then rolled over. Falon climbed on the bed then climbed on top of Beth's back. She started rubbing her neck real slow and applying pressure at the right spots. After about a minute Falon said

"Now I'm bout to start using the oil, I ain't did shit yet. Take this off so I can get your whole back" Falon tugged at her tank-top then reached over and grabbed the bottle off the ground. She watched Beth think about taking it off, then slowly take it off and toss it on the floor. Falon poured the oil in her hands then started massaging her neck again

"Hmm" She heard Beth moan a few seconds later

"This shit feel good huh? You got a lot of knots in yo neck and shoulders. You gotta stop stressing so much and enjoy life"

"I know, it's just so hard. Oh that feels good" Beth replied then moaned the last part. Falon started dripping the oil on the back of her neck and shoulders. She started rubbing the neck first then made her way to the shoulders. She increased the pressure where she felt the knots at and started pushing her thumbs into them

"Oooh that feels good, stay there for a second" Beth moaned and demanded

"I thought I didn't know what I was doing?" Falon taunted her.

She started pouring the oil down her back and felt Beth tense up. Falon began rubbing her back in circular motions then moved to her ribs. When she started applying pressure on the side of her ribs that's when the moaning started. She could feel Beth tense up a lil bit on certain spots so she started rubbing her thumbs over them. Next she started rubbing her hands from Beth's neck all the way down to the bottom of her back. Then she started only using her thumbs to find tense spots and apply pressure on them. The whole time Beth was letting out small moans. When Falon made her way back down she asked

"You want a full body right?"

"Yea" Beth whispered back.

Falon pulled down her pajama pants to her ankles then threw them on the floor. Beth was wearing yellow lace panties to match her bra

"You got a nice lil plump booty. It's all firm and toned"

"Everybody can't have a big juicy ass like yours" Beth replied back sarcastically

"No I was being serious. It's nice and athletic looking and you got nice skin too" Beth didn't reply this time. Falon poured some oil on the bottom of her back then started rubbing it in. She kept moving towards her hips back and forth. She started dropping oil on her ass cheeks, thighs and legs. She gripped her ass with both hands then started massaging it one cheek at a time. Falon tried to see her facial expressions but couldn't because her whole face was buried in the pillow. Falon moved on to her thighs and was rubbing them real slow and soft

"You like that?" She asked. Beth just nodded her head. Falon got to her legs and rubbed them from the outside to the inside real slow. Then she moved her hands all the way back up real slow and under her panties to massage her cheeks, that was covered by the panties the first time. When Beth didn't protest the touching, Falon decided to make her move. She started rubbing her neck again then asked

"It still feel good?" Beth nodded her head in the pillow

"Did everything feel good?" She nodded again. Falon unstrapped her own bra then tossed it on the floor. Falon started rubbing her hips and thighs again real slow

"Your skin is so smooth and beautiful" Falon got down to her legs

"And you got long sexy legs" Beth still didn't comment, she just let out a moan every few seconds. Falon moved her hands back up to her ass and started massaging it. She started sliding he panties down, when she got them half way down her ass Beth finally spoke up

"What are you doing?" She started working on her neck again

"I'm doing what you want me to do" Then she laid on her back and made sure Beth could feel her titties. Falon started whispering in her ear

"You know it feels good. Just lay here and enjoy the feeling mixed with the wine. You deserve to feel good, or do you want me to stop" Beth didn't respond so she started rubbing her back again and making her way back down to her ass. Her panties were still half way off. Falon slid them down real slow and threw them on the floor. She grabbed the bottle of wine and started dripping it on the bottom of her back. Beth sucked in air

"Cold" She said. Falon made sure some dripped by her ass hole. Then started licking the middle of her back and moving down real slow

"Umm" Beth moaned

"You want me to stop?" Beth shook her head no.

Falon continued down and licked up the wine that was around her ass crack. She knew it was time, she gripped her cheeks and spread them open. Falon waited a second to see what Beth would do, she just laid there. She started sucking on her pussy then Beth flinched and started moaning

"Ohh! What are you doing?" She didn't answer with words, she stuck her tongue inside the pussy instead. Beth was moaning and squirming like crazy. Falon kept on attacking her pussy, licking and sucking it with expert skills

"Bitch take that bra off" Falon demanded her. She kept her tongue on Beth's pussy while watching her snap off the bra and toss it

"Umm, don't stop. It feels good" Falon stopped eating her pussy and got on her knees

"What are you doing, why you stop?" Beth started yelling at her

"Roll over" Falon instructed her. Beth turned over on her back and Falon laid on top of her

"You ever fucked a bitch"

"No" She answered

"Well you have now and your bout to be my bitch, you hear me?"

"Yes" She answered again. Falon started kissing her on the lips then told her

"Can't no nigga make you feel better than I can" Then she stuck her tongue in Beth's mouth. Beth started rubbing and gripping Falons ass

"It's so fat and juicy and hella soft. I've been wanting to grab it since day one" Beth said them palmed it hard as she could. Beth started trying to pull her panties down. Falon finished the job and threw them. She had one of Beth's titties in her mouth and was sucking on it hard while rubbing the other

"Oh baby! Let me eat yo pussy!" Beth yelled and moaned. Falon rolled off of her and laid on her back

"Climb up here, we gone sixty-nine"

"No you get up top. I wanna be able to grab your ass and have it in my face" Falon got on top in the position.

"I don't know what it is about this ass but niggaz or bitches can't get enough of it." Falon said then stuck her tongue in Beth's pussy. Beth was rubbing and gripping Falons ass. She was fascinated by it and couldn't stop touching it. She finally began sucking on her pussy.

A few minutes later she was fully into it and was licking like a pro

MARCELLUS ALLEN

"I'm bout to cum!" Beth took her face out of Falons pussy for a moment to announce. Beth stuck two fingers in her pussy and started fingering her. When she heard Falon moaning she felt extra freaky for some reason. She started licking around her ass hole then stuck it in. Beth started cumming harder than she ever did in her life. She wanted Falon to feel the same way. She kept eating her ass like her life depended on it. The whole time she was rubbing Falons clit to add extra pleasure. Beth moved her tongue back to the pussy and began trying to lick all the juices that came out. Falon started grinding her ass on her face. Beth grabbed it and pulled it closer to her face. She started rocking her ass on her tongue and this was driving Falon crazy. Falon had had enough and jumped off of her

"What are you doing!?" Falon crawled close to her face and straddled it.

"You eat pussy way too good for this to be yo first time" Beth couldn't respond due to Falon sitting on her face. Falon gripped her own titties and started grinding on her face. Beth gripped her hips to control the pace and was sucking her pussy like it was the best thing on earth. Falon leaned forward and started grinding faster and harder

"I'm bout to cum!" After a few more seconds she was cumming all over Beth's lips and face

"Aghh shit that was some good as head" Falon admitted then climbed down. She went and grabbed some towels from the bathroom and handed Beth one. Beth was exhausted. She wiped her face then laid back with her eyes closed. Falon grabbed her phone and took a picture of her laying naked. She texted

"Bitch give good head" Along with the picture and sent it to O-Dawg. She climbed back on top of Beth

"That was the best massage of yo life huh?" Beth started smiling

"You seduced and tricked me. Gave me alcohol and weed then turned me into yo plaything" Falon kissed her on the lips

238

THA LAST OF MY KIND

"You're not my plaything but the rest is torture. I told you your about to be my bitch" Beth palmed her ass

"This feels good. Having somebody bigger than me lay on top and I get to grip their ass. I could probably get used to this" Beth admitted

"So you gone let me make you feel like this all the time?" Falon asked then kissed her on the forehead.

"How you gone be with me and you got a man?"

"Because you don't got a dick so he ain't gone care. Shit he probably gone like it and start tryna come over more" They both started laughing because they knew how men were.

ࢤ

O-DAWG'S HOUSE

ࢤ

O-Dawg started smiling as he read Falons text and looked at the picture

"If she make you that happy, why don't you go be with the bitch!" Tamia snapped at him from across the room. They were sitting on couches in their front room when he got the text.

They were in the middle of having a heated conversation about their relationship when he started smiling

"You don't even know what the fuck you talkin bout, that's yo problem. You always talkin and being insecure. Trust and believe if I didn't wanna be here, I wouldn't have come. But on some real shit, that mouth gone get you fucked up. I've been putting up with yo mood changes and

239

attitude cause you pregnant. But you need to start realizing who the fuck you talkin too" O-Dawg checked her

"Well you need to realize you can't just treat me any type of way. I'm not one of those stripper bitches yall be running trains on. You're disrespectful but then expect me to respect you" Tamia shot back

"First off, you gone respect me or get killed like the ones who didn't. And what the fuck you mean I don't be respecting you? You get every fuckin thing you want and more. I treat you better than I do everybody else, so what the fuck you talkin bout?" He asked getting frustrated

"So you think blaming me for setting you up was respectful? You bring a bitch in my house that your fucking is respect? Nigga I'm pregnant with your child and you barley come home, is that respect? I mean I can keep on going, in the last 10 years I'm sure I can write a book"

"If I'm so disrespectful then why the fuck you want me here all the time? You don't even make since, you're contradicting yourself. You sit here and claim I'm disrespectful, then say I'm not here enough. That's the pregnant shit I be talkin bout blood. Why you tell me to come over if all you wanna do is argue. You starting to stress me the fuck out! Ain't you the one told me to do whatever I have to do so I make it home? You told me to finish this shit so we ain't gotta be looking over our shoulders"

"Yea I said that, but you're forgetting the key word! So you can make it home at night. You ain't been here so where the fuck you been at?" She questioned him.

"Tamia, lower yo voice and stop cussing when you talk to me. I'm not gone tell you again"

"Who do you love!?" YG's voice blasted through his jeans. He took his phone out because he knew it was Gotti calling

"What's mobbin?" He answered "What the fuck you mean nigga!!" O-Dawg yelled "I'm on my way! And for the sake of everybody's life, this better be a mistake!"

"You there right now? He's gone?" O-Dawg asked holding his breath. A few seconds later he hung up without saying a word. He ran to the bedroom and almost yanked off the closet door. He pulled a duffle bag out and started going through it. He took off his white t-shirt he was wearing and put on the Teflon vest he grabbed out the bag

"Baby what's going on?" Tamia asked from the doorway.

"Go grab my gun off the table and bring it to me" he demanded her with pure malice in his voice. When she came back in the room he had a hoody over his vest now. She watched him load up a 12 gauge shotgun then drop it by his feet. He had a chrome .45 sitting in his lap with a couple clips. She walked over and handed him the gun. She watched him release the clip and put in one of the longer ones that was in his lap. When he cocked it back She couldn't resist it any longer

"Marshawn what's wrong? Can you please talk to me?" She pleaded with him. He put the gauge in the bag and both his .45 was in his hoody before locking eyes with her. There was tears building up in his eyes and she'd never seen him look more evil

"Stay in the house and keep your gun close to you. Don't worry bout nothing, you know you're safe here. Some shit just went down and I gotta go see what's up" He responded coldly

"Baby can't you wait until tomorrow? Your too mad right now and don't forget you got a child on the way" Tamia said trying to convince him to stay home. O-Dawg let out a deep breath

"Tamia, baby it's not the time. Please get out my way before I do sumn I can't take back" When she seen the look in his eyes again she stepped to the side.

ⵔⵔ

BEFORE THE PHONE CALL

MARCELLUS ALLEN

☙❧

"This shit low-key dry tonight huh?" Boobie asked Jersey Joe. They were chilling at a strip club called Mystiques

"Yea son, this shit wack tonight yo. It's probably because we always in here and we done fucked all these bitches ya heard? Ima take you to some spots back home son. Yo, the shit don't even compare ya heard?" Joe replied

`"What's up with my blood niggaz?" Overdose asked as he took a seat at their table

"What's brackin blood?" Boobie responded while shaking him up

"Shit just moving in slow motion, tryna knock a new bitch to the team. These bitches already know if they ain't paying the most, they can't fuck with the Dose" He replied making everybody laugh

"What's good with that nigga Lonnell?" Boobie asked him because they were from the same hood

"The lil homie doing aight, he called me a few days ago. I guess some crabs just shot up his baby mom house, so he hot about that

"I ain't heard shit bout that on the set"

"I thought you would've been knew since him and O-Dawg is brothers. He Gucci though, he from Failing block so he ain't got no choice" He stated showing pride for his hood

"Yo why yall west coast niggaz always shootin up houses son?"

"Shut yo ass up blood, don't nobody feel like hearing that Death Row vs Bad Boy shit tonight" Boobie cut him off before it all got started

"Ain't that those brand niggaz right there?" Overdose nodded his head in the direction of the door. They watched Pull out, Half dead, Ron and Gucci ty walk into the club

"That's the bitch nigga right there yo!" Joe said rubbing the scar on his face and standing up. Boobie grabbed his arm and yanked him back down

"Not in here wait 'till we get outside. It's only two of us, we gotta at least call Burnside" "Fuck that shit yo, you got two guns on you so that means it's three of us"

"Nigga I'm riding with yall on the 'F', what I look like walking away when it's bout to pop off" Overdose jumped in

"Look at them bitch ass niggaz! Yo on everything I'm worth this Desert Eagle is poppin off tonight" Joe growled while mean mugging them.

The Gutta Squad was sitting at a table with a bunch of groupies surrounding them. 20 minutes later Joe was still keeping his eye on them.

He couldn't tell if they noticed him or not. He watched two females walk his direction

"Blood them bitches was rockin with the crabs then moved around for a minute, now they on the way over here yo. I think the crabs is tryna play us son" Joe informed them

"Nigga stop acting paranoid you just looking for a reason to pop it off" Boobie said. The two dark skinned females walked directly over to their table

"Hi, can we sit down with yall?" The female with the biggest titties asked

"Hell yea, what's yall names?" Overdose spoke up

"I'm Shanae and this is my home girl Tee-Tee" The same female said while they sat down. While Boobie and Overdose were conversing with the ladies Joe kept peeping at the crips to see what they were doing. On three different occasions he seen Ron look over at him. Joe made eye contact with Boobie the last time to see if he saw what he was seeing. Boobie gave a slight head nod

"So what's up, is yall coming back to our spot with us?" Shanae asked

"Yea son yall go head. I'll catch up with yall tomorrow, I ain't bout to be no third wheel yo"

"You can come too, that's not a problem. You won't be no third wheel, I promise. C'mon let's go" Shanae stood up and touched Boobies shoulder. Joe seen out the corner of his eyes that the crips were leaving also. They stood up and looked around discreetly. When Pullout gazed at him. That set Joe on fire. He picked up the bottle of Cîroc off the table and busted Shanae in the head with it. Before she hit the ground Joe grabbed his .50 cal. off his waist and aimed at Pull out. Pull out was in the middle of pulling his gun out. Booyow! The desert eagle sounded like a cannon going off. From that moment it was pure pandemonium inside the club. Everybody who didn't have a gun hit the ground. Boom! Boom! Boca! Boca! Boca! Boc! Boc! Bak! Bak! Bak! Booyow! Both the crews started shooting at each other and ducking for cover. Overdose grabbed Tee-Tee and used her as a shield as he let his .40 cal bark off. Boca! He was moving with her and she was screaming at the top of her lungs. He felt a powerful impact hit him and he flew back on the ground. He crawled behind a table that was turned over.

He seen Tee-Tee on the ground bleeding out her chest. Boobie jumped up firing both of his 9 mm handguns. Boom Boom Boom Boom Boom! He watched a man fall that joined in helping the crips when the shooting started. Booyow! Booyow! Joe started letting off with his eyes locked on Pull out. Pull out started ducking and shooting back. Bak Bak Bak!

"Stop hiding bitch ass nigga!" Joe yelled. Boca Boca Boca Boca! Ron started firing at Joe. Boca Boca Boca Boca Boca! Overdose got on Ron from the side

"Aghhh!" on yelled and ducked behind a table

"Where you hit at cuz!?" Gucci ty asked

"Left shoulder, I'm good cuz!" Boom Boom! Gucci ty let off sending Overdose back ducking. A security guard had caught Pull out slippin from behind and had his gun aimed at his back. Pull out put his hands up a lil bit to show he gave up. Gucci ty ran up from behind. Boom Boom Boom! He shot the guard 3 times in the back until he fell.

Booyow Booyow Booyow! Joe shot at them while they were slightly distracted. Gucci ty hit the ground

"Grab that nigga gun!" He told pull out

"C'mon blood we gotta get out the back before the boyz get here" Boobie told the group. The backdoor was down the hallway that was right behind where they were ducking at. They all got up and started walking backwards towards the door. Ron got curious on why everything was quiet. He poked his head from around a table. Boom Boom! Overdose tried to take his head off

"Cuz they going out the back!" He shouted.

"Good let those niggaz go so we can get up outta here" Gucci ty said. They made it out the back with no other problems

"You need a ride blood?" Boobie asked overdose. They heard sirens and started rushing towards the parked cars

"Naw I'm good my shit parked over here" They watched as groups of people rushed out of all directions to their cars. Bak Bak Bak! Somebody was shooting at them from across the lot. They ducked down

"Fuck that we outta here blood" Boobie yelled at Joe while hopping in his car. They all got in their own cars and sped outta the lot. Joe was following right behind Boobies car. When they reached the first red light, Joe pulled up on Boobie's passenger side

"Let me get a banger mines is empty!" He shouted then hopped out the car. Boobie was leaning over to grab a gun off the seat. Joe speed walked around to the front door

"Here blood take this shit, hurry up" Boobie said then watched Joe point his cannon straight at his face

"I knew you" Booyow! His words was cut short by being shot in the face. The impact made his body fly half way to the passenger seat

"You ain't know shit bitch ass nigga!" Booyow Booyow! He stuck the gun in the car and shot him twice more

"One for tryna take over, one for my bitch, and one cause I never like yo ass" Joe jumped in his car and sped off. He called Boobies phone 3 times just to show that he tried to call him in case anybody ever got suspicious.

THA LAST OF MY KIND

ॐ

102ND/STARK ST.

ॐ

When O-Dawg got to the crime scene he felt in his gut that every-thing was lost. After he jumped out of his car he made eye contact with two females that were crying. He could tell by the hurt in their eyes that the worse had happened. He refused to believe it, even after he recognized Boobies red Impala just sitting there, with paramedics and cops surround-ing it. More than 50 people had already got to the scene and was standing around looking defeated. O-Dawg finally made it over to Gotti and the look on his face said everything that didn't need to be said

"They got Boobie, they killed my nigga" Gotti said shaking his head and looking ready to cry

"What happened" O-Dawg growled

"Him, Joe and Overdose got into a shootout with them niggaz inside Mystiques. They had a shooting in the parking lot too, then everybody left. Then one of those crabs caught em at the light" Gotti nodded his head in Boobies direction

"Who have you talked to?" Gotti hesitated before he answered because the look he seen in his younger cousin eyes put even a lil fear in him.

"I talked in detail with Joe after 100 bitches called me crying"

"Get the fuck out my way!" They heard somebody yell and turned their heads to see Burnside walking up on them with murder in his eyes

"Tell me my nigga ain't dead!" Burnside said then started biting his lip waiting for an answer.

"Have everybody at the warehouse tomorrow night and send me Overdose number ASAP" O-Dawg said in a low and chilling voice as he walked away

"Did he just say the warehouse?" Gotti asked because he thought maybe he heard him wrong.

O-Dawg hasn't attended a large meeting in years, let alone been to the warehouse. That was the spot they used to plan every move they made when they was on the come up, especially murders. If everybody was going to be there that meant it was time for an all-out war. Usually the heads would meet at his or O-Dawgs house, then they would pass the orders down the line. But at the warehouse, that meant one person would be doing all the talking and everybody that claimed their hood would be there

"You heard what that nigga said blood. You know what time it is too, so don't try and talk em outta it."

"We shoulda been killed these niggaz!" Burnside said, when Gotti didn't respond he walked away and jumped in his car. Gotti pulled his phone out and made a call

"Everybody be at the warehouse tomorrow at 7 o'clock. Call everybody and tell em, whoever don't come, might wanna leave town" He hung up the phone and watched them take Boobies body out the car. A tear escaped his eye before he turned around and got in his car.

ᘒᘍ

NEXT NIGHT AT THE WAREHOUSE

ᘒᘍ

The warehouse was exactly what it was called. They leased it awhile back and had it furnished with TV's, pool tables, couches, and a mini bar.

Over 20 people was there sitting around talking and waiting for the meeting to start. Everybody had the look of death on their faces and was talking about nothing else except that. When O-Dawg finally walked into the room all the talking stopped. He was wearing some black Nike sweats with a black hoody and everybody could tell that he had a vest on. He wasn't wearing his glasses and had a look of stone on his face

"I'm not about to waste a whole bunch of time doing no talking. Yall know what we here for and what's about to happen. So if there's anybody here that don't want to kill or get killed then leave right now before it's too late" Nobody moved an inch.

"It's a whole lot of shit that's about to change starting right now. Don't think I haven't heard the rumors. Niggaz talkin bout I done went soft and don't wanna beef with nobody. Niggaz think I won't kill no more! So with that being said, niggaz start losing respect, even my own niggaz" Joe was standing on the wall next to Burnside and was sweating bullets

"Burnside! What's the only thing niggaz respect?"

"Murder!" He yelled back.

"Murder! So I guess it's time for niggaz to start respecting and fearing me again right? Well first we must start with the inside before we can make others do it" O-Dawg walked up on Dute Fly "You only respect murder right?"

"Yup!" Dute answered

"What about you bleed?"

"Same thing blood" He replied

"Same thing, I can dig that" He walked up to Kaylin who was sitting in a chair

"What about you my nigga, what you respect?"

"I only respect real niggaz and murder" He said meaning every word

"Consider yourself murdered then" Then O-Dawg pulled out his .45 and shot him in the head before anybody could blink. Boom Boom! He shot him twice more once his body hit the ground. Everybody looked at him like he was crazy and everybody was confused

"This bitch nigga stayed with my name in his mouth. Nigga talkin bout he gone take over soon. Then to top it off, this ho ass nigga is family with Pressha. Why yall niggaz ain't kill em when yall saw that picture on Instagram! We in the middle of war and this nigga taking pictures with the enemy! Shooter, why yall ain't kill em?" He asked and stared him in the eyes waiting for an answer

"That's his blood cousin" He responded

"From now on, I'm not gone respect nobody that don't murder" He tossed Burnside his gun. Burnside took the one off his waist and tossed it to O-Dawg

"You know what to do with it." Everybody meet back here after Boobie funeral. By that time we'll have everything planned out. Until then, Every time I turn on the news, I wanna see somebody dead!" He looked everybody in the eyes before he walked out the warehouse.